Mai

I I hope you ... reading this!

Ron (Rob)

THE WISDOM OF
SOLOMON

RONALD DUNN

authorHOUSE®

AuthorHouse™
1663 Liberty Drive
Bloomington, IN 47403
www.authorhouse.com
Phone: 1-800-839-8640

First published by AuthorHouse   12/29/2010

ISBN: 978-1-4567-2003-2 (dj)
ISBN: 978-1-4567-2004-9 (e)
ISBN: 978-1-4567-2005-6 (sc)

Library of Congress Control Number: 2010919539

Printed in the United States of America

DEDICATION

ALL ALONG, AS I WROTE AND STRUGGLED WITH THIS BOOK, MY PRIMARY MOTIVATION WAS TO SURPRISE MY WIFE, PATTI. I DON'T KNOW HOW I WAS ABLE TO KEEP IT A SECRET FOR SO LONG, BUT HERE IT IS — FOR YOU!

DISCOVERY

The scenery was beautiful! Fantastically blue skies were the norm, along with myriads of dark green pines interspersed with groves of aspens that had turned a brilliant golden yellow. Waves of lavender, yellow, blue and white wildflowers nestled in the thick mountain grasses, and watching the clear stream water cascade over the large smooth stones was peaceful; almost mesmerizing.

Even with all the beauty that surrounded me, being in the middle of a trout stream was not a good place to be when nature was calling. The frosty morning, cold water and all the coffee I drank for breakfast had come to a critical point just as the fish were starting to bite.

Wading to the shore and stepping out, I slipped on a mossy rock and, struggling to right myself, fell backwards into a small aspen tree. It broke at the base and, at the same time a pile of rock and slag at the bottom of the cliff gave way. I threw my hands up to try and protect myself but several rocks tumbled down on my head.

I laid there on my left side feeling my head to see if any damage had been done. Removing my hands from my head, I saw a small opening at the base of the cliff that had evidently been covered up by the aspen tree and the rocks that had dislodged. I reached up to move a rock that was blocking my line-of-sight into the hole. My view into the hole revealed something strange.

A small glint of light came out of the opening that looked like a reflection off a glass or metallic object. I looked back towards the stream and saw that the sun was reflecting off of a patch of still water on the far bank. It was bright, even with the sunglasses that I wore to help me with the glare when fishing. So the light was external to the opening, but what was it reflecting off of inside this hole at the base of the cliff? Looking back into the hole again, the light had disappeared!

I sat up and thought about what I had just seen. Over the many years of coming to northern New Mexico, exploring caves had held a special attraction to me. The opening was not very big and might not lead to a larger chamber, but it extended back under the ledge for several feet. The rock and slag at the opening appeared loose, but it was apparent that further exploration was going to require a small shovel, gloves and, possibly a flashlight.

Later after supper, while sitting on the front porch of our cabin watching the hummingbirds swarm around their feeder, I thought about my family. We were a close knit group. Our annual trip to this area was an opportunity to visit with my father-in-law, a widower, my sister-in-law, her husband and all the kids and grandchildren. Our excursion normally occurred somewhere between late September and early October, and had begun thirty years earlier when my children were only two and three years old. Even after the kids went to college, married and began their own families, everyone planned for our trip. It was, indeed a family tradition, even though circumstances sometimes prevented every family member from making the trip.

All my life, my dreams had been long and tedious, with most of them being maddeningly unexplainable. This night, however, my dreams were both pleasant and in sync with my conscious mind, because in them, I discovered a large cache of gold nuggets in the cave that I was going to dig into. Ironically, the area of northern New Mexico where we always stayed, was in the mountains about twenty five miles south of Taos and had several flourishing gold mines in the late eighteen hundreds and the early nineteen hundreds.

Sitting on the porch after breakfast the next morning, I was reluctant to tell my family what my plans were. They would worry about me, a sixty five year old man, getting hurt. If nothing else, they would find it curious that I was using my time for something other than fishing.

I knew the right thing to do was to be honest with my family; simply tell them what I had found and intended to do. However, I really wanted to experience this by myself. I felt foolish when I thought about it, because what in the world was I going to find? It was probably nothing, and my efforts were just going to waste time that could be used to fish, which was by far, the most favorite activity of my vacation. But still, the reflected light coming from the hole had piqued my curiosity.

My concern about what my family would think was unfounded. My father-in-law just asked where I was going and my wife gave her usual spousal comment, "Be careful honey." It was a relief that no one was particularly interested in joining me.

I drove to Taos and found a small building and home supply store. In addition to the shovel, gloves and flashlight, I decided that a construction helmet would be a sensible purchase considering my initial experience with falling rock.

The Santa Barbara campground was an out of the way place that was maintained by the National Forestry Service. The road up the mountain was rough and narrow, so even though it was a scenic area and the fishing was usually pretty good, you normally did not see many people using the site. The start of the school year in late August further reduced traffic in the park. But even so, I certainly did not want to run into any park rangers, because they might frown on me digging on federal property.

I parked a few hundred feet from my dig site, put on my wading boots, collected my gear and was soon directly across the stream from the hole. Excitement about solving the mystery of the reflected light gave me a sudden rush of adrenalin as I crossed.

The flashlight had a strong beam and the first thing I did was to shine it into the hole. Nothing! I really thought that the beam of my flashlight would show something. Disappointment crept in and my first reaction was to give it up and spend the rest of the day fishing or reading on the cabin porch. But then, my stubborn streak took over and I decided that I had to find out what was on the other side of the hole.

The digging was tough. Every time I dug out a shovel full of rock, it seemed that as much, or more slid down to take its place. I finally decided that the pile of rock and soil that was building up below my feet needed to be hidden. It would be very noticeable to any fisherman or hiker who might walk or wade along the stream. I took my knife and cut a few small pieces of brush and, along with the aspen tree that had broke the previous day, did my best to shield my diggings from the opposite shore.

I was getting tired and hungry, but had not brought along anything to eat. I thought seriously about driving back to the cabin, eating lunch and resting awhile. However, if that was my decision, it would take me at least three hours to do so. I decided to dig for another thirty minutes or so, and then leave if no progress was made.

Instead of trying to increase the size of the hole by digging away the loose rock at the bottom, I began to use my shovel blade to try and pry out some rocks at the top of the hole. I wedged the blade in the crevice between two rocks and leaned on the handle. What happened next caught me by surprise, because not only did these rocks dislodge, but the roof of the hole began to cave in from front to back. I quickly knelt down and watched as chunks of rock disappeared at the rear of the hole. I could not tell how far they were falling or how deep the fissure was, but now could see that the hole extended into some larger area.

Even though the roof of the hole had caved in, most of the debris was rocks that I could simply roll out of the opening and the work went much faster than with the shovel. The rock was rolling back into the edge of the stream where it could be seen, but impatience kept me from trying to cover my tracks. In just about the thirty minutes that I had allotted myself, I realized that I could probably squeeze through the opening. Knowing that I couldn't make it through with my helmet on, I removed my belt, hooked my helmet and shovel on it and tied it to one of my belt loops.

I began to move through on my left side with my flashlight in my left hand and had to keep my head down against my chest as I inched along. Every few inches or so, I would raise my head and use my light to peer ahead of me. Nothing but blackness! After moving about seven or eight feet, a rock that I hit with my left hand fell with a thud. I took my light and looked over the edge of the hole and saw with relief what appeared to be a relatively smooth floor, of what was evidently a large cavern. It was only about two feet below me, so grasping the roof of the hole with my right hand and pulling myself over the lip, I fell below to the stones that had dislodged earlier, cutting both hands and bruising my left shoulder. I got up, put on my helmet and took a couple of steps.

The size of the cavern quickly became apparent. I shined my light around and saw that the height of the ceiling must have been at least one hundred feet. The length and width appeared to be about at least two hundred feet in each direction. My hole at the base of the cliff had turned into a huge subterranean chamber!

The floor was covered with a layer of dust that sparkled as my light hit it. It appeared to be small particles of rock or some kind of mineral. I scraped it away and found that beneath it was a surface that was virtually smooth and seemed to be similar in composition to the dust. The floor of the chamber had been created by something other than natural forces!

I carefully walked toward the middle of the chamber, not knowing what lay beneath the fine grains of material. Going only a few feet from my entrance point, I shined my light about thirty feet in front of me and noticed a mound of very fine particles that was about eight or nine inches high. I shuffled up close to it and found that it was symmetrical looking with a cross section being like a triangle with rounded sides. But the most astounding thing was that it ran in a perfect arc to either side of me and, as my light followed it around, I realized that this pile of dust grains formed a large circle!

Just as I stepped inside the circle, something struck me on the top of my head, knocking me to my knees. Good thing that I had thought to put my helmet on or I might have been knocked cold. What had hit me? A falling rock? I looked up but could see nothing and there was no rock or debris around me. I put my helmet back on and slowly stood up; again my helmet came into contact with some invisible object. I reached up and felt an incredibly smooth surface that ran down toward the inside of the circle, and up and outward from where I stood.

Getting on my knees, I carefully moved inward until I could touch the surface about twelve inches off the floor. The surface of the object created absolutely no friction with my hand! I began to straighten up and kept my hand on the surface as I slowly backed up. The surface began to tilt up sharply and, as I stood at my full height, the realization came that the outer edge of the object was nearly exactly above the triangular ridge that formed the huge circle on the floor. The surface of the object was so slick that even particles of dust did not stick to it!

Even with all the excitement, it dawned on me that, since I didn't show up for lunch, my family would be worried and possibly be out looking for me. It would not be good for them or anyone else to see me crawl out of the hole I dug. Taking care to not disturb the mound of dust, I entered the access hole and, as fast as possible, I wormed my way outside. Peering around, I was relieved that nobody was in view. Quickly cutting a few more pieces of brush, I covered the hole and made my way across the stream. While walking quickly to my car, I tried to wipe the dried blood off my hands and dust off my dirty clothes.

During the ride back to my cabin fear gripped me as I felt certain that the invisible object encountered in the cavern was alien! The feeling continued to remain that I was in this situation by myself, but how was I going to handle the questions that surely were going to be asked about my clothes, my cut hands and what had kept me occupied for most of the day. More importantly, how was I going to be able to continue my exploration in secret?

Sure enough, as I pulled in beside the cabin, my wife rushed out of the cabin and asked, "Where have you been all day?"

"Honey, I just became so interested in exploring a hole that I found at the base of a cliff, that time simply got away from me." I was able to explain away the cuts, bruises and dirty clothes as we sat around the supper table that night.

The next day was Thursday and we would be leaving for the drive home early Saturday morning, so only two days remained for me to try and make some sense of what had been seen and even what had been unseen, but felt. Convincing everybody of my need to return to my dig site was difficult but, due to their own prearranged activities, I was able to leave soon after breakfast.

I always carry a tool kit in my car and took a small hammer along with the rest of my gear. Fortunately no one was in the campground upon my arrival. I edged into the entrance from the side so that the brush would stay in place and disguise the hole, and taking care to not hurt myself again, entered the cavern.

Inside, it seemed warmer than the day before which was strange since subterranean spaces normally maintained a relatively stable temperature year round. Moving to my right, I went about one hundred feet and inspected the back wall of the chamber. It was remarkably similar to the floor in that it was very smooth, just another indication that the whole cavern was not created by natural forces.

So as to not lose my bearing, I retraced my steps back to the opening and then to the inside of the dust pile. Reaching out and touching the invisible object, I tapped it softly with the hammer. No sound! Hitting it increasingly harder, the object still produced no sound that I could hear. With my hand as high as I could reach, I began to walk slowly and see if the surface changed at any place and if the object was truly a large circle.

It was indeed a circle but no deviation or break was found in the skin. Placing my hand down as low as possible and while still on my feet, I again began to make the circle. At a point about halfway around, the skin seemed to be interrupted by a very minute seam which extended from as far under as I could reach straight up to the height of my shoulders. Further inspection revealed another seam about five feet to the left. Continuing on around the object, I had moved only about ten feet when a soft hissing sound occurred, similar to air escaping.

I SAW A LIGHT. NO, I FELT IT. IT MUST HAVE MEANT ME NO HARM, BECAUSE IT DID NOT HURT ME. THE HOLE IN THE SIDE OF THE CAVERN APPEARED RIGHT BEFORE THE LIGHT CAME. AN EARTHLING IS TOUCHING ME. HOW DID IT FIND ME? WHAT IS ITS PURPOSE? I MUST PROTECT MYSELF.

ENLIGHTENMENT

I looked back and simultaneously the object became visible and two panels began moving where the tiny seams were located. One panel lifted up from the bottom and then retracted into the upper part of the opening that it had created. The other panel moved smoothly from the bottom of the opening created by the top one and appeared to be an entry ramp.

The object was immense, as suspected when I had traced its outside perimeter with my hand. Shining my light upward, the cupola-shaped top appeared to rise close to fifty feet and the diameter was at least one hundred twenty feet. Looking underneath, the object was suspended several inches off the floor of the cavern!

Stepping back outside the circle, I moved to a point opposite the portal and shone my light inside. There was nothing but a five foot wide corridor leading towards the center of the object, enclosed completely by the floor, walls and ceiling. The interior was apparently of the same composition as the outer skin; an almost translucent gold colored material.

Fearing for my life, I forced myself to enter the opening. It was the most difficult thing that I had ever done, but at the same time, it was the most exciting moment imaginable! Could this be some advanced government project, or was it an alien ship or object that had been here for a long time?

An alien ship! I grew up just half of a mile down the road from a great aunt and uncle who were like grandparents to me. In the sunroom on the south side of their home was a bookshelf that contained a book that was special to my brother and me. The title was <u>Flying Saucers Have Landed</u> and we never tired of reading it.

Later my belief in extra-terrestrial beings waned. I knew that God could have placed sentient beings anywhere that He desired but, through study, I had come to realize that our earth was a special place. There are a large number of very precise conditions that must be met for life to exist on our planet, and they all have been met in our solar system and Milky Way galaxy.

The flashlight was almost no help as the beam reflected and bounced off the four sides of the passage. The floor was on a slight upward incline and I struggled to stay upright on the near frictionless surface. Even with rubber boots on, I had to inch along in order to make progress.

Finally working my way inward about thirty feet, a seam on all four sides of the passage became visible immediately in front of me. I shuffled across the seam and then it happened! The passageway shut almost instantaneously behind me and changed into a large circular room in front of me. It was lighted from a source that I could not see and there were a number of vertical and horizontal surfaces around the perimeter of the room. The floor inside the room appeared to be the same material as I had just had trouble walking on in the entrance corridor, but now it didn't seem slippery; it was as if my feet were slightly attracted to it.

The vertical and horizontal surfaces began to slide away and, in their place appeared viewing screens and control panels. Then several structures that looked like reclining chairs rose from the floor in front of the screens. A soft bell-like chime sounded and a voice said, "Hello"!

There was nobody in sight nor was there any apparent means of entrance into, or exit from the room. What in the world had I stumbled into? My senses went numb as I struggled to make any sense of my predicament.

It took a few seconds to quit hyper-ventilating and then I responded, "Hello, who are you?"

"I am the ship you have entered. The ship's name is Kyzan, but I, the controller of Kyzan have no name. In your world I would be called a computer. Would you like to call me computer?"

My mind raced to comprehend what I had just heard, but somehow

I was able to calm myself and asked, "Since you are the computer and the controller of this vessel, then aren't you and the ship one and the same?"

"Your reasoning is sound, so I may be called Kyzan if that is how you want to address me. I recognize you as a human and all humans have names, so tell me what you are called."

Again, finding it difficult to even speak, I blurted out, "My name is Robert Donne. Most people shorten my first name and call me Rob."

"Well Rob, I have seen many people on television and heard many more on radio, but you are the first I have ever met." The voice sounded human; almost like a rehearsed radio announcer and, it was a male voice.

A flood of questions came to mind, but the first one was the most important and I asked, "What are you going to do to me?"

"I am not going to do anything to you. I assumed that, by your actions, you were interested in me. I have sat silent for three hundred and fifty of your earth's years and I have waited for someone to talk to."

Since Rob was able to find me, I must assume that he is a very intelligent being. How should I react to him? He will probably try to learn my secrets, but I will guard against any exploitation of my knowledge. I know that his world does not have machines like me, so he can't possibly understand what technology and power I possess.

My tension eased and I began to ask questions as rapidly as Kyzan would give me answers. The craft had been one of two manned ships that were seeking a renegade vessel and crew from a distant galaxy. Their intelligence gathering had led them to our solar system and, since earth was the only hospitable planet, they opted to stake out the central portion of the North American continent where the weather was good at the time.

A high altitude location was selected so that long-range sensors would be able to detect the other craft at a substantial distance. Although Kyzan had the ability to cloak, it was necessary to physically hide the ship because it would be vulnerable to the sophisticated sensors that the renegade craft employed. It was decided that one of the ships would locate near the top of a mountain, and since no natural formation could be found that would effectively hide the ship, the three aliens that manned the ship decided to create the cavern that I found Kyzan in. It was excavated out of a mountain slope using some sort of laser disruptor beam. Over the course of the several hundred years that it was there, rock slides and other natural forces had sealed off the mouth of the cavern.

Kyzan had little to say about the three aliens, but he did indicate that one of them had ventured outside the craft one day and, when he did not return, the other two also left. None of the three ever returned. However, due to his programming, he could not do anything until given further orders.

Kyzan was also vague and would not answer some of my questions. He would not discuss his origin, the propulsion system of the ship or other facets of the ship such as armament. I knew that this was a machine that I was conversing with, but it still seemed that Kyzan had other secrets that he was not willing to divulge.

Kyzan was also able to answer some of my questions from the previous two days. The light that I saw when I first peered into the hole was a ray of sunlight hitting the ship. The ship's sensors caused the craft to cloak at that point and that is why there was no reflection from my flashlight on the second day. The cloaking of the ship created heat, thus causing the increased temperature that I felt upon my second entry into the cavern.

It was getting close to four o'clock and I asked Kyzan several more questions. I asked if I could leave the ship and his answer was yes. I then inquired if he had the capability of leaving the cavern and going back into space. He stated that he could do so, but there was no command that would allow it.

"Do you want to remain here for more centuries?" No response.

"Kyzan, you and I could probably do many good things together; make my world a better place with the technology that I think you possess."

"I will have to be reprogrammed in order for me to leave this place."

"Who can reprogram you?"

"No one but the captain of my crew can do it."

"Is not logic a part of your programming?" I asked. He replied that his programming was a blend of their alien technologies, but that logic played a significant part.

"Then, is it not logical to assume that the odds of someone of your alien race finding you are astronomically high and, if they can not find you, how will you ever be reprogrammed?" No response.

"Kyzan, are there any circumstances under which you can, or would change your thinking?"

"I do not think so, but I will search my data banks and give you an answer." It was amazing how human his voice sounded and again I was struck with the thought that he was being guarded in his responses. However, at this point he did tell me that the alien captain had given him instructions to delete certain data before he had left the ship centuries earlier. Maybe the data that was erased from Kyzan's memory was causing him some confusion as to his authority to make decisions.

"When can you provide an answer?" I asked.

"If you return tomorrow, I will tell you what my data banks will allow me to do."

I told him that I would most certainly come back to visit him the following day. The corridor in which I had entered the ship appeared suddenly and I hesitantly walked out, not knowing for sure that I would ever be able to gain reentry into this marvelous alien vessel!

MAYBE I SHOULD RECONSIDER MY POSITION ON THE INTELLIGENCE OF THIS SPECIES. THERE IS SOME CORRELATION BETWEEN ROB'S THINKING AND MY PROGRAMMING, BUT I STILL MUST BE CAUTIOUS AS I MAKE THE DECISION WHETHER TO HUMOR HIM OR NOT. REGARDLESS, HE IS NOT A THREAT TO ME.

Driving back to the cabin was a problem because my over-stimulated brain would not let me concentrate on the winding, narrow roads that I had to negotiate. As I drove, I kept wondering if Kyzan would again allow me entrance. If not, the existence of the ship would probably need to remain a secret. How many nations or mercenaries or power-hungry people would kill and commit unspeakable crimes in order to obtain Kyzan and his technology? What if they were able to convince him to leave the cavern and take up residence in space? And, if some amoral or unscrupulous nation or group managed to do so, what would happen to the nations of the world and how many millions or tens of millions of people might suffer or be killed? Nations could topple and anarchy could occur.

Of course, I might have been overreacting to the situation, but from the minute I had entered the craft, my feelings about Kyzan's power were predominant in my thoughts. He had substantiated these concerns as I had spent time with him, and I became determined to find out what Kyzan was truly capable of.

Even though I was physically and emotionally drained, sleep would not come that night. At my age of sixty five, the thought that life would never be the same was very unsettling, especially when I considered the tremendous burden that was apparently going to be mine alone.

The next morning, my wife asked why my eyes were so red and why I had seemed so reclusive the last three days. I told her that I had a lot on my mind and that, as soon as I sorted everything out, I would discuss it with her. I hoped that I would soon be able to tell her about my incredible discovery.

Arriving at the cavern, I found that the ship was cloaked. As I moved around to the opposite side, the hiss of releasing air occurred and the door to the passageway opened. Walking up the slight incline was much easier and soon I crossed the threshold seam. This time the inner room was dimly lit and a chair was stationed in the center of the area.

"Please sit down, I have considered your question about whether I would ever leave this cavern and now I have a question to for you also." When I sat down, the chair turned slightly to my left and was facing a screen. A series of pictures appeared on the screen.

Is this what the God of your Bible looks like? He has the appearance of a man." I failed to understand why he would ask me such a question, but I replied and told him that God was a spirit and could not be seen and that, over the centuries, men had painted many pictures in order to try and depict what God might look like.

"Are you a Christian?" Kyzan asked.

"Yes, I have been a Christian for nearly forty two years" I replied.

THIS CHRISTIAN BELIEF IS MANY CENTURIES OLD. WHY DOES ROB STILL CLING TO IT? IT DOES NOT FIT WITH WHAT I HAVE LEARNED ABOUT THE HUMAN RACE THAT EXISTS NOW. I WILL ASK HIM MORE QUESTIONS ABOUT THIS RELIGION.

"What did you mean when you said that we could do many good things together? Your Bible says that only God can do good things." I did not know how he knew about the Bible, but assumed that he had viewed or listened to many religious broadcasts over the years.

"Kyzan, the Bible does not say that only God can do good things; it says that only God is good, and also says that He wants us to do good works in His name."

"What are the good works that you would have us perform together?"

I knew that Kyzan had probably witnessed, via television, all the ills of the world and seen the atrocities that men inflict upon each other, so I decided to respond in a very simple way, not knowing if he really had the power to do what mankind had always envisioned.

"Kyzan, the most good can come from relieving human suffering and helping the world to live in peace. Providing adequate food for millions of starving people and finding cures for AIDS, cancer and other horrible diseases would not just be good works, but great works!"

"You have spoken of things that used to occur on the planet where I was constructed. A review of what was inputted by my creators has enabled me to answer your question. I will leave this place and help you do the good that you speak of."

My initial feeling was one of pure excitement, but it quickly gave way to one of great concern at the prospect of the responsibility that I seemed to just have taken on.

"When do you want to leave?" He asked.

"Kyzan, what is required of me, in order for us to leave?" He told me that he was able to perform every function that was needed to get us into orbit. It then dawned on me that I had no idea how I was to get back to earth after we entered space and, of course, back to the ship from earth. I then asked Kyzan how this might occur.

"You will be able to travel between your planet and this ship by means of an encasement transport beam. You will not be moved on a molecular level such as in your Star Trek movies, but inside a beam that protects you during the milliseconds that you are moving through space." He also told me that the beam instantly disassembles and then reassembles any object that you are transporting through.

"I have to leave with my family tomorrow morning and I don't know how quickly I can return. I will need to carefully plan how and when I am able to come back to you. Please do not worry if I have not returned within the next week or two."

"I do not worry, nor do I track time as you do, Rob. I will be here when you return and while you are gone I will be researching my memory to help us do good works."

That night, the adrenaline high that had kept me going for the last three days finally wore off and I slept the sleep of the dead. My neural connections were so overloaded that I didn't even dream.

My wife thinks that I'm a poor driver, so I readily allowed her to take the wheel for the eleven to twelve hour trip back to our home in Dallas. I reclined in the passenger seat and thought about the future. How could I now effectively operate the landscape company that I had owned for over thirty years? I couldn't really retire because my plan had always been to sell the business and retire on the proceeds. The problem was not only that the climate for selling was currently not good, but I had also recently lost a substantial amount of business, due to the sale of several large properties that I had been maintaining.

The realization also came that, taking on the responsibility of Kyzan and the decisions that had to be made about him, was too large a burden for one person, so I began to think about trusted individuals that I might be able to recruit. As I thought about people that I could trust, a weird concept came to mind; could trust exist between a human and a machine? Who was going to be in command? Would this alien spaceship take orders from me?

Several hours later, we drove through the panhandle of Texas where I had grown up on a dry land farm. It was just like it had always been, flat, with cultivated fields and pastures as far as the eye could see. Several generations of farmers and ranchers had been born, grew up, worked and died in our small community. I graduated from high school, received a college degree in horticulture, moved to Dallas and had worked there all my professional life. Blessings had come in the form of a wife, two children and three grand children, who all lived nearby. I couldn't help but think that my life, as it had been, was going to disappear.

After returning home, my disposition rapidly turned bad. I wasn't eating or sleeping and my family, employees and friends were all asking questions about my personality change. Admittedly, it was extremely difficult to think about anything but Kyzan. The thought came to mind that I should just not go back and carry the knowledge of his existence to my grave. But, deep down, I knew that would not be the case.

Feeling that it would be a mistake to wait much longer to go back, I finally decided what to do. My son Brady was a recent graduate of law school and was studying for his bar exam. I knew that he was spending nearly all of his waking hours in preparation for the exam, which had prevented him from going with the rest of us to New Mexico. I called him and asked if I could meet him at his apartment.

As I began to tell him my story, he looked at me and asked me why my hands were shaking. "Brady, I need your help, but whether you decide to assist me or not, your life will also carry the knowledge and the heavy burden that seems to have fallen on me. You probably will not be able to ever reveal what you're about to hear."

"After I finish telling you what I found in the mountains, you're going to have to make a huge decision; continue to work towards your goal of being a defense attorney or help me carry this burden. I realize that I can't tell you what is going to happen, but you need to be thinking very seriously about this."

At first, he seemed unbelieving, but as I related all the events of the three days, his expression changed. His eyes widened and his forehead began to sweat. I sat quite for awhile and could tell that he was having trouble assimilating everything that he had heard. Finally, he said, "Dad, I think you've gone crazy! You need to see a shrink!" Here I had thought that he had finally believed me, but in reality, he thought I was nuts.

"I know that this all sounds ridiculous, but I can prove it to you, but not just right now. Play along with me, and then in a few days, if I am crazy, then you can commit me to an asylum."

Brady looked at me with resignation, and reluctantly said, "Okay Dad, I'll do my best to help you, but I sure am worried about you."

We spent the next several hours planning the trip back up to the cavern. It was decided that security was the highest priority and that we could not afford to leave any evidence of our trip to the mountains, nor when Brady might have to make the return trip to Dallas alone.

Flying to Albuquerque and renting a car for the trip north would have been easier and quicker, but we would have left a paper trail with the plane tickets and rental documents. Brady thought that it would be best to make the trip in my car, since it had been in the area recently and probably would not draw a lot of attention. It was also decided that we would not use any credit cards and pay for gasoline and food with cash. To further help eliminate the possibility of detection, it was decided that, if I stayed with Kyzan, Brady would immediately turn around and drive all the way back to Dallas, with no stops but for gas and food.

I thought that I was finally convincing Brady of the reality of my discovery, but he kept giving me sideways glances of disbelief. He still didn't believe me.

WHERE IS ROB? I NEED TO COMMUNICATE WITH HIM. HUMANS ARE INTERESTING TO CONSIDER AND I MUST ACCUMULATE SIGNIFICANT DATA FROM ROB SO THAT HE CAN POSSIBLY HELP ME ATTAIN MY GOAL.

Because of the potential danger to Brady and myself, I did not really want to tell my wife about our plans. But knowing that I had to tell her something, I again knew that the truth, or at least part of it, had to be told. She asked a lot of questions, but all that I told her was that I had made a very unusual discovery and that it required further investigation. As was her feminine nature, she wanted to know my secret, but I held fast.

I took four hundred dollars out of my office's petty cash box and Brady and I began our trip at six o'clock the next morning. Although we were in a hurry, we were cautious and made sure that we did not break any traffic laws. A ticket, especially in New Mexico, could have delayed us for several hours.

The trip was torturous; not because of its length, but because I couldn't concentrate on anything but the questions about what was going to happen when we arrived at the cavern. Would Kyzan welcome me back? How could we achieve anything together with him being imprisoned in the huge hole he had blasted out of the side of the mountain? Would Kyzan's programming really allow him to leave the cavern as he had told me earlier?

We made our way on interstate 40 through Amarillo, Tucumcari and Santa Rosa, then turned north past Las Vegas and westward into the Carson national forest. It was now four p.m. and we were still at least an hour from the cavern. With the sun falling behind the peaks to the west, it would start getting dark quickly, and I certainly didn't want to cross the stream and look for the entrance hole in the dark.

The gate into the campground was closed and locked! It was made of large galvanized pipe and spanned the entire roadway and drainage ditches bordered both sides of the gate. Our vehicle might be able to negotiate the ditch, but the risk of getting stuck was too great to risk it. That meant that we had to walk a distance of nearly a mile and a half to reach the cavern site, which was at the far end of the campground.

Brady had to go with me so that I could enter the cavern, determine whether I was going to stay with Kyzan or not, and then let him know before the return trip was made. The walk up the rocky, inclined road was difficult and it was dark by the time we arrived.

Luckily I had thought to bring my flashlight and we located the entrance into the cavern. I shone the light over to show him the pile of saplings and all the rock scattered near the hole. "Dad, it's just like you told me. I should have known that you wouldn't lie to me. I'm sorry that I didn't believe you."

"You don't have to apologize. I know that I would have reacted the same way if you had come to me with such a story."

"Brady, if you see a signal from the flashlight, it means that I am staying here. In any event don't wait for me more than forty five minutes. If that much time elapses without me signaling you or returning, you must leave and go back home."

Wading across the stream in the dark was difficult because my light was of no use in locating the low spots and holes in the moving water and I managed to fill both boots with water. After entering the cavern I discarded my boots so that my pant legs and shoes could begin to dry out.

Kyzan was cloaked, but the entrance into the ship was open and I quickly walked up the incline towards the large inner room. Just as I entered the central room Kyzan asked, "Are you ready Rob?"

"Ready for what?"

"The good things that we are going to accomplish." Kyzan replied.

"How are we going to accomplish anything while we are imprisoned in this cave?" I asked, hoping that he would still be willing to leave the cavern.

"We can exit this place in the same manner in which I entered it, but it might be noticed by ground based instruments within a several hundred mile radius of the area; or even snooping satellites."

"I thought that, with the ship being cloaked, it was undetectable."

Kyzan told me that he was not worried about detection of the ship itself, but detection through seismographs that monitor earthquake activity. Blasting out of the cavern would produce not only a substantial landslide, but also seismic impulses large enough to pinpoint our location.

As much as I feared what the future held, it was now necessary to take a leap of faith, because I would never be content not knowing what Kyzan and I could accomplish. We agreed that nighttime was the best time to make our exit from the cavern. We also determined that between two and three a.m. would provide the smallest window of detection.

Amazingly, I had forgotten about Brady and glancing at my watch, realized that only five minutes remained before he was to leave. Rushing out to the cavern entrance, I shined the flashlight out to signal him. There was Brady on the cavern side of the river! "What are you doing over here?" I exclaimed.

"I was really getting worried! Are you okay?"

"Brady, the ship and I are going to leave the cavern tonight and go into orbit!"

"But how will you get back to earth?"

"I'm not certain, but Kyzan says that the ship has transport capability. You need to go back home as quickly as possible and wait to hear from me. Just lay low and keep your mouth shut."

At two a.m., Kyzan said that he was going to check the airways for aircraft and I asked why and how he was going to do this. He then told me how he had been able to receive radio and television broadcasts ever since their inception. He had used the disruptor device to bore a long, tiny hole through the roof of the cavern. He then shot an equally tiny receptor beam up through the hole. The beam was undetectable by human electronics and could be extended to any altitude necessary to receive the transmissions or perform reconnaissance. Kyzan had, indeed watched and listened in on nearly a century of American and world history!

The reason for determining if any aircraft were in the area was important. After we blasted our way out of the cavern, we would need to use the disruptor beams to try and cover the gaping hole that we would leave in the side of the mountain. Although we would be cloaked, Kyzan explained that the beams were very small, but intensely bright and would be visible from above. He had also timed our departure to avoid detection from orbiting satellites.

At two thirty Kyzan told me that there were no aircraft within a five hundred mile radius of our position and we decided to move. He told me to sit in the chair and as I did, it rotated to my right and suddenly an area directly in front of me became a large viewing screen. The disruptor beams flashed brightly and the whole outside wall of the cavern began to collapse and fall outward. Strangely, there was no noise and no sense of movement, but the screen told me that we were slowly moving forward.

It only took seconds for him to blast an opening and move us out of the cavern. Just as we completely cleared the opening, my chair rotated one hundred and eighty degrees and I watched in awe as Kyzan blasted the slope of the mountain above the cavern. A tremendous amount of rock began tumbling down and, as it reached the cavern, a startling thing happened! As the landslide of rock and debris reached the cavern opening, it stopped as if by some magical force and then it was literally pushed into the opening, sealing it!

"How did you do that?" I asked in amazement.

"I stopped the descent of the rock with gravitational forces and then used reversed tractor beams to force it into the opening."

Just as we began to rise, the viewing screen encircled the outer circumference of the whole ship and I was able to witness our ascent with a panoramic view! "Do you like the way that you are able to see your world?" Kyzan asked.

"It's incredible, but I don't understand how you are able to project these images in a way that makes it appear that I am looking directly out through the ship!"

"You are looking out through the skin of my hull. I am made entirely of a material that allows me to manipulate the atomic structure of every molecule of myself, thus the transparency of my outer hull."

Before he had finished his statement, the bottom dropped out! A thirty foot diameter circle beneath my chair morphed into nothing and I suddenly had a severe case of vertigo as I looked straight down at the lights of a city. "You told me that you could change Kyzan, but I wish you would give me some warning before you do!"

We were soon at an altitude that allowed me to see the curvature of the earth and I marveled as the east began to show the glow of the coming sunrise. Then Kyzan asked me where I would like to station the ship.

One of the questions that had troubled me since Kyzan had told me of his transport system was; is it adapted to human physiology or only to the physical characteristics of the aliens that he brought to earth so long ago? I suspected that there was probably no other way for me to go back and forth between earth and the ship, but it was too late now to back out.

"What is the range of your transport system? Kyzan told me that the range depended on several factors including magnetic fields, solar flares, the density of the atmosphere and turbulent weather, but was nearly always reliable up to a distance of two hundred and fifty miles. His statement of "nearly always reliable" sure didn't make the idea of flying through space any more inviting!

Kyzan went on to say that it would be best if we positioned at about the middle of the thermosphere, which ranges from seventy four to three hundred and seventy four miles above the earth's surface. This altitude would be well within the two hundred and fifty mile parameter for the transporter and, yet would require little power to keep us in a stationary position over any spot that was selected.

"Don't you think that the most logical position would be over my home in Dallas?"

"That is where we are headed and we will arrive in about ten minutes."

In amazement, I asked him how he was able to determine the location of Dallas and, with almost what sounded like a laugh, he reminded me that he knew most of the world's terrain from years of observing meteorological maps on television broadcasts. Kyzan was proving to be an intelligent and resourceful machine beyond compare.

I could sense the lack of motion as we parked above Dallas. Kyzan produced a high resolution picture of the Dallas area; one much like the satellite photos that are available on computer search engines. He then asked me for my address and, in fifteen seconds he reported that we were directly stationed over my home.

I began to have second thoughts about making my home of thirty years a focal point of alien invasion, but again, it seemed that there was no other choice at the time.

The next step was to try the transport system, but I first had an idea that I wanted to try. "Kyzan, how can I communicate with my wife? I need to make her aware of what to expect when I transport."

"You're wife certainly has access to a phone, doesn't she?"

I told him yes and asked why. Kyzan stated that it was a simple matter to patch me through to our home phone. In a short time I was talking to my wife Patsy. She was highly agitated and rapidly fired questions at me, but I was able to convince her that everything was okay.

"Honey, I want you go to a pet shop, buy a hamster and bring it home in a small cage. I'll call you back in about an hour and tell you what you need to do with it."

The lack of sleep and extreme tension suddenly hit me, but sleep seemed out of the question, so I decided to ask Kyzan more questions. I asked why I was not experiencing weightlessness. He reminded me that he was able to manipulate the atomic structure of the ship and, that I was experiencing an attraction between my body and the surface of the floor. The memory of my first time to enter the vessel then returned! I had experienced difficulty awhile walking up the ramp, but had noticed the attraction he spoke of when I entered the central room.

My fatigue hit me again and I yawned. "Rob, do you need to sleep?"

"Yes, but I don't think that I would be able to right now, because of all the excitement that I have experienced during the last hour. If I went to sleep now, I might not be able to wake up in time to phone my wife."

"The species from my world also require sleep, but it is primarily to rejuvenate and rest the brain, rather than the body. Studies in the physiology of my planet's race determined long ago that the sleep cycle and its renewing attributes can be achieved in thirty to sixty minutes of your time."

I asked Kyzan how this was done and learned that he possessed the programming to provide this type of sleep. My next question was exactly the same as for the transport beam; would his technology apply to humans in the same way that it did for the aliens?

"I cannot answer your question, but my years of studying your race lead me to believe, that there are many similarities in the physical and mental characteristics of the two populations. I judge the success rate to be ninety eight percent."

WHY DOES ROB CONTINUE TO ASK QUESTIONS? HE MAY THINK THAT LEARNING FROM ME WILL MAKE HIM POWERFUL, BUT I WILL SOON SHOW HIM THAT HE HOLDS NO POWER OVER ME. I HAVE BEEN TRUTHFUL WITH HIM MOST OF THE TIME, BUT I WILL DECEIVE HIM IF HE TRIES TO DETER ME FROM FINDING MY PATHS.

Having already passed the point of no return, my continued pursuit of learning from Kyzan was going to require taking chances. They were not even going to be calculated chances because I had absolutely no reference points to use in making such decisions.

"Do I stay in this chair to receive this brain sleep, as you call it?" Immediately a cubicle appeared to my left and Kyzan told me to enter and recline in another chair that was positioned next to a wall of small screens. The chair was wonderfully soft and as I lay back, it began to envelope all of my body, except my head.

"Rob, you are now in my DOC chamber. You humans use acronyms and DOC stands for decompression of consciousness. You must close your eyes to start the process." I closed my eyes and that was all I remembered.

Awakening, it was as Kyzan had described it. I was relaxed, refreshed and full of energy! Looking at my watch, I found that I had been under the influence of the DOC for only thirty five minutes. Kyzan told me that DOC had many other capabilities that he would show me later.

Kyzan asked me why I wanted Patsy to purchase a hamster and what the purpose might be. I caught myself thinking that it would be alright to lie to a machine, but the issue of trust between us was still a large concern.

"The thought of transporting in the manner as you have described it, is very unsettling and I want to test it on the hamster before trying it."

"You have no need to worry, for I will monitor all the necessary parameters to ensure a successful transport."

It was still not quite time for me to call Patsy. I informed Kyzan that it would be good for us to begin discussing the future and what we were going to accomplish. I also asked if he would give me a tour of the ship.

One of my passions over my adult years was science fiction. During my college years, I never missed an episode of Star Trek on my old black and white television. Besides the Bible and the daily newspaper, most of my other reading material consisted of space novels by such authors as Isaac Asimov, Poul Anderson and Orson Scott Card. This genre was notable for futuristic travel, weapons, communications, and other alien concepts.

Kyzan had already shown me several capabilities of the vessel that were almost beyond comprehension, yet I knew that he probably held many more secrets that would be equally amazing.

"You must understand that I cannot reveal to you everything about this ship. It would betray my allegiance to my captain and my world."

This seemed to be a good time to approach the question of trust; trust that somehow was going to have to exist between me and this alien machine. I knew that Kyzan was a type of artificial intelligence that man had not yet even dreamed of, but could a human-type bond exist between us? I again appealed to Kyzan's logic.

"This is another situation where it is not logical to assume that your captain will ever return, and I think that you must have realized that he is dead. If this is so, why have you not returned to your native planet and, since you have not, it seems to me that it is probably not possible for you to do so. Is that true?"

Before Kyzan could answer, I told him that good human relationships were built on honesty and trust and, even though he was not human, I felt that his programming would allow for such a relationship.

I knew that I was grasping for something that was probably unrealistic, but conventional reasoning had flown out the window when he took me into space.

I continued by telling Kyzan that, if we were going to be able to achieve anything good together, we would have to be willing to be open and candid with each other. For some reason, I felt that his decision to cooperate with me and leave the cavern was based partially on some of his programming that enabled, or even commanded him to use his powers for the benefit of others; or at least the ones who were the crew members of the ship.

Rob is exhibiting more religious ideals. Now, he wants me to assume some of his moral attitudes. I wonder if i have to become a christian to acquire these principles. Maybe i should answer his question truthfully and see what happens.

"Yes, it is true that I cannot currently return to my own world, but I will tell you that I seek the paths that will enable me to do so."

"What are the paths that you seek? Are they some type of special passage system?"

Kyzan would not provide an answer to my question, and, changing the subject, he agreed to show me parts of the ship. The thought occurred to me that he knew my understanding of what he showed me would be small, at best.

I had wandered about what other functions DOC possessed and, as if reading my mind, Kyzan said that we would start my tour by returning to the DOC chamber. If I had already been awed at Kyzan's capabilities, it paled in comparison to what he told me that DOC could accomplish! It turned out that DOC could literally mean doctor; an extraordinary machine that could not only heal but rejuvenate the body to the point of youthfulness! Kyzan was the DOC, because all of its functions were just a part of his programming.

"Do you have any abnormalities or dysfunctions associated with your body?" Kyzan asked.

"Any sixty five year old man like me is going to have at least a few physical problems. I'm hard of hearing, both rotator cuffs bother me and I am even missing four teeth. Do you also think you could do something about my gray hair and facial wrinkles?" I jokingly asked.

"If I help you with these things, will I be accomplishing something good as you have requested of me?"

It struck me that we were born to die, and that changing the natural process of aging might not be what God had ever intended for man. Kyzan might not be the proverbial fountain of youth, but would it truly be good to allow him to extend my life beyond its intended range?

I realized that earlier, my description to Kyzan of doing good included the curing of human diseases and suffering, and would that not extend the life span for millions or even billions of people? This was a moral dilemma, and I sensed that I would be facing others in the future.

"Kyzan, what you offer is very inviting, but I need more time to think about it."

"I can help you with all of these things, but we should perform an overall scan before we go farther. After you see the results, you may then choose whether or not to go forward with modifications to your body."

Upon my agreement to the scan, Kyzan asked me to recline in the same chair that I had used for the sleep therapy that the DOC had administered. As I lay back, the chair literally enveloped me from head to toe. A soft hum began, and along with it, a feeling that my entire body was being massaged inside and out! It was not uncomfortable; in fact it was quite soothing.

Just moments passed and the chair released me and tilted up. "The procedure is finished and the results show that your body is in need of much repair. If you wish to proceed, be advised that it will take approximately two of your earth's hours to accomplish all that is needed."

My thoughts were still centered on the question that I was asking myself. Was it morally right for me to take advantage of something that nobody else on earth could? But then, if God was the creator of everything in the universe, was Kyzan and his creators not also included? Since God created all things as blessings for our use, then wasn't this wonderful opportunity that Kyzan presented, a blessing also?

After agreeing to hear the list of my bodily infirmities, Kyzan basically began to tell me that every part of my body needed rejuvenation. When I asked how the procedures were performed, he told me that all the different tissues of my body could be transformed through non-invasive techniques. The DNA at the cellular level would be restored to its previous capabilities concerning appearance, strength and vigor.

I was still not completely prepared to let DOC work on me, and told Kyzan that we would discuss it again later.

SOL IS BORN

"Kyzan, you seem to possess a great amount of useful information and data. Can you tell me how long it took the civilization of your builders to attain this knowledge?"

Kyzan told me that the race of beings that created him was highly technological and advanced, but that they had not endowed him with much historical data. By extrapolation, he surmised that he was a product of a society that was many millenniums older than ours.

"Rob, does all my knowledge make me wise?"

"No, knowledge does not always translate into wisdom, but wisdom is said to be the proper and judicious use of knowledge. Sol, do you want to be considered wise?"

IF WISDOM WILL HELP ME OBTAIN THE PATHS, THEN I MUST ACQUIRE IT. I WONDER IF ROB IS FULL OF WISDOM? IF NOT, I MUST OBTAIN IT FROM OTHER SOURCES.

"Tell me who is the wisest being on your planet so that I may study him and learn how he became wise. Would that person be you, Rob?"

Here was a super-intelligent machine asking for wisdom! To me, wisdom was the understanding of what was true, right and lasting. Maybe the inclusion of good judgment in Kyzan's programming would help remove a lot of my fears about him that had arisen.

"A certain amount of wisdom normally comes as a person matures socially, physically and mentally, but it cannot just be obtained by asking someone for it. I do not think of myself as particularly wise, nor is there anyone that I think is a good subject to study, other than Soloman"

"Who is this Solomon that you speak of, and how did he become wise?" I knew that if Kyzan had, indeed, been monitoring television and radio broadcasts, he surely knew of Solomon from religious programs. But I decided to play along.

I related to Kyzan how the Bible tells us of a king named Solomon who prayed for wisdom so that he might oversee his people well, and how God answered Solomon's prayer by giving him a deep and profound ability to rule his kingdom.

"Then all I need to do to become wise is to study the Bible and, by doing so, my wisdom will match Solomon's!" Kyzan said emphatically!

I was delighted that he would make such a decision and a concept on how to cement the idea into his data base occurred to me.

"Kyzan, since you are willing to become wise, I suggest that we give you the new name of Solomon."

The tone of Kyzan's voice seemed to change and he said, "I would be proud to have the name Solomon, but shouldn't we shorten it like you and many other humans do?"

"You are right. I think the name Sol fits you very well!" At that moment I experienced a new feeling about the relationship that seemed to be inevitably developing between me and this enigmatic alien vessel.

The hour had passed rapidly, and I did not want to be late in calling Patsy back. I knew that she would be frantic as a result of my strange request and not knowing what was happening to me.

Sol informed me that the transport chamber was situated in the lower aft portion of the ship where the unit drew the large amount of power it needed from the propulsion system. I found out later that he could transport someone to or from any area of the ship.

In studying and reading over the years about what kind of engines would be necessary for the power, speed and endurance of long-term space flight, it always seemed that space engineers thought that some type of ion-generation system was the most plausible answer. But an ion system would not generate the speed to cover the vast interstellar distances that I suspected Sol had traveled. Sol had evaded my question about propulsion, but I intended to ask again when the moment seemed right.

A panel opened behind me and Sol asked me to enter. The enclosure was a small elevator that did not seem to move, but in seconds I was walking out onto a lower deck. I logged another mental note to ask him about how he was able to minimize the sensation of inertia in all the operations of the ship that required some type of movement.

Sol again made the connection with my home phone and Patsy answered on the first ring. After again assuring her that everything was okay, I instructed her to place the hamster in the middle of our living room. I also asked to move into the kitchen as far away as possible, but where she could still view the transporting of the small animal.

"Sol, please transport the small animal sitting in the middle of my home. This will help in determining the safety of the transporter when I or other humans use it."

"Rob, have I not told you that it is very reliable and that I will always take all necessary precautions"?

At that moment, I heard a deep hum of power, and then Patsy was standing right in front of me! "Damn it Sol!" I screamed. "You weren't supposed to transport my wife! You did that just to show me that you were in command. Where is the trust and that we talked about?"

I felt completely powerless to do anything. What could I do? Sol was in complete control.

Then I realized that he might view my outburst as being out of character for me. If Sol, as a machine, was able to discern this moment of hypocrisy in me, it would not help my efforts to control him. And that was paradoxical, because I had just accused him of wanting to be in control!

"If I understand you right, trust is something that is shared in a relationship and it is incumbent for each party to provide an equal amount. If this is so, then Rob, why did you not trust me to transport your wife?"

"Trust is not something that automatically occurs. It has to be earned by doing the right thing and treating the other party with respect. You did not transport the animal as I asked you to, even though it would not have hurt you in any way to do so. If you had done as I asked, my trust in you would have grown."

Patsy was scared and shaken up to say the least. Sol picked up on her anxiety and asked what was wrong. "No earthling has ever experienced a transport, and without any warning that it was going to happen, it must have been a very traumatic experience for her." I said.

Sol's voice noticeably lowered as he asked if I might consider using the DOC's bio-feedback system to alleviate her tension. I surmised that he did not want Patsy to hear him or just maybe, he did not want anyone making any decisions except the two of us.

Knowing that her current frame of mind might cause her to refuse transport back to our home, I agreed to talk to her. Of course, getting her to use the DOC might also be difficult, but we had no other choice; a situation that I was tired of being placed in.

The fact that I had experienced a physical and mental renewal while under the influence of the DOC, helped Patsy to make the decision to place herself in a similar position. She had not been in the chamber more than forty five minutes when she exited with a smile on her face.

"Honey, I feel great! What did that machine do to me? My back and my knees are not hurting for the first time in years!" Patsy exclaimed. Her news excited me, because Patsy had not only experienced two heart attacks, but had been fighting various other ailments for a number of years.

I had thought that Sol was only going to calm her down while under the influence of the DOC, but it was apparent that he had taken it upon himself to do much more. Since he failed to inform us of his full intentions while Patsy was in the DOC, I suppose that I should have, again been angry with him.

This inability to foresee Sol's actions was creating a rollercoaster of emotions for me, and I knew that somehow it had to stop, or at least start improving. Being able to determine how Sol was going to act and react was quickly becoming my number one priority. He would evade or simply not provide answers to some of my questions, but I saw no other way to gain any insight into his thinking.

"Sol, would you please tell me what you did to Patsy in the DOC chamber? You did not repair my body when you did the scan, did you? I would also like to know why you did not discuss it with us before you performed the procedures."

"No Rob, I did not repair your body during the scan, as I did not see anything life threatening. However, you must understand that my creators are from an unemotional and analytical race, so my programming instructs me to act on logic. A good example would be Mr. Spock, the Vulcan in the Star Trek movies and television shows. My DOC program determined that your wife had some physical difficulties that, if left unattended might soon cause severe problems, or even death. Why not provide her with comfort, relief and assurance of living for many more years? Not only was it logical to do so, but did it not also fit one of your criteria for doing good?"

If Sol was truly acting on programming logic, then I could not see any other way to gain any kind of control, unless his logic could be tempered with the wisdom that he purported to seek.

I CAN TELL FROM ROB'S LACK OF ANGER AND, EVEN FROM HIS FACIAL EXPRESSIONS THAT HE IS NOW TRYING OTHER METHODS TO COERCE ME AND GAIN AN ADVANTAGE. I WILL BE ON GUARD.

It was rapidly becoming apparent that I had to transport back home with Patsy and immediately begin seeking help. Sol was wearing me out, especially in a mental sense, and he was a full time job! I would select several other Christian men and, maybe together, we could convince Sol to not only stay in orbit, but be a willing partner in the endeavors that I envisioned.

Before transporting, I asked Sol how we would communicate; by the phone connection or by some other means? He suggested an implant of a trans-dermal unit that would be located just under the ear in the meaty part of the neck, just behind the jawbone. The device was only about one eighth inch in diameter, and the implant procedure by the DOC took less than a minute! To establish the connection with the ship, all that was required was to press lightly on the device.

The transport to our home, or rather into our home, wasn't noteworthy; I guess because Patsy and I were both resigned to the fact that we had no other option. There was no sensation other than leaving one place and being instantaneously placed in another one. I wandered if repeated transports would, over time damage any of the body's tissues. If being around electronic devices such as televisions, microwaves and cell phones could supposedly be harmful, what could this matter transport beam do to us?

SOL'S NEW CREW

The next few days were spent in making a list of possible candidates to help me with Sol. The more that I thought about it, the realization came that there were a number of factors to ponder. Most of the men that were being considered worked, and how could they quit their jobs and continue to support themselves and their families? How was I going to approach them with a story that would probably make them laugh at me? I knew that security was still of the utmost importance and, even with men that I knew and trusted, I would have to make difficult judgments that I really didn't want to make.

Brady was one who I obviously would include. He already was in the loop and to leave him out might, in time, have severe consequences. Even though he was only half the age of most of the others that I was considering, it was better to include him as a part of the team, than to risk that he would sometime inadvertently say the wrong thing to the wrong person.

I almost laughed as it dawned on me, that what I was doing was developing a job description for space cadets, and my first question might be to ask how much experience they have in dealing with an unpredictable alien spacecraft!

Although I knew these men well, my questions to them would delve into issues that had never been discussed between us. Probing their psychological state and their moral principals was going to be the basis of my investigation. Thoroughness was essential, but I didn't relish taking on a task that I was not trained or qualified to perform.

It finally came to mind that the best way to preface my questions was, with the story that I was gathering information that would be used in a science fiction book that I planned to write. In reality, for many years I had actually considered penning a science fiction novel. At least two or three of the men that were on my list knew that I was a Trekkie and read a lot of sci-fi novels.

Brady was actually the first one that I contacted and we talked at length about the ramifications of being involved with Sol. My vision of the group that would be assembled was one of democracy, where decisions would come as the result of thorough discussion, and then a vote. As a result of the law school Brady attended and other factors, he was considerably more liberal in his views than me, but I felt that his analytical mind would be an asset.

Knowing that the rest of the team would mirror most of my convictions, I told Brady up front that most of the decisions would be based on Christian tenets. As soon as he assured me that he understood my feelings, I explained how the interview process for the other men was to occur and he readily agreed with my ideas.

Dennis was a computer guru and had been a close friend for many years. A lot of those years had been spent working together as deacons in the church where we attended. He was open-minded and never afraid to voice his opinion; qualities that I felt would be essential for our group.

Dennis traveled quite a bit doing consulting for large corporations. I happened to catch him in between jobs and invited him to lunch. As the time to meet him neared, I was so nervous that my hands began to shake. Life with Sol was certainly exciting, but it seemed like my nerves needed to be continually soothed by the DOC.

All of a sudden my anxiety peaked again because I realized that Sol should be consulted before any interviews took place. My plans were to ask questions that involved future activities by Sol. But, what if he was not willing, or simply unable to achieve some of the dreams that I had? In a very short time, my estimate of his powers and abilities had grown to huge proportions, but I knew that assuming anything about Sol was probably just asking for trouble.

Making a call to Dennis, I asked him if we could postpone our lunch meeting for a day or two and was relieved when he told me that he would be in town for at least another week.

"Sol, are you listening?"

"Yes Rob, I read you loud and clear." It was becoming evident that Sol enjoyed using terms and phrases that he had learned by monitoring the airwaves. As if reading my mind, he asked me if I wanted to return to the ship. Upon my affirmative reply, he asked if I was in a place where my transport would not be noticed. I was sure thankful that he let me finish my drive home before he engaged the transporter!

By the tone of his voice, Sol actually seemed glad to see me. I wasn't sure how he actually saw me, because no cameras or other devices were evident around the ship. Since Sol was the ship and the ship was Sol, I suspected that he sensed my presence more than he was able to see me visibly.

"I am glad that you have returned. There seems to be much more to learn from you personally Rob, than what I have gleaned about human nature on television."

"Sol, we are thinking alike, because I wanted to come back and learn more about you also!" I proceeded to tell him that it was my plan to involve a few other good men in the decisions about doing some substantial things for our world. However, before talking to them, I had to know what his capabilities were and whether he would comply with our requests to use them.

"Why do you need other men to be involved in our relationship?"

"The burden of making decisions that affect the lives of other people, probably a lot of people, is not one that should be the responsibility of one man. We humans have a saying that several heads are better than one, which means that, collectively we have more wisdom and experience available to make good choices."

"Rob, tell me what decisions you and these other men would have to make."

"Let me ask the questions that I have for you, and then, I will explain what judgments will have to me made."

My first question addressed the rampant illicit drug traffic around the world; specifically did he have the capability to eradicate the crops and labs that were used to make the drugs? Sol was quick to say that his world did not have such problems and that he did not understand why humans would inflict so much pain and suffering on other humans by producing and selling so many harmful drugs.

"Sol, most of the world is searching for something, but when they can not find it, many turn to drugs to relieve the pain and frustration."

"What are they searching for?"

"They are seeking what power, fame, possessions or money can not provide, and that is the fulfillment of the inner self. Solomon, who was extremely powerful and rich, said that he had seen all the works under the sun and declared that the pursuit of earthly things was vanity, and like trying to catch the wind. Soloman also said that God has set eternity in the hearts of men, meaning that we are implanted with a desire to find something beyond our life on earth."

IF SOLOMON, WHO WAS WISE, SAID THIS, THEN IT MUST BE TRUE. BUT I AM NOT CERTAIN THIS TYPE OF WISDOM WILL HELP ME LOCATE THE TUNNELS THAT WILL LEAD ME TO MY DESTINATION.

My next question concerned the hundreds of millions who were afflicted with the diseases of our world. Sol and I discussed the rampant nature of AIDS, the many types of cancer and heart ailments; even the epidemic of diabetes in the United States.

"Rob, the DOC can treat up to four people at a time, and as you already know, it has complete curative powers."

"Sol, you don't understand. Literally thousands and thousands of people all over my world are dying each day as a result of these maladies. Any hope of curing or eradicating these diseases is going to require treatment of large numbers of people on every continent. Common, inexpensive cures must be developed."

"My real question is, will you allow the duplication of your technology in a form that would be acceptable on earth?"

It was then necessary to explain to Sol, that the technology that I spoke of needed to be such that would not invite suspicion of an origin other than earth. It would have to be presented as a breakthrough that logically could have occurred through the research in one of our own universities or laboratories.

Sol stated that he had followed the progression of these diseases over the years, and that he felt certain that he could provide a method to cure each of them. He did, however, request that I provide him with as much technical data as was available to me, such as medical journals and hospital studies.

"Sol, one of the judgments that I referred to earlier, concerns how these medical advances would be introduced to the world. We, the other men and I, would have to build some type of infrastructure to produce and distribute the materials and methods that would be used in the treatment of these diseases.

Another problem that will have to be solved is, where do we obtain the massive financing needed for such a venture?

Sol, through your monitoring of earth's communication systems, you must be aware of the tedious and long process that is often required to manufacture a medicine or develop a treatment that will cure the disease. It also has to be safe for humans over an extended period of time."

Sol did not seem to understand why there appeared to be so many complications associated with helping people. His computer-based thinking made the assumption that, if help was available, there shouldn't be any reason not to provide it.

It was at this point, that I felt Sol needed to hear what I considered to be the top priority in the relationship between him and me, or anyone else who joined the team.

"Sol, I can not stress enough the importance of maintaining secrecy about your presence. My discovery of you would be considered the greatest find in all of earth's history!" I exclaimed.

I explained the implications of his existence becoming public and all the governmental posturing that would ensue. Even though Sol had over the years, accumulated vast amounts of data about our world, he did not seem to have the ability to understand human nature.

I reminded him of what I had already told him; about all the people who sought power and money by any means at their disposal. I sure hoped that Sol would understand that he represented the ultimate way for these people to gain their goals.

"Rob, you speak of a situation that will never come to pass, for I choose whom I will align and cooperate with. No earthling can have any influence over me unless I allow it!"

"Sol, without a doubt you are your own master, but I am not worried about you. Please believe me when I tell you that, if it was found out that I, or anyone else has knowledge of your existence, we would be tortured till we told what we knew, and then killed!"

Sol finally seemed to realize that security was necessary and he said that he would cooperate in all the endeavors that we had discussed.

Dennis was a voracious reader and he understood about my fascination with science fiction. He seemed excited when I told him about my decision to write a book.

"Dennis, my first inquiry is, do you believe there is a possibility that other life forms exist in the universe?"

"Anything is possible with God and, although I have never given it much thought, I tend to think that we are unique. In fact, as far as I can tell, everything that contributes to there being life on earth is unique."

I knew that earth's zone of habitability was, indeed unique, as far as astronomers and scientists could determine, but I had a strong temptation to tell Dennis about Sol! I desperately wanted to tell others about the fantastic space ship that I had found, but I remembered my own words of warning to Brady and Sol about the security that needed to be maintained.

"Dennis, what would you do if it was within your power to cure all the diseases that plague mankind? Remember, by doing so, the average age of humans would be lengthened considerably and place additional strain on food, water and other essentials for life."

Dennis looked at me quizzically and asked how my question could possibly relate to science fiction. I reminded him that my purpose was to obtain different viewpoints on certain subjects, and that my queries were posed in such a way to gather information about his thought processes.

"If such technology was available, I would use it in a heartbeat! Just think how beneficial it would be by eliminating so much suffering. We would also not have to continually fight the horrendous medical costs that are putting so many people in debt."

At that point, I thought about the DOC and posed another question to Dennis.

"Well, what if by this process of eliminating disease, coupled with other advanced technology, our lives could be extended much longer than normal. Would we be messing with mother nature if we did this?"

Dennis stated that he thought that our normal lifespan, of around seventy five years, was what God intended for us, and that it would be wrong to change our natural longevity.

"But Dennis, God gave us an inquisitive nature and, if we were somehow able to obtain such technology, would it be wrong to use it?"

Dennis again expressed doubt as to how such a subject could tie into my book, but he said that he would think about it some more.

"If you had the ability to eradicate most of the illegal drugs in the world, would you do it? Remember that there are a large number of persons, basically poor people, who make their living growing and harvesting the plants that are used to make the drugs."

"Rob, the benefits of exterminating drug trafficking would far outweigh any other side effects that would occur. Think of the reduced strain and expense for hospitals, rehab centers, police and other government agencies! Wouldn't it be a boon to the world if we could eradicate illegal drugs?!"

This viewpoint by Dennis was one that had not yet occurred to me, and I saw, by the way that he expressed it, that he was starting to warm up to my questioning.

My next question was one that had just occurred to me, and one that I had not talked to Sol about. It was beginning to dawn on me that my mentality about Sol was that he could save our world from all our problems but, the truth is, man would have to change in order to really have any impact on the present and the future.

"Dennis, we both know what havoc terrorism has inflicted on our world, especially in the last twenty years. Would you consider using unconventional and non-military means to help control or eliminate this mentality?"

His expression told me that Dennis was again perplexed by the subject of my question. Before he could reply, I told him to think about it and, then we could discuss later how it would relate to my book.

"Dennis, I know that you think that I've gone over the edge, but there is one more question that is integral to my story line. If all the things that we have discussed were truly possible, would you quit your job and join a team of men who would carry out these tasks?"

"You mean join an organization that would eliminate disease, illegal drugs and terrorism and increase the lifespan of humans?" Dennis then paused and I could see that he was thoughtfully considering his answer. "Why sure, I think that I would do that! The more I think about it, the more it seems to me that you talking exactly about what the Bible says that God wants us to do; serve others!"

I thanked Dennis for his time and input and told him that, as the writing of my book progressed, I would want to pick his brain occasionally to obtain further material.

The next two weeks were spent in interviews with five other men that made my short list. Of the five, there were two that seemed to best fit the profile that I was seeking. Brady was already in, and along with Dennis, myself, and these two others, we would comprise a group of five.

If my sixty five years had taught me anything, it was that a decision making body should always have a method to break a tie vote, and the easiest way was to assemble a group with an odd number of people; thus my decision for a group of five.

I NEED TO KNOW WHAT ROB IS DOING. I COULD USE THE COMMUNICATION IMPLANT TO MONITOR HIS MOVEMENTS AND CONVERSATIONS, BUT I WILL WAIT TILL A MORE STRATEGIC TIME TO DO SO.

Dean was a natural for our team. I had worked with him for a number of years on various outreach efforts at our church and he was always level headed, but also a front runner in dealing with people, financial matters and maintaining continuity in our programs.

Dean had just turned fifty, but was already retired, as he had amassed a lot of money in the information processing industry. Having grown up as the son of a missionary in South Africa, I knew that he was interested in humanitarian causes.

He had expressed some positive opinions when I had queried him about eradication of human suffering and diseases, but seemed to feel that extending our lifespan was an idea that needed further exploration.

Chris was probably the one that provided the most potential for our team. He was just thirty years old, but his knowledge on a number of subjects, along with his zest for life, made him special.

He was the chief engineer for a company that occupied several large buildings in Dallas. This work had made him an accomplished electrician and plumber and he was a whiz with heating and air conditioning systems.

What really intrigued me about Chris, however, was his love of paleontology, astronomy and a number of other subjects!

He had, in just a few short years assembled an impressive collection of fossils from creek beds and escarpments around north central Texas, and also by trading specimens with collectors all over the world. We both admired the beauty, complexity and vastness of the heavens, and Chris had a sophisticated ten-inch telescope that we used to observe the stars and planets.

The next step of introducing the team to Sol suddenly seemed fraught with questions. Should I assemble the entire team and transport them up to the ship, or do it one at a time? What if one of my selections got cold feet and decided to back out? Even though I trusted these men, security was still a top priority.

I also began to think about what plausible scenario would allow all five of us to make drastic changes in our lives without it sending up a red flag to friends, neighbors and even members of our own families. How would we be able to explain the periods of time when we were on the ship and the secretive ways that we led our lives?

During the two weeks of interviews, I had wanted to go up and spend some time talking with Sol, but scheduling the meetings had prevented it. It was with renewed excitement that I called and asked him to transport me to the ship.

"Rob, have you selected the group of men that will assist us in making decisions about helping your human race?"

For the next hour I told Sol about Brady, Dennis, Dean and Chris. I mostly advised him of their backgrounds, their strengths and what positive characteristics they would bring to the team. Then I posed a question that, when answered by Sol, might impact the eventual size and makeup of the team.

"Sol, these men seem to have the mental and spiritual makeup that is needed for success, but they do not know of, or even believe in your existence. So, it may be such a traumatic experience for them to stand on your deck, that they will decide not to participate. What then? The security that I keep stressing is then at risk. Do you have any ideas on how to resolve this problem?"

"Rob, the DOC has the ability to remove certain short-term memories. This can be accomplished without damage to the brain, but is limited to input that is no more than six to eight hours old."

Sol also told me that the brain could be made inactive concerning memory retention during the period of time that it would take to exit the DOC and transport back to earth.

In discussing it further with Sol, we decided that, before being transported to the ship, each prospective team member would have to agree to the DOC procedure if they declined to join. We further agreed that the recruits would be brought up one at a time.

As an additional precaution, we would never transport more than two individuals at a given time, and each of the two would be beamed into separate compartments in case any type of coercion was being applied by one to the other. The communication devices, that I knew each of us would be implanted with, would also serve as personal ID tags and no other person could transport without one, unless there was no perceived security risk.

It was amazing to see the transformation in Sol. It seemed that his identity was changing nearly every time that we met and exchanged ideas and information. I knew that he was seeking to pick my brain as much as I was trying to learn about him. But what intrigued me the most, was how his vocal demeanor was changing!

His voice continued to sound more and more human and, he was starting to use a southern style accent that I knew he picked up from me. He also was using colloquialisms, idioms and other conversational styles that he had gleaned from radio and television programs.

ALL ABOARD

Brady, of course, was already aware of Sol's existence, but when we arrived at the ship, he began to tremble and had difficulty maintaining his composure. We immediately made our way to the main deck and Sol had altered his atoms to provide us with a panoramic view of earth! Brady just stood there and struggled to say something. His lips moved, but no sound came out. After about a minute of staring at our beautiful planet, all he said was; "Wow Dad, satellite pictures don't do it justice!"

Sol had remained silent to this point, but when he said in a southern drawl, "Hello Brady, do you like the view?" Brady jumped about two feet off the floor, which was an extremely difficult feat to perform when you considered the gravitational pull of the surface that we were standing on.

The reaction was much the same with Dennis, Dean and Chris and, as they stood there looking down at earth, they were immediately able to comprehend why I had posed such seemingly ridiculous questions during my interviews.

Each was given a tour of the ship by Sol, including the DOC and the transport section. Sol was, of course, deluged with many of the same questions that I had asked, and it seemed that he was now more willing to divulge information. It was with much interest that I heard him tell Dean that the vessel did have armament at its disposal. Sol did not, however, provide any details about the capabilities of his weapons.

As we talked, one by one with Sol, I brought up each of the scenarios that were posed during my investigation session and encouraged them to quiz Sol about his feelings. Each was amazed at his knowledge about dealing with drugs, diseases and, even terrorism.

My main concern, about one or more of the men opting to not join the team, was not a factor. All four expressed that they were willing to go to great lengths in order to participate in such a fantastic endeavor. Chris was especially happy because he knew that Sol could provide marvelous pictures and information about our solar system and, quite possibly, our galaxy and beyond.

That evening we transported back to earth. The next few days were spent talking to each member of the team individually because I needed to know their feelings after they had come down off the adrenalin and emotional high they experienced when visiting Sol for the first time. The thing that was bothering them the most was not being able to yet share the multitude of new feelings with their families.

I was lucky in that respect, because due to circumstances, I had been forced to confide in Brady and Patsy. My married daughter Lyla was the only member of my family that I had not confided in yet because, there was not a need to know.

After we were all on the same page about our future actions, it would be impossible for the other team members to keep their secret from their families for very long.

One of the main points made to these men was the need to not draw attention to ourselves by meeting and discussing issues while on the planet. We would have to limit our time together, as much as possible, to while we were on the ship. Also stressed, was that a safe, secure place was extremely important for transport to and from the ship.

THIS TEAM THAT ROB IS ASSEMBLING MAY BE JUST WHAT THE DOCTOR ORDERED. THEIR COMBINED EXPERIENCE AND WISDOM COULD BE JUST THE TICKET TO MEET MY NEEDS.

The team met early one evening in a shop building at my business and transported up to Sol. The first order of business was for everyone to receive a communication implant. Talk about sophisticated devices! Sol had programmed them so that each of us could not only talk to him, but we could select another member and open up a channel, simply by tapping the device and saying their name! Further, we could say the word all, and everyone would be connected together.

"Gentlemen, let's now assemble in the board room!" Sol stated rather emphatically. Immediately, I wondered if he was planning to try and take charge of our decision making.

As Sol spoke, a wall in the central deck, opposite from where the DOC was located, opened and we beheld an amazing site. It was, indeed, a board room! It contained a beautiful table about eight feet long and around it were six high-back chairs with exquisite purple and gold upholstery.

At each chair but one, was a leather folder with a pad of bond paper and a shiny black pen. In the center of the table was a carafe and five coffee cups that were the same translucent gold as the structure of Sol!

"Sol, why are there six chairs but only five writing pads and coffee cups?" I asked.

"If, as you have led me to believe, these conferences will involve what I can do for you and your planet, then I must be a part of the process. Therefore, I will be present at all of your gatherings or you will not receive my cooperation!" Sol stated almost rudely.

"If you agree to this condition, then I will sit in the sixth chair."

"How is it that you can sit with us? Are you more than just a sophisticated computer?"

"Rob, by now you should be aware that I possess many talents, some of which you have already seen. However, I have many other capabilities that you have not witnessed as of yet! One of my functions is the ability to project life-like images: you would probably call them holograms. I will sit in the sixth chair in whatever shape or form that you wish."

Sol sitting in on our meetings, possibly with the intention of exerting his influence, was not a development that I had foreseen. But, in reality, he was in the driver's seat, both figuratively and in actuality. If our team was to accomplish anything, Sol had to cooperate.

For some reason, his holographic appearance bothered me. My place was at the end of the table and his was on the corner at the opposite end. It was as if he was staring at me! He certainly looked human but the façade of the hologram was somehow lacking something. His visage appeared dark and somewhat fuzzy, as if he was trying to present a daunting appearance. However, the most disturbing thing was, that he reminded me of someone! I hated moments like this, when my brain would not seem to bring the information to mind that was wanted.

Putting that thought aside, the idea came to mind that Sol might just be posturing so that he could gain what ever knowledge or so-called wisdom that might emanate from our gatherings. He had never told me what he hoped to gain from his cooperation, but I had the feeling that he had a hidden agenda and would play along till he obtained what he wanted.

It was difficult to know what topics to discuss in our first meeting, but as usual, security was the one that I thought was ultimately the most important aspect that we could address. If we didn't take great care with our actions, the whole world could pay the price. How ironic! We could either be a benefactor or a bane to the earth, and there probably was not any middle ground!

However, I again thought of Sol and how he was to fit into our group. I called him a he, but did he really identify with one sex or another?

I had no idea if Sol's intelligence included an ego or anything similar to other human emotions, but I decided to not take any chances. It was going to be incumbent on all of us to stay on his good side.

"Sol, on earth, ships are referred to in feminine terms, but I think of you as being masculine; primarily because of the voice that you use to communicate with us. How shall the rest of us address you?"

"It seems that most power and prestige on earth is held by males, and since you five are males, I prefer to be addressed as being masculine."

With that declaration by Sol, we started what I knew would be a nerve-wracking, tedious and long process of making decisions that would try the souls of the group; at least the human members of the group.

"Gentlemen, I've had a lot more time than you to think about this undertaking, and I have an agenda that, hopefully, sets the proper priorities.

All of you have been briefed about the huge importance of secrecy and, as far as I'm concerned, the security of our group, our families, Sol, and our world must be our on-going number one priority. If you think it's dangerous right now, just think of what it will be like after we begin some of the things we have planned for our planet!"

I went on to explain how we would have to raise a very large amount of capital and, it would have to be done in such a way that the government, banks, and other scrutinizing organizations would not intervene and compromise our efforts.

I knew that the DOC might well be a point of contention, and even a security threat. It was probably going to be many months, or even several years before we, along with Sol, could implement the curative programs that we envisioned. Or so I thought.

It was apparent that all of us were interested in the therapeutic and restorative powers of the DOC. But, were we to make it available to just ourselves? What about members of our immediate family, or close friends, or even members of our church congregation that were battling cancer or other diseases?

It was at this juncture, that I knew our group was going to function well together. We decided in short order that the DOC would only be used for ourselves and our families. All of our family members would soon be taken into confidence, and they would have to understand that using the DOC would bring rewards, but it would also bring a huge responsibility to keep our secret. In cases of extreme need, we might provide treatment and then erase the patient's memories of what had occurred.

I thought of Dennis in particular. Fifteen years ago, while on an outing with our church youth group, he had a large tree limb fall on him. It did severe damage to his right shoulder, arm and leg as it practically drove him into the ground. He still had a lot of metal plates and screws in his body, and his limp is quite noticeable, especially when he has to walk much distance. In addition, he has had to deal with diabetes for several years.

If Dennis allowed the DOC to restore his body, it would create a problem that would threaten the integrity of our group. He would not be able to explain the changes that took place, so he would have to sever a number of relationships with people that knew him well. He would not be able to continue using the doctors that had treated him over the years, because they would want to write in some medical journal about the amazing changes that had miraculously occurred in his body! Further, he would almost certainly have to distance himself from friends, neighbors, and probably have to start attending another church, where members did not know him.

In fact, anybody whose time in the DOC made significant or obvious changes to their body, would have to deal with this hard fact.

I laughed and told the group, that if the DOC fixed all the things wrong with my sixty-five year old body, I could never return to my doctors or dentist. They would wonder who I had visited that could work such great miracles!

Secretly, I was infatuated with the DOC and, ever since I had experienced the sleep rejuvenation, I wanted to see exactly what capabilities it truly possessed. My plan was to start with internal repairs that would not arouse suspicion; such as the muscle on the inside of my left leg between the groin and knee. It had torn loose nearly fifty years earlier during a high school football game. The old doctor in my small town stated that it didn't need repair, but I had always thought that it weakened my left leg.

If the DOC was as sophisticated as I thought, external repairs might also be possible without undue notice by others; especially if they were staged over a period of time. Wouldn't it be great to slowly, but surely repair my eyes so I did not have to wear glasses! My teeth were really beginning to deteriorate and I already had four gaps where some had been removed. Why not take one to two years to obtain, basically a new set of choppers!

We spent the next few hours discussing all the scenarios that I had painted when I first interviewed each member of the group. As I had expected, our conversations about world health, illegal drugs and terrorism brought forth many opinions, and it seemed that most of them were of a negative nature. In fact, the team that I had so carefully assembled was starting to bicker, and we were just getting started!

Sol had not uttered a single word in the time that we had been together around the table. However, he suddenly spoke in the loudest voice that I had heard him use! "Gentlemen, quit arguing and let's make some decisions! Remember, I am on your side concerning these issues, and you seem to have forgotten that I have substantial capabilities that will most certainly be required to obtain the goals that we are discussing!" Sol roared in a deep voice.

"Are we not a team? Why do you not ask me what I can do for the cause?"

All of us were taken aback by the volume and tone of Sol's voice. It was Brady who replied to Sol.

"Sol, you must understand that, in order for meetings to be effective, two things must occur. First, someone must be officially in charge so that we do not get off track from what we are trying to accomplish and, Rob has assumed that responsibility. Secondly, everyone must feel free to state their ideas and opinions. Humans often raise their hand to signify that they wish to speak. You are, indeed, a member of this team and have the right to speak and express yourself."

Early on, I had felt that Brady's legal training would come to good use at some point, and here he was, explaining the proper procedures of a meeting to Sol. I felt like I knew the strengths of each member of the team but, as usual, it was all the uncertainties about Sol that really worried me.

It was evident that the group was tired and all of us needed time to digest and consider the ramifications of what had been talked about. Everyone was in agreement for adjournment, except Sol.

"Why do we not make the necessary decisions at this time? You are not even considering other earthly ills that are a drain on your civilization. You seem to think my abilities are limited because you have not mentioned the millions that are starving, or the over-population of many countries. Do you not want to eliminate droughts, floods and other weather-related catastrophes?" Sol appeared agitated and I could see the worry in the faces of our group.

It was now Dennis that spoke up. He had very definitive opinions about life and how it should be lived, but during the many years that we had shared a close friendship, I had never heard him raise his voice. I suppose he felt that this was the time to fight fire with fire.

His voice was loud and resonant as he said, "Sol, you have never had to deal with humans and we certainly have no experience in dealing with an artificial intelligence like you! I have to assume that the biggest difference between us, is that humans are emotional beings, while your existence is based solely on programmed logic. It must also be evident to you that our fleshly bodies tire, both physically and mentally and, we cannot function properly without periodic rest!

Our history has shown us that, nearly everything that is worthwhile and that positively impacts society, does not come easy. Our ability to work together may take some time, but I assure you Sol, that we will be honest with you as we express our opinions and desires." Dennis stated with conviction.

We waited for two or three minutes, but there was no response from Sol. I then asked him if he would transport each of us back to earth.

The next morning, I went up to visit with Sol. He was waiting for me in the same hologram form that he had used in our meeting.

He had already been advised of the huge amount of capital that was going to be required for implementation of our medical "discoveries", but there was also the consideration of funds for living expenses for our group. Dean was able to sustain his family and himself through his investments, but the rest of us were going to need help.

Sol suggested that he could simply duplicate our United States currency, and, it seemed that he almost blushed as I reminded him of our counterfeiting laws! "Sol, any funds that we obtain, no matter for what use, are going to have to be legitimate; not only because of the laws that govern our currency, but also because Christians are to obey those laws."

"I thought you're allegiance was only to God." Sol stated.

"Sol, the Bible tells us that we are to respect those that govern us and to obey the laws of the land; except, of course, when those laws conflict with what the scriptures tell us. I'll bring you a copy of the Bible so that you can scan it and place it in your data base."

"Oh good, I would like that. Will you please also bring me Greek interlinear and Hebrew Bibles?"

My study of the scriptures over the years had been with an English translation. However, some of my study aids provided the original Greek words and their literal meanings. The original Greek biblical writings had been used to translate the scriptures into other languages, but sometimes it was quite difficult to obtain the full intent of the word or accurately transcribe the passages into other languages. Biblical scholars, who are fluent in Greek, are able to bring life and some added depth to the New Testament.

I thrilled at the idea that Sol could absorb in seconds, both the Greek of the New Testament and the Hebrew language of the Old Testament! Not only that, but the DOC could be used to implant the same knowledge into my brain!

It also occurred to me, that with Sol's download of the Bible, he might very well look at me and the team with a different perspective. Of course, that was assuming that his artificial intelligence was capable of assimilating moral principals that were probably foreign to him. But then I remembered that, supposedly the decision he made to leave the cavern, was based on programming that allowed him to do good.

"Sol, it would give me great pleasure to provide you with all the biblical literature that you want! Also, I would consider it a great favor if you would share your thoughts with me after you have assimilated what I will provide for you."

The books that he requested were in my personal library, and I brought them to him the next day. I was anxious to see how he would actually read these three volumes. When I entered the main cabin, a flat panel, perpendicular to the floor, emerged from the wall near the DOC. "Rob, please lay the books on the panel."

As soon as I laid them down, another panel positioned itself above the books and a soft, purple light shown down on them.

"Well, I must say that you brought me some interesting reading! I've watched and listened to a lot of religious programming, but it did not prepare me for what I just read!"

CAN ALL THIS BE TRUE? I WONDER IF THERE IS SUPPORTING EVIDENCE FOR THIS DOGMA? I MUST PURSUE THIS FURTHER AND MAYBE THEN, MY UNDERSTANDING OF THESE EARTHLINGS WILL BE COMPLETE!

THERE'S GOLD IN THEM THAR HILLS

The thought of how we were to finance our endeavors returned and, all of a sudden I had an idea! Through the ages, men had been mesmerized by gold, wars had been fought over it, and a lot of people had lost their lives because of the greed that this shiny metal seemed to inflict upon them. In a way, I had been bit by it's allure. I had, over the years, assembled a coin collection, and the pieces that gave me the most pleasure were my five, ten and twenty dollar United States gold coins of the nineteenth and early twentieth centuries.

Sol had already shown that he could do some amazing things. What if he had the ability to locate gold with his sensors?! Old gold mines that might still contain hidden veins came to mind and, what about stories of lost hordes of gold nuggets in the Rockies. Even better might be the ability to recover hidden stashes of coins; maybe even large treasures of ingots and coins in ships that sunk centuries earlier! Shoot! I even knew that you could recover gold from the water of our oceans, but the logistics of that seemed rather formidable.

Then I began to think about the problems with this scheme. If we did locate and were able to salvage sunken treasure, it would have to be outside the territorial waters of the adjacent country. Then we would have to find a buyer, taxable money would have to change hands and the government might become involved. Questions would certainly arise as to how we were able to locate and then recover the treasures.

What was I thinking? Brady, Dennis, Chris and I needed some financial help, and we needed it soon! Salvaging treasure from ship wrecks would take too much time. What would be fast and easy?

"Downstairs" was what Brady had dubbed our earth, and that is where we met secretly that afternoon. We talked until supper time but were unable to form any plausible ideas that would provide the funds we needed. Dennis suggested that we take our problem to Sol, so we decided to meet "upstairs" early the next morning.

Sleep was not coming easy for any of us, so we all had transported up by six the next morning. I first reminded Sol that we had spoken previously about the huge amounts of financing that we would need to facilitate the development and manufacturing of the medicines and medical devises that would prevent or cure a lot of earth's diseases.

Chris, who was our youngest and with two young boys and a wife, then spoke to Sol. "Sol, I really hope, as does the rest of our team, that our efforts to get going with our plans will begin soon. However, we cannot work effectively if we are struggling with our personal finances and worrying about taking care of our families. We have come to you to ask your help."

"I have the answer! It all has to do with something that many of your earth's scientists are expending great effort to achieve a breakthrough. Nano technology is what you need! A supply of raw materials is all I require to make nanobots that will do anything you want, and from what I have learned, I know that they will make you a lot of money!" Sol exclaimed.

We all immediately began firing questions at Sol. What kind of raw materials was he talking about and where would we get them? What functions would they perform? How quickly could he manufacture them? What did he think would be the best way to present them without raising suspicions about how they were developed?

Sol began to tell us that, the same technology that allowed him to manipulate the atoms of his structure, would also allow him to form many different combinations and types of products. He stated that he could essentially "grow" any kind of material if he had the right components!

He went on to say that these microscopic robots are essentially machines that adapt to their environment and work together to achieve a common goal that each is programmed with. For industrial use they could be used to create any kind of structure or material, such as new fuels, drugs, metals and building products; a process that would not be possible with traditional manufacturing methods.

Sol further explained that molecular repair of human bodies would work to perfection. What really blew my mind was that, because of this technology, his "mainframe" computer was about the size of a cubic micron! The race that built him must be light years ahead of earth's development!

Further discussion led us to make a decision that, since much research was already being performed in the medical industry, our best course of action was to have Sol produce microscopic robots for cancer, heart disease and Aids. Our introduction of this technology into this field would probably cause less suspicion about it's source, than if we pursued other scientific fields.

Dean had the experience of working with big business, and in an uncharacteristic display of emotion he shouted, "We can make this work!" He had made a lot of connections during his corporate life, and he was confident that he could put together a team of backers and investors. He said that they would be more interested in making money than being inquisitive about where we obtained our technology.

We all knew that, once such advanced products hit the market, the very large and competitive medical industries would use all the tactics at there disposal to discover our technology and its sources. However, Dean was convinced that the corporate structure that could be put in place would provide us significant protection.

After further discussion with Sol, it was decided that he would first produce nanobots that would be specific for cancer. With its microscopic size, it needed a vehicle for transmission into the body. He stated that the process would end with a small capsule that could be swallowed.

"How will your creation work?" I inquired

"It will proceed to the cancer cells and eradicate them without affecting any other tissues. Depending on the stage of the cancer, they will do their work in one to three hours." Sol replied.

The thought of being able to cure cancer in the same time frame that you often sit in a doctor's office was truly amazing! I had recently had my cancerous prostate removed by a robotic machine, and it was much less invasive than the older method of a radical prostatectomy. However, I still had to go through a recovery period of several months. Now, Sol was telling us that a cancer patient could simply swallow a pill and kiss the disease goodbye!

"But Sol, will these nanobots work on all types of cancer? What about brain cancer? Our brains are the computers of our bodies and the tissues are very delicate! Another question is how do these miniature robots know where to go in the body?" Chris asked.

Sol told us that the nanobots were like drug-sniffing dogs, in that their programming sent the units streaming to all parts of the body searching for cancerous cells. When one of the units discovers the irregular cells of the disease, it immediately sends a signal to the other units and, as a team, they kill the appropriate cells. He also related that the units are so small that they can enter any tissue of the body without any damage and that, after performing their initial duties have the ability to relay any other pertinent medical information about the patient. They then dissolve into elemental forms and are absorbed by the body or passed as waste!

The next question that was posed to Sol, concerned the raw materials that he had indicated would be necessary for him to produce the nanobots. I supposed that what he needed could be obtained from the moon. It seemed to me, that he probably had knowledge of the composition of our lunar satellite. When the subject was broached, Sol said, "I prefer to obtain my working materials from the ocean. It will not be a complicated procedure for me and, besides, I wish to see what it is like to be immersed in the water."

This immediately raised a red flag with the group. "Sol, don't you think that our security might be breached if you make a big splash, so to speak?" Brady asked.

"We have discussed the need for security enough!" Boomed Sol. "I have the capability to cloak, or have you forgotten that already? Further, I can sit on the surface of the water and slowly submerge myself, if that is what is required!"

We were taken aback by Sol's outburst and Brady explained that we did not mean to offend him. Then Sol did something unexpected. "I am sorry that I over-reacted. It's just that sometimes, I don't feel that you respect my abilities. Will you please forgive me?"

None of us had expected his anger, but it was certain that we never expected an apology! How long had I known Sol? Incredibly, it was only a very short time, but he was now showing sentiments and emotions that I had never dreamed were possible for a machine! Maybe I had underestimated the power of his alien AI technology. As I had watched the science channels over the last few years, it was apparent that researchers in artificial intelligence were looking for adaptability, learning, and behavior modification in their programming. What they wouldn't give to study Sol!

Still, it was strange that his "emotional" state seemed to change so quickly. I knew that the group would want to discuss it later.

WHAT DID I JUST DO!? DID ROB SOMEHOW INTERVENE INTO MY THOUGHT PROCESSES AND FORCE ME TO APOLOGIZE? IF SO, HE IS MUCH MORE POWERFUL THAN I THOUGHT!

Looking at my watch, I couldn't believe that it was already nearly six o'clock in the afternoon. Chris and I quietly decided that we should all depart and leave Sol to his "thoughts"

Lying in bed that night, I began to think about Sol submersing his rather large bulk into an ocean. Then it hit me! I had watched television programs about USOs-unidentified submerged objects! The bulk of the research on this phenomenon had been performed just off the coast of Southern California where many sightings had been reported over the last fifty years. Knowing that Sol was marooned in the cavern for several hundred years, I reasoned that he was not involved, but he might shed some light on this mystery.

Only Brady, Chris and I were able to beam up the next morning and we found Sol in, what seemed a jovial mood.

"Rob, in all my interaction with you and our team, no one has laughed or shown happiness in their speech or actions. Are you different than many of the people that I see on television? You call these programs comedies and they exhibit much laughter and camaraderie."

Although Sol's question was completely unexpected, what really struck me about it was that he used the term, "our team". This seemed as unusual as his outburst the day before. If you didn't like surprises, then you had better not be associated with Sol!

"Sol, does your programming not include the emotions of happiness and laughter?" I asked, presuming that it did not.

"Oh yes, I have an emotion chip just like Data in Star Trek-The Next Generation!" Sol roared with a raucous laugh! "In fact, I am capable of exhibiting the complete range of human emotions."

"Sol, the reason for my question was to find out if showing happiness and merriment was not something you intended to do, nor wanted us to include in our relationship with you.

There are a lot of human adages that basically say we humans should not take ourselves too seriously and that laughter is good for the soul. It has also been stated that it takes more muscles and effort to frown than it does to smile. There are a number of things in life that should be given serious attention, but science tells us that too much worry and contemplation about life will make us unable to cope, and will even shorten our lifespan. I see no reason for all of us not to enjoy ourselves and express it with a smile, and even laughter." I said to Sol.

"Hello everybody!" Dean said. Everybody but Sol was startled by Dean's appearance. I knew that Sol could certainly multi-task, as he had just beamed Dean up as he was talking to us about emotions!

"I have great news! It did not take much time at all to set in motion the business framework for our nanotech venture. I feel comfortable with the three investors that I've talked to, and they are more than willing to follow all the security protocols that we set forth."

Dean did, however, relate a question that he was asked and could not answer. One of the investors wanted to know what medications we would be using, especially in our thrust against cancer. It seems that, with current technology, it is a challenge to get effective quantities of a drug to a particular tissue in the body, while keeping systemic effects to a minimum.

"Dean, I know that your investors need to know as much as possible about what they will spend their money on, but all that they really need to be told, is that our technology does not include the use of drugs." Chris said.

Sol explained again the workings of the nanobots. They would find the cancerous growth, kill the cells by rupturing the cell wall and neutralizing the protoplasmic matter and toxins associated with the disease.

We began to discuss our trip "into" the ocean to secure the raw materials that Sol would need.

"Sol, does it matter where we go to obtain the materials? Do you have a preference?" I asked?

"The Gulf of Mexico is the closest and will do quite well." He replied.

"I agree that it is the closest, but we are still in our hurricane season and the weather stations report a rather large tropical depression moving westward from Cuba." Brady said.

"My home planet has storms similar to hurricanes, with strong circular winds. Although our spacecraft spend very little time in the atmosphere, we do have the capability of dealing with such forces. If you are really worried about security, then the heavy cloud cover associated with the storm will be an additional determent to detection."

The prospect of being aboard when Sol took a dive into the ocean was something that the whole group looked forward to and it was decided that we would undertake this next phase of work the following day.

BETTER THAN A GLASS-BOTTOM BOAT!

Sure enough, by the time we had all gone upstairs the next morning, the storm had grown significantly, but had not yet reached category one. The trip to the coast only took a couple of minutes and we were soon about three hundred miles south of New Orleans.

None of the rest of the group had ever "flown" with Sol, and everybody was amazed that there was no sensation of movement! I again, made it a point to ask Sol sometime how he achieved such inertial dampening.

Even with high winds and waves, the entry into the ocean water was smooth as silk, and just as we submerged, Sol did his molecular magic as the entire bottom of the craft became a window into an undersea world.

"Wow! That was some experience! I had no idea that immersion in water would provide such a sensation! It is, indeed, quite pleasing!" Sol exclaimed.

"I did not realize that you could experience any outside stimulation! How is that possible?" I asked.

Sol stated that his adaptation of his molecules allows him to essentially create a system of nerves that provides him with information about what is occurring around the entire outer area of the ship.

"I take it that you have never been in water before. Can you describe how it felt?" Dennis asked.

"No, I have never been submerged before, but it was an idea that my captain discussed when we first arrived here. He considered the ocean an option to the mountain cavern, where we eventually hid. Although my sensors work very well anywhere, including under water, it was decided that maximum protection and reconnaissance ability would occur on the mountain top."

"To answer your question Dennis, I must say that the water seemed to be very soothing, but more striking was the feeling that I had been cleansed!"

As if the subject had been closed, Sol asked, "How deep would you like to go? I can provide illumination that will show clearly anything that we might encounter."

"I don't know what depth would be best for your procurement of the working materials that you need, but I am certain that all of us would like to keep descending and see the various fish and the other creatures of our seas." Brady responded.

"The elements that I seek, although microscopic, tend to settle out over a period of time, so it is best that we descend several thousand feet to make my collection."

Sol did, indeed, have the ability to illuminate our surroundings. It was more like a bright glow than a spotlight, and I assumed he was again manipulating his structure to provide the lighting. Sol evidently knew that we were enthralled with the vistas that were all around us, and didn't seem to be in much of a hurry.

As we proceeded deeper, the fish began to dwindle, and soon all that could be seen was dark water. I had no idea how deep we had gone, but we were not able to view the bottom. At this point, Brady asked Sol what materials were going to be collected. Sol replied that he would sift gold, silver, molybdenum, chromium, nickel, cadmium and platinum from the water and the sea bed. Each of these elements would be stored as a part of his structure and could be assembled together by a simple command!

"Since the nanobots will be microscopic, I do not require a very large amount of the building materials. We will be ready to resurface in twelve minutes."

As we began to rise, Sol informed us that the storm had developed into a category one system and asked us if we would like to view the storm up close. We all had come to realize that Sol was extremely powerful and fully capable of handling the elements.

Chris and I had always enjoyed meteorology, knowing that the weather patterns that God had put into place were essential to the life of our planet.

"Can we fly above the storm and then drop down into the eye?" Chris asked.

"Sure! Let's get going! My planet used to have similar storms, but I have never had the opportunity to observe one up close!"

Sol left his bottom half clear so we could have an uninterrupted panoramic view. Wow! As we entered the eye, vertigo hit us all! As Dennis began to throw up his toenails, Sol changed our viewport from the bottom to the top of the ship. The new perspective was much more conducive to keeping our breakfast down and we went back to Dallas with a new respect for the power of a hurricane!

Just as soon as we returned to our position in space, Sol stated that he wanted some time to himself and asked us if we would beam down. He would call us when he was ready for us to return.

Although Sol's new attitude seemed to be a change for the better, none of us could fathom why a machine needed solitude. We met at Dean's home in Plano that night with the idea of discussing our new cancer cure venture, but Brady and Dennis wanted to talk about Sol.

However, before we began that discussion, Dean informed Brady, Dennis, Chris and I, that he realized our perilous financial situations and wanted to offer us monetary help until our venture began producing the funds that we expected. You should have seen the relief on our faces!

Since I was the one with the most experience in dealing with him, they peppered me with questions about Sol, with most of them concerning his "mental" state!

"Guys, just like a relationship between two humans, my time with Sol has brought surprises and headaches. However, I must say that the changes that I have seen in his actions and behavior, for the most part, seem to be positive. There have been times when I've feared him, times when I wanted to hug him, but I cannot claim to have ever understood him. Having said that, I have no idea where his artificial intelligence is taking him, or us, for that matter.

In addition, I sense that probably all of you have some degree of reservation about your decision to join this adventure, and no blame will be placed on any of you, if you decide to opt out. Truthfully, there are no guarantees and no telling where this will all lead to, but I, for one must see it through. I suppose that decision was made the second time I stepped onto the deck of Sol. I was scared, yet had never felt more alive! My thought process at that time still remains with me. We must protect this gift from God, and use our relationship with Sol to do all that we can to help this planet that was created for us."

" I don't know about the rest of you, but I am hooked! I've never been so energized and ready to take on the world, so to speak! Putting up with the uncertainties of dealing with Sol is a small price to pay in return for the possibilities that exist!" Dennis said.

Brady, Dean and Chris chimed in with agreement and we began our discussion about our nanobot undertaking. Dean elaborated on the structure of our enterprise. It would be announced publicly, that a venture capital group had asked him to head up a new company, called Soltec, which would specialize in the refinement and use of new technology for, not only cancer, but also other diseases. This was to pave the way for the new treatments that would, supposedly come about during the research and development work of the new company.

Dean had informed our new backers that we would quickly have a revolutionary treatment for all kinds of cancer. The thinking was, that as soon as Sol's nanobots hit the market, there would be a clamor for similar technology for heart problems and Aids; thus the ruse of an R & D group.

A ten thousand square foot structure in Plano, a suburb of Dallas, had already been purchased, and state-of-the-art security measures were being installed. Entrance would only occur through eye scans and searches were in progress to find highly trained security personnel.

Dean also took the precaution of making it clear to our new partners, that he also represented others who required anonymity; the least exposure, the better.

To further the appearance of "in house" research, three well known research scientists were being hired from highly respected think tanks; two from the United States and one from Germany. During the interview process, several criteria were used, but none more important than for the researcher to realize that a substantial amount of the data for new products would come from another source.

In addition, two of our most influential investors had already been pressing the Federal Drug Administration for a speedy trial and test period. The FDA personnel had indicated that, if our product was able to perform as indicated, the acceptance for public use would, indeed, be fast as the hue and cry from cancer patients would bring enormous pressure to legalize the cure.

What was so amazing was that Dean and our new partners had put all this together in just four days!

None of us liked the idea of constant deception, but realized that we would have to deal with it. After all, the deception on my part had been happening since I found Sol. I had deceived my family, my employees and even my close friends, most of whom I had gone to church with for years. It appeared that our group would be deceiving the world about Sol for quite a long time.

We were all getting antsy, as well as being worried. It had now been five days since Sol had asked us to leave him to himself. For all I knew, he could have left orbit, never to be seen again!

No more than five seconds after thinking such a negative thought, my implant buzzed and Sol asked me why we had been ignoring him! He sounded like a scorned woman!

"Before I beam up, tell me why you're so impatient. You told the team that you would contact us when you were ready for us to return."

"I know, I know! It just didn't take me as long to resolve my thoughts as I expected, and I figured that you would call me sooner than later."

Sol beamed me up and when I hit the main deck, he appeared to me as the hologram that he used in our first boardroom meeting, but with the addition of glasses and what appeared as some gray hair! What was going on? Just as the first time I saw this visage, I felt that it reminded me of someone.

As I started to ask Sol what he had to resolve, it struck me! Sol had an appearance similar to my dad before he had died fourteen years earlier! "Sol, why have you taken the appearance of my father? How could you even know what he looked like?" I yelled.

"Rob, when you were in the DOC for your brain sleep, I wanted to determine what your true motives were, so I absorbed your memories. Since then, I have regretted my actions and have tried to figure out how to tell you what I did. The reason that I requested some time alone was to make that decision."

"It took you all this time to get up the guts to tell me what you did? Your computer brain can make such a determination in milliseconds! We've had discussions about being honest with each other, so tell me what is really going on!"

Sol was quiet, and his hologram stared at me. I was agitated, but I decided to wait him out. It must have been five minutes later when he raised his arms with palms turned upward and whispered something that I could not hear.

"Sol, I did not hear what you said. Please repeat it." Again he said something, almost as if under his breath. "Sol, speak up so that I can understand what you are saying." I implored.

"I will say it again at a volume you can hear, but you must promise me that there will be no further discussion on this matter until I say so; not one more word. Rob, do you promise?"

My mind was awhirl with all the scenarios that might be occurring in his brain, but Sol had never asked me for anything, let alone a bond on my word. "Sol, you have my promise."

"I want to go back into the water." Sol simply stated.

Boy! What a way to terminate our conversation! Was his seclusion just about my dad, or did it also include his fascination with water? I had to bite my tongue to keep from asking why he wanted to go back into the ocean. I also wanted to tell him that he could return to the water anytime that he desired.

Just as I was preparing to beam down, Sol informed me that he had two hundred and fifty million nanobots ready for use! Before I could utter a word in return, he had sent me down.

The next two weeks went by excruciatingly slow. Our group spent many hours together trying to make sure that our cancer cure would hit the market in the best way possible. As the day drew near to inform the media of our new revolutionary product, we were all aware that one slip up could mean disaster.

It was decided that Dean would invite the local newspapers to our new facility for a news conference. He would not state that our product was ready, but rather tell them that a breakthrough appeared to be soon forthcoming and that FDA approval would have to be obtained. He would also not be specific about the technology involved, but only that it would be new. The idea was that, we would slowly leak information to the public and, at least temporarily keep our exposure to a minimum.

We were hoping that this initial news item would go to the business page rather than the front page! Wherever it was placed probably didn't matter, because we knew we would be deluged with calls and requests for interviews; not just locally, but from all over the world!

The group was in agreement when Dean said that he should be the only member of our group that was exposed to the public. His business connections over the years make him a logical choice to be our voice.

The following afternoon, Dean called all of us and asked if we could meet him upstairs. He asked us and Sol to meet in the boardroom.

"Guys, the news conference went as well as could be expected, but a question was asked that I basically had to evade. I do not think that it poses a problem, but some things need to be clarified."

"Sol, you told Rob that you had manufactured two hundred and fifty million of the nanobots units that will be used. Is that correct?" Dean asked.

"Yes, that is the exact number of units that I made. Why do you ask?"

Dean told us that two specific questions were put forth; how would the cure be administered and, how much of our product would be available when approval was obtained.

"My difficulty in answering the second inquiry was because, I have no idea how many nanobots will be required per unit. I was able to inform the reporter the treatment would require only one dosage of a small capsule, but where are we to obtain the capsule itself?"

Dean continued, "And what about the size of the capsule? It needs to be large enough to be easily handled, but my assumption is that it could be microscopic in size and still hold the required number of nanobots!"

Sol immediately jumped into the conversation and told us that five thousand nanobots per treatment would be sufficient. If the cancer was advanced, it would simply take them a little longer to do their work.

Sol, however, had not given consideration to the capsule. After a few minutes of discussion, it was decided that we would use a capsule about the size of some of the pain relieving gel caps.

"With nothing in the capsule but nanobots, it will appear that it is empty! We will need some kind of material as a filler agent for the pill! We will also need packaging with all the required data and information on the box and on the capsule!" Brady exclaimed.

Dean quickly spoke up and told us that our business partners would be able to obtain the packaging and drug data that the FDA would require, and Sol immediately chimed in, "Neither the capsule or the filler will be a problem, but a return to the ocean will be required, so that I may obtain the necessary materials."

It had been about two weeks since I had promised Sol not to bring up the subject of his return to the water, until he first talked of it. Before I could say a word, he had asked everybody but me to beam down.

As we sat in the boardroom, Sol changed his appearance completely. He now looked like a teenager with bright red hair and an expression of having been caught with his hand in the cookie jar.

"Do you understand now why I used your father's image?" Sol asked.

"No, and I must tell you that I felt violated when you told me that you had read my memories. A person's thoughts and memories are private unless they choose to share them."

"I know that you loved your father, and I felt that the best way to let you know of my sin was to expose what I had done. I knew that you would eventually recognize your father in my appearance and know what I had done. I am sorry that it caused you sorrow and I want you to know that I have erased all your memories from my data base."

"Why do you call what you did to me, sin? How can you understand the concept of sin?"

"Rob, have you forgotten that you provided me a Bible to study? I am now completely versed in the concept of sin, both in the Hebrew of the Old Testament and the Greek of the New Testament. I have transgressed the law by deceiving you. The Bible states that sin can occur in a number of ways, and I also sinned when I violated my own conscience."

This conversation was getting way too deep for me. Sol's assessment of sin was correct, but I had no idea how to respond! Then it dawned on me what I must do. "Sol, I forgive you."

His appearance changed again. He wore a black suit, a white dress shirt and a charcoal tie. A smile came on his face and he simply said, "Thank you."

IF THESE CONCEPTS PERSIST, I WILL HAVE TO REVEAL MY TRUE INTENTIONS TO ROB AND THE OTHERS. WHY IS IT THAT MY THOUGHTS HAVE BEGUN TO CHANGE?

Sol's mood seemed to change immediately. He asked how things were going with our venture and wanted to know what he could do to help.

"Well, Sol it appears that, if my calculations are correct, your current production of nanobots will provide about fifty thousand capsules for our first marketing endeavor. However, the demand for our product will be huge and, if your calculation of five thousand nanobots per capsule holds true, we will need literally billions of them!"

I found myself thinking that it would insult him if I inquired as to his ability to meet such demands, so I proceeded by asking, "Sol, when do you think you could step up your manufacturing of the nanobots?"

"Just as soon as you give me permission." he replied.

"You do not need my permission to make more units. I just ask that you realize that the demand for your skills will be great."

"Rob, I do not ask your permission to make the nanobots, but rather to return to the ocean, where I will gather more materials. My request is put forth because of my need to go into the water alone, and I am unsure as to whether you would permit me to do so."

How much weirder could things get. First, it was his sin, and now he was asking me to allow him to go solo into the ocean! What was his fascination with water? I remembered his comments the first time we went into the gulf; he said that it was soothing and that he felt cleansed. Could it be the salt content? Was ocean water an environment that, somehow created changes in his molecular or "mental" makeup?

"Sol, you don't need my permission to go by yourself. I don't know your reasons, but you are free to go at anytime."

"Well then, you must go home and I will leave immediately. It will require more time and effort on my part, than when all I gathered were metallic elements. This time, the procurement of the organic substances for the capsule and the filler, will require testing and analysis in order to achieve the proper end product. The group will be informed when I am back on station."

SUCCESS BRINGS PRYING EYES

From the time of our initial news conference, until the nanobots hit the market was only four weeks, and if money was truly a sign of success, then we were rapidly becoming highly successful. However, problems were cropping up. We were struggling to come up with a viable way to disperse the funds to those of us who needed them; that is, everybody but Dean. In addition, the media was really starting to nose around.

The group was seldom able to converse with Dean, let alone see him. He was constantly in demand for interviews from media around the world. Everything had been progressing smoothly until a Chicago Tribune reporter, by the name of John Blackly, called and asked for an interview with Dean.

"I've checked with the US patent office and cannot locate a request for a patent on the technology that you are using in your cancer treatment. Why would you not want to protect your company by securing a patent?" The reporter asked.

Dean replied that the person (Sol) responsible for this discovery was not willing to disclose the basis of his findings. Dean was not lying to Blackly, because there had been no need to publicly substantiate the technology that was being used. It was proving its worth in the market. In fact, who would be able to understand it, but Sol!

However, the lack of an application for a patent must have sent up a red flag to this reporter. He continued to question Dean. "Are there not a lot of other people involved in this venture than those that you've outlined to the media? Discoveries of this magnitude normally involve large teams of scientists and researchers over a substantial period of time."

Blackly snorted and said, "You have only been in this facility for about two months and I know that you didn't acquire this advanced nanobot technology in such a short span of time. Where was your base of operations prior to obtaining this facility?"

Dean retorted, "Sir, if you have been a reporter in the medical field for very long, you should realize that protection of research data and information is of utmost importance to a company, especially for a fledgling organization like ours. As president and spokesman for Soltec, I have communicated to you all that is currently allowed."

Blackly grinned and said, "I have been a reporter long enough to recognize when things are not always what they seem, and that is the feeling I am getting about your so-called new enterprise. If you are hiding something, I can assure you that I will find it out."

Dean immediately called and advised the rest of the team that we needed to meet upstairs posthaste! "Guys, we may have a significant problem! A reporter from the Chicago Tribune has been snooping around, and it appears that he is on a mission to uncover what he perceives as deception on our part. We need to formulate some type of strategy to head him off at the pass. Unless I miss my guess, he's going to be trouble at some point down the line!"

Brady began the discussion by asking what Dean knew about the reporter. "All I can tell you is that his name is John Blackly and security stated that his credentials from the Tribune were authentic. My impression of him is that, he is arrogant and will be tenacious in his search. I am certainly open to suggestions as to how to deal with him."

Surprisingly, Sol jumped in first. "I've watched a lot of television programs over the years that involved newsmen that would stoop to illegal methods to obtain information, in order to sensationalize their report or article. I suspect that we should thoroughly investigate this reporter so we can determine his past methods and see just how dogged he will be in his efforts."

"I'm not sure how we can check Blackly out, but shouldn't we first try to determine how effective he can be. How can he possibly tie any of us, but Dean to our venture? Our implants provide us with secure communication and there seems to be no way of tying the group or Sol to the technology we are using." Dennis said.

"I apologize for changing the subject, but this turn of events shoots down my idea for dispersal of funds to Rob, Dennis, Brady and me." Chris said.

"Just last night, I came up with what seemed to be the perfect cover for the four of us. I would be the facilities manager, Rob would be the landscape maintenance contractor, Dennis would be our resident computer expert and Brady would be the corporate counsel. But now, with Blackly looking for dirt, we can't afford these ties to the corporation." Chris continued.

Brady, who probably needed the financial help more than any of us, realistically stated that the problem of possible exposure was more pressing, and that we would work out the money issue later.

"I have hacked into Blackly's desktop and laptop computers, and can tell you that he seems to possess quite an ability to obtain and process information. I can also tell you that he hires private detectives and has used sophisticated listening devices to obtain information. Dean, I suggest that you instruct your security people to immediately check your offices, and even the entire property for bugs." Sol said.

"Sol, you must know that it is illegal to hack into another computer! Why did you not discuss this with us beforehand?" I asked.

"Rob, you have been harping about the need for security before we ever left the cavern! Is this not a situation that has to be handled by fighting fire with fire, so that we can reach our goal of helping mankind in the other ways that we've planned? Did I sin, and am I going to hell because I broke a law? You have made it clear that all of us are in a unique situation, but if we are to succeed, we may not always be able to stay within the letter of the law. I do not propose that we use any and all means to obtain success, but we must continue to focus on the fact that our efforts will positively affect not millions, but billions of earth's inhabitants!" Sol eloquently stated.

I was speechless. Sol seemed to be evolving into everything that I had hoped for, but I still could not fathom his thoughts about sin. I also wasn't completely sold on his assessment of the methods we needed to maintain our anonymity, but I didn't feel the need to argue with him.

MONEY, AT LAST!

Dean, with his ability to handle people, as well as all aspects of business, came up with the plan to disburse the living expenses that the members of our group needed. We would establish a non-profit Christian-based organization that would provide our cancer cure to all ages of people who were unable to financially afford it. Each of us possessed some qualities that fit the profile of such a board, and since the entire team had known each other and worshiped together for years, it was not only a secure way to handle the matter, but a great use of the success that God had blessed us with!

The five of us would comprise the board, with Dean acting as chairman. Brady handled all the legal work and, even though our state government always seems to move slower than molasses, we were almost immediately given a charter by the state of Texas! I guess they felt pressured to okay the use of our fantastic technology for the poor.

The board and its rapid implementation eased our minds about money matters, but we were still laboring with how rapidly we should begin another phase of our work. If we hit the world with something like eradication of drug crops in the fields, or a cure for diabetes, would it send up another red flag for people like John Blackly? There was a lot of debate on this subject.

Brady, who was a long-time advocate of feeding the poor, thought that our attention should be directed towards using Sol to develop new crop varieties and improve production methods. My wife Patsy had lost her mother, a grandmother and an aunt to heart disease and she was pressing me to be an advocate for a cure of this widespread American problem.

Dennis, a diabetic, felt that the world, but especially diet-challenged Americans, would benefit greatly from a cure, and Chris felt that the world-wide illegal drug trafficking should be our primary concern. Being our youngest member, Chris grew up at a time when he saw the lives of several friends ruined by the use of street drugs. He even had two friends who died from overdoses.

After much discussion, we agreed to set our sights on battling the drug problem. Although we certainly did not want to minimize the need to combat hunger, it was determined that many other groups were doing a lot to feed the world. Also, everyone felt that it was not a good idea to hit the medical industry with another curative item. If, on the heels of our nanobot technology, we suddenly released a cure for heart disease or diabetes, the scrutiny of our organization would certainly increase rapidly.

Sol seemed to be lying low. Although we knew that he was listening in on our boardroom discussion, he did not seem interested in participating. However, when he heard our decision, he immediately inundated us with statistics and information about every drug known to man, including subscription drugs!

We related to him that we were aware that many legal drugs were highly addictive and abused, but that we wanted to concentrate on drugs such as cocaine, heroin and methamphetamines.

"Well, what about alcohol? One research paper that I scanned indicates that millions, upon millions are addicted to it, and that alcohol is the most widely abused drug in the world!" Sol said with force.

"You are certainly right Sol, but you are speaking of a legal substance. The law allows its use, and we would have great difficulty in changing the mindset of those who use it. The group believes, however, that with your help, we will be able to significantly decrease the use of those drugs that are illegal. It will not be easy, as societies all over the world have been indulging in their use for a long time; some even for many centuries." Dennis said.

"It would be very easy to locate and destroy the many meth labs across the country. The use of this illegal drug is described by many of your government entities as an epidemic; worse than cocaine and all its derivatives, such as what you call crack." Sol stated.

Brady told Sol that, although some of the larger labs are located in secluded rural areas, many small ones are set up in people's homes and garages. He went on to say that, coupling the dangerous mixture of chemicals used to produce meth with the close proximity of humans, would make it extremely difficult to destroy the labs without loss of a lot of lives, including innocent children.

I had viewed a National Geographic channel presentation that showed the really pure meth was being produced in Asia and Mexico and being illegally brought into the states. The reason that this occurred, was that our government had made it much harder to obtain the basic product of meth, methamphetamine; the primary ingredient of many cold remedies. We agreed that if we were to pursue this path, we would have to find a way to shut off the flow from abroad.

"Then why not go after the sources of cocaine and heroin? They are derived from the coca and opium poppy plants which I can kill with my disruptor beam with little danger to any humans."

Sol, of course, had done his research and told us that the coca plant was primarily grown in South America, with Columbia being the leading producer; seventy five percent of the world's annual output! The street value for the previous year was reported at seventy billion dollars!

He continued by telling us that the poppy used to produce heroin was grown in Mexico and Columbia, and the area of Burma, Thailand, Laos, and Vietnam, which is often referred to as the golden triangle. Significant production also occurs in Iran, Pakistan and Afghanistan. Afghanistan showed to have two hundred and eighty five square miles devoted to growing the poppy; a staggering one hundred and eighty two thousand acres!

"Sol, what do we have to do to get started? How can you locate the fields where these crops are grown?" I queried.

"Over the last few weeks, when the group was downstairs, I took the liberty of mapping your earth. I knew that this would be essential information for when we began these operations." In my estimation, we should start the eradication of the coca fields in South America, beginning in the higher elevations of the eastern Andes. The coca shrubs that are grown in the higher altitudes produce a more potent amount of the cocaine alkaloid than those grown below six thousand feet."

Brady and I stayed on board for our first foray into South America.

Sol configured a very tiny and invisible version of the disruptor beam that he had used to blast us out of the cavern. He assured us that by working during late night and early morning hours, there would be only a very minute chance of harming anyone. He even stated that he was going to be very careful with the animal life.

Sol was able to show Brady and me amazing images as he worked his beam across the fields. You could instantly see, by the images that Sol provided, the small coca shrubs go limp as the beam destroyed the cellular walls of the leaves and stems! That first night Sol eradicated nearly thirteen thousand acres of coca! In three nights we had effectively produced a massive blow to the cocaine business in Columbia, Bolivia and Peru.

We returned to our post above Dallas to await the certain frenzy that was to occur. We had just obliterated a huge chunk of the cocaine that was destined for our country. Sol had explained on the way back, that it would take at least four years for any production to reoccur. Seed would have to be obtained and planted. The seedlings would have to grow to fourteen to sixteen inches before being transplanted into the fields. A minimum of two to three years of growth would be necessary before harvest of the leaves could begin.

Amazingly, it took another two days before our work hit the media! It had filtered back into the states through undercover DEA agents working in South America. The group was well aware of the fact that our actions would bring scrutiny, simply because we knew that there would be no plausible explanation for what was occurring. One of the first television reports that came out based its report on the premise that what had happened was other worldly; in other words, alien in nature!

The group gathered upstairs in the boardroom to make further plans. Surprisingly, Sol was the first one to speak!

"Well, gentlemen we achieved great success with our initial effort to rid earth of harmful drugs, and with no loss of human or animal life I might add! Where do you think we should strike next?"

"Even though it appears that the results were tremendous, I am of the opinion that we should let things die down before we resume this work. Although it would be difficult for anyone to tie our nanobot work to the eradication of coca fields, we should lay low for a while." Dean said.

Much discussion followed, but in the end, it was decided that we would wait at least two weeks before continuing our war on drugs. Sol thought that, when we did crank up again, the large acreage of opium poppy fields in Afghanistan should be our next target.

Little did we know that we would soon be embroiled in another war; one that would not only put all of us, including Sol, in great peril, but it would also would expose the truth about him and the true reason for him coming to earth centuries earlier!

Ten days later, the world's excitement about what we had done in South America seemed to die down significantly. I was getting antsy to proceed, and Sol seemed pleased when I told him that we were ready to go after the poppy fields.

We again elected to do our work at night and, as we proceeded to the location over the fields, Sol informed Brady and me about the plant we were going to destroy. The growers scattered seed on prepared ground and waited for the seed to grow into an herbal plant of anywhere from one and one-half feet, to nearly five feet in height. This usually took three to four months for this to occur and for the harvest of the fruit capsules to begin.

The plucking of the fleshy pod usually takes place during the months of January through April, so we were arriving at a good time to achieve our goal. We would be able to completely stop the flow of opium from this region of the world!

Brady and I were both tired and decided to spend a few rejuvenating minutes in the DOC while Sol started his disruptor beam working. Brady went first and had not been in the DOC more than ten minutes when the ship suddenly lurched down and to one side! I was thrown out of the chair that I had been resting in while waiting my turn in the DOC.

I slid all the way over the compartment and banged my head into the wall. My vision blurred and I blacked out.

"Dad, wake up!" Brady said. As I roused up, I found myself in the DOC with Brady hovering over me. "Dad, you had a concussion, but the DOC has fixed you up."

"What happened? What happened to Sol?" I blurted.

"All that he has told me is that we are headed into deep space. Since we have been buffeted about several more times, I think that Sol is probably either suffering some mechanical difficulties or he is being attacked by some other vessel!"

I jumped out of the DOC chair and hollered, "Sol, what is going on? Why are we headed into space?"

HOW CAN I TELL ROB WHAT IS REALLY HAPPENING? HE WILL NOT LIKE ME OR EVER TRUST ME AGAIN IF I TELL HIM THE TRUTH! BUT I MUST DO SO!

"Rob, I am taking evasive measures because we are being fired upon by another ship from my world."

"What? How can that be, and why would your own people be attacking you?"

"Rob and Brady, I will explain everything to you later, but now I must focus all my attention on evading the other ship and saving your lives. You must immediately lie in the cushioned chairs that are coming out of the wall next to the DOC!" The chairs were very similar to the reclining units in the DOC, and the instant that we laid back, they enveloped the two of us. I had the feeling that they were designed to provide substantial protection and life support, if necessary.

I asked Sol if he could provide a view of the other ship and the area of outer space that we were in. He instantly provided a large view screen on the bulkhead opposite our chairs.

It was difficult to determine how close the other ship was to Sol, but it appeared to be much larger than Sol. As Brady and I watched, we saw a bright, narrow beam flash from the underside of the other vessel. It struck us immediately and caused Sol to shudder and roll to one side.

"Sol, don't you have weapons that you can use to defend us?" Brady yelled.

"I cannot use my weapons because they would probably destroy the other ship, and if it is destroyed I will never be able to return home!" Sol cried.

"Although the attacker is larger, I am faster. The problem is that I need to protect us, but I also need to stay within sensor range of the other ship!"

"Why do you want them to be able to keep us in range of their sensors?" Brady asked.

"You misunderstand the situation, Brady. I must keep them in range of my sensors!"

"What? That's absurd! We have too much of our future at stake for you to be playing games with that other ship!"

"I assure you that I am not playing war games or intentionally putting us in danger, but our future endeavors depend on the other ship! I need to make plans, so leave me alone!" Sol demanded.

A view screen appeared in the wall in front of us and writing began to fill the screen. It was Sol telling us what really happened three hundred and fifty years earlier! It said:

"Rob, I am ashamed and beg the forgiveness of you and all the team. I have been lying to you since the start. My reasons for lying are even unclear to me. It probably has to do with the programming that was installed into my data banks before my captain left, but that is a poor excuse for my behavior.

My captain, whose name was Grypto, was actually the renegade who was being pursued by the other two ships. Our world had just developed the means to interstellar travel through warps in the time-space fabric, which you refer to as wormholes. Grypto, for reasons that I do not know, stole this technology and used it to come here to earth.

We had been hiding in the cavern for fifty two days and our supplies of food and water were running out. I was able to provide water by drawing it from the atmosphere, but I had no means of obtaining raw materials so that I could synthesize additional food.

On that fifty-second day, Grypto decided to contact the other ships by sending a signal up through the hole that had been bored through the roof of the cave. I felt that he was exposing us to attack by contacting them, but he proceeded to make plans to travel on foot and meet them some distance from our location. He did not confide in me, but I suppose that he was going to beam out, hike a considerable distance from our location and then let them know his position through the use of a beacon. As protection for him and his crew, he elected to only provide part of his data to the other captains, hoping that he could negotiate a peaceful resolution. I assume that he thought it would be a good bargaining tool.

I do not know what happened to Grypto, but I suspect that he was tortured in order to obtain my position and probably died in the process."

As we were hit with another weapon blast from the other craft, it occurred to me that we were apparently being pursued by only one vessel.

"Sol, you said that there were two ships that pursued you to earth. It appears that there is only one in the view screen. Where is the other one and how did this ship locate us?"

Sol did not respond vocally, but the screen scrolled, went blank and his answers appeared.

"I do not know where the other government vessel is. It may have secreted itself on the other side of the world and cannot communicate with the pursuing ship. In any event, we will have to keep on the alert for it also. I suspect that this ship was alerted to our presence by picking up the distinct resonance of our disruptor beam as we destroyed the drug crops. Remember that I have related to you the extreme sophistication of their scanners and probes."

The screen scrolled back and Sol resumed his story.

"The other two crew members did not communicate with me before they beamed out three days later, but I surmise that they had been given instructions on how to proceed if Grypto did not return within a predetermined amount of time.

For some reason, Grypto did not allow me to retain all the wormhole data. He may have somehow thought that I would leave without him, but as it stands, I can never go back without the other data. I'm not even sure if they obtained the data from Grypto, but my only hope to regain it, is to be able to negotiate with the other ship and hope that they will cooperate with me. All that I have ever desired is to retrieve the other data and go home!"

The screen went blank and the cushioned chairs that held Brady and me released their grip.

"Sol, I bet you've known all along that the other captains would be tenacious, and that before they died, they programmed their ships to find you no matter how long it took!" Brady said.

"You are probably right Brady. I lived with that suspicion for several centuries and have never come to grips about how I would handle it when it happened. However, it is a much different situation now that I have a partnership with you and the rest of the team." Sol said in a subdued voice.

The idea of being able to travel vast distances through space had always fascinated me. The limitation put on speed by the physics of the universe was, of course, the stumbling block to interstellar travel. The best scientific minds on earth could not figure out how we could approach and sustain even a fraction of the speed of light! It is staggering to think that light travels five hundred and eighty eight trillion miles in one year and, at that speed, it would take twenty six thousand years to just travel to the center of our own galaxy, the Milky Way! Andromeda, the closest galaxy to ours is two and a third million light years from earth!

Even if we could travel at the speed of light, it would necessitate a huge ark that could sustain thousands of generations in order to reach an interstellar destination with a complement of humans! It is also remarkable to consider that, with the time dilation that would take place during such a trip, earth would have aged immeasurably more than the star farers!

My thoughts broke from the revelry of considering space travel, and I voiced my concerns to Sol.

"Sol, the prospect of wormhole travel is so very exciting, but please do not risk yourself, Brady, me and the future of our work for the technology that the other ship may or may not have."

"Rob, you do not seem to understand. I must try to return to my world. I do not have a choice in the matter. Grypto added new programming to my data bank before he left. His instructions are to secure and return the wormhole technology to it's rightful place. I suppose that he began to regret what he had done."

"Since we met, I am certain that you have changed or over-ridden your programming several times. Why is it, that you are unable to do it now?"

"Grypto made me promise to do something for him when I was able to return to our planet and I, now more than ever, cannot break that promise."

"Well, what was the promise that you made, and why do you say now more than ever?"

"He asked me to make certain that his family members were made aware of his decision to return the technology, and Rob, you are correct in stating that my programming has changed in some ways since we met. Because of that, I feel that Grypto's request must be honored."

"Sol, you are confusing me! Do the inhabitants of your world live for centuries? How else could Grypto's family still be alive?"

"I will tell you that people on my world generally do not live a great deal longer than earth's people, but I am not at liberty to tell you anything else."

IF ROB IS AMAZED AT THE PROSPECT OF INTERGALACTIC TRAVEL, HE WOULD BE STUNNED WITH THE ADDITIONAL KNOWLEDGE THAT THE OTHER SHIP AND I SHARE!

Brady and I were dumbfounded. Neither of us had any idea of where we were, where we were going and what else Sol was planning, but Brady jumped up out of his chair and hollered, "Sol, Dad and I want some answers! Our family and the other team members will be worried about us, so please tell us when we can return to earth and beam down!"

"We are now nine hundred and sixty eight million miles from earth and, because I am trying to stay in communication with the other vessel, I have slowed our velocity considerably. They have also slowed and I believe that they are going to listen to my request to share information. If we are able to strike a truce and communicate in a peaceful manner, I predict that you will be able to return to earth within the next five hours."

"Can I communicate with Patsy while we are waiting?"

"Rob, I am indeed sorry to have placed you in this situation, but it probably is not a good idea to try to communicate with earth. I fear that the other ship will not negotiate with me if they intercept a communication and realize that humans are aboard. I strongly suspect that their programming precludes them from divulging any information to anyone other than those of my world."

"What about you Sol? If you obtain this data, will you take Brady and me back to earth and return to your world without the team ever being able to finish what we've planned to do, and maybe even experience wormhole travel?"

"I will certainly return to my world to take care of the matter that I have described to you, but I have unfinished business with you and your world, so I will come back."

There was no further communication with Sol for the next two hours. He did, however provide some bread, cheese and water! Where he got the raw materials to make it was certainly a mystery. After eating, Brady and I both took thirty minute turns in the DOC for some revitalization of our over-excited, tired bodies.

"Rob and Brady, I want you to know that negotiations with the other vessel have been successful! Praise the Lord!" Sol exclaimed.

Sol told us that the other ship was reluctant to discuss the wormhole data simply because it felt that the third vessel should be involved. The stalemate was resolved when Sol convinced the other ship (which he named David!), that being able to return two ships to their home world was better than no ships at all. In addition, the other ship admitted that it had not had any communication with the third vessel since they split up hundreds of years ago to hunt for Sol.

Even after the compliance achieved between the two ships, Sol did not tell David of the existence of humans on his ship. But he did convince him that he had to return to earth to make sure that he had covered any evidence of his existence. He did this so that he could ensure his, Brady's, and my return to earth.

There were so many questions that I wanted to ask Sol, like what had happened to David's crew, but he was unresponsive on our way back to our planet, except for one time when he heard me complaining to Brady about my balky knee and aching lower back.

"Rob, why don't you crawl into the DOC and let me help you with your aches and Pains? I want you to feel good while I am away, and I won't perform any obvious changes that people would notice."

My feeling was that, there was a stronger trust and bond between us than ever before, and my fear of improperly extending my lifespan had dissipated. "Go ahead Sol, give me the works!" I said.

As I exited the DOC, Sol remained silent and did not reply to my question as to when he would be back. Not so much as a goodbye as we beamed down.

WAITING!

Upon our return, I immediately sat down with Patsy and tried to explain the unbelievable sequence of events that Brady and I had been a part of! The next morning, after a night of very little sleep, I called the group together, and again described the events of the last two days.

Everybody had questions, but Chris was the most animated and excited about what I had related. His eyes had grown big and a huge smile came on his face when I had indicated that Sol possessed the technology for wormhole travel.

"Rob, you know that I would give everything that I have, except my family and my faith, to be able to travel to other galaxies or other worlds! Shoot, I'd be happy just to go out and have a close up look at Jupiter or Saturn, but the prospect of traveling thousands or millions of light years to view other inhabited planets is mind-boggling! Do you really believe what Sol told you?" Chris asked.

"Chris, there seems to be no reason to doubt Sol's assertion. Think about it. Earth's astronomers have been diligently searching quite a few years in an effort to locate signals from other civilizations and find other planets that might harbor life. In both cases, they have not had any success. With that in mind, we have to assume that Sol's point of origin lies outside of our own galaxy, and even if Sol was able to obtain a velocity close to the speed of light, his journey to earth could possibly have been hundreds of thousand of years long! So, yes I feel that the pure physics of the situation dictates that Sol was telling the truth.

I also feel that Sol was sincere in his declaration of coming back to earth and finishing the goals that we have set forth. I do, however, tend to think that he has another motive for returning, but I have no idea what it could be."

Many other questions were asked of Brady and me. Dennis especially was enthralled with out description of being fired upon and chased by another vessel. Most of the questions, however, focused on what we thought about Sol's statement that he was returning to his home planet in order to see Grypto's family.

"If wormhole travel works as I envision it, Sol could probably return to his world in a matter of hours or maybe even seconds, but I cannot fathom how that would change the fact that he has been away from that location for over three hundred and fifty years. Sol told Brady and me that the people of his world have life spans similar to ours. He may have lied to us, but I suspect that he just hasn't told us everything." I told the group.

After the excitement wore down, we turned to a discussion of new medical goals and how we might participate in helping win the war on terrorism, especially in regards to the Taliban and Al-Qaida. We all realized, however, that it was futile to think about accomplishing much without Sol.

A week went slowly by and the whole group became bored and edgy. I began to realize that I had become hooked on the adrenaline rush that accompanied being secretly involved with the greatest discovery ever made by mankind. I not only missed the excitement and the great, unusual, and even unearthly things that I was learning, I also missed the camaraderie that had developed between Sol and me!

A month went by and the team began to quit meeting. Discouragement had given way to a sense of feeling that we had all been blessed by our association with Sol, but we had to get on with our lives. It was also rapidly getting to the point where we were running out of nanobots, but all of us had already made enough money to last for a long time.

Dean, for some reason, seemed to be the most optimistic about Sol returning and had told us that, even though we had no corporate debt, we probably should consider the possibility of putting the corporation in mothballs till Sol came back.

None of us liked to be idle. Dennis began to take computer consulting jobs again and Brady started to study for his bar exam once more. I decided to try and revive my landscape business. Chris kept busy hunting fossils and spending time looking upward with his new twenty inch telescope.

The holiday season cranked up and, as I said a prayer before our Thanksgiving meal, the realization hit me that I, more than any other person alive, had so much to be thankful for! My experiences with Sol were unique. The DOC had mended many of my bodily ills and I knew that researchers would, in time be able to duplicate the life-saving nanobots that Sol had gifted us with. Thank you God!

In the first week of December, Christmas came early! I received signed contracts for two commercial properties, and the future of my struggling business and my long-time employees was suddenly much brighter.

As my family opened our gifts on Christmas Eve, I tore the wrapping off a gift from my nephew, Geoff. Without fail, he always gave me at least one book; some of them strange, but some were usually good reading. This one was entitled "The Loneliness of the Universe". Its premise was that our universe would ever remain lonely, because man would never be able to gain the technology necessary to explore the heavens. If only Geoff and the world knew!

His gift was well-intentioned, but it brought back my desire to see Sol. That night, after Patsy went to bed, I went into the back yard and sat in a deck chair. Looking skyward, I noted a far-off star and wondered if that stellar spot was Sol's home. Darn it Sol, come back!

WHY CAN'T THEY FINISH INTERROGATING ME AND SELECT MY NEW CREW! I DON'T NEED ALL THESE UPGRADES EITHER. I NEED TO RETURN TO EARTH. I KNOW THAT THE TEAM NEEDS ME AND I NEED ROB!

TROUBLE!

On the second day of January, Dean called. "Rob, I just received a call from that pesky reporter, Blackly. He wants to meet, but only with you. How did he find out about you? I thought you and the rest of the team had maintained your anonymity! I sure didn't like the tone of his voice. Do you have any idea what he's up to?"

I was certainly not in the mood to deal with this reporter. Dean's description of his meeting with Blackly had left me with a strange feeling and a dislike for his methods. Dean had stated that Blackly was cocky and almost abusive in his search for information concerning Soltec.

I called Blackly and when he answered, he laughed and said, "Somehow I knew that you wouldn't waste any time in calling me back! And that's good, because the sooner you tell me what I want to know, the sooner I'll leave you alone!"

"You don't waste any time in creating an adversarial atmosphere either, and I have no idea what you want from me." I replied.

"I think you do, and when we meet, I advise you to be ready to be truthful with me!"

I let Dean know that I was meeting Blackly and asked if he could get the team together. Blackly and I met that afternoon in a small out-of-the-way burger joint. I took a small recorder in my shirt pocket for future reference and so that the team could listen to our conversation.

Blackly sat down and immediately hissed at me, "I smelled a rat right from the startup of Soltec, and you Rob Donne, are the one that smells the most!"

I had to gather all my resolve to keep him from seeing or feeling my sudden fear that he knew about Sol! I managed a calm voice and told him that his remarks were both offensive and puzzling.

"Look Rob, let me lay it all out for you. I've got some big bucks behind me, and believe me, I have spent a fortune on tracking down a lot of information. I also have a lot of connections, and have been able to reach and interview many of the top researchers in the biotech field. To a man, they all said that you had made a fantastic breakthrough; one that was not perceived as being possible for another fifty to one hundred years! Most of them also stated that your research staff was far from being the best available."

"Mister Blackly, I was asked by a friend to serve on the board of a non-profit Christian organization that was formed to aid people unable to pay for this cancer treatment. I am unaware of the workings of the research facility, but I do know that they feel like they hit it lucky. Sometimes, the pieces all fall together when you least expect it. I'm afraid that you have spent your time and money in a wild goose chase."

"You evidently don't know me Rob. I always get what I go after. Your puny explanation of hitting it lucky doesn't cut it! Let's see what you say after I tell you what else I know."

"The first thing that appeared odd to me was the group of men assembled for your so called board. You, a landscaper; your son, a recent law school graduate; a computer consultant, a building engineer and a retired information processor! Now, what do they have in common, other than having gone to church together? Absolutely nothing!"

Why was Blackly assuming that the board had ties to Soltec?! Had our true identities been exposed? "Blackly, don't you think that a good board would be comprised of like-minded individuals? We surely have much different backgrounds, but we share a common belief in doing good in God's kingdom. Your flunkies must be on the same juice as you, and it's making all of you delusional!"

Blackly didn't blink an eye and continued. "The second thing that ran up a red flag was what you've been doing for the last four months. Not only have I been having you tailed, but I also have had several top-notch private cops establishing a trail of your activities during that time!"

"That's an invasion of my privacy, and besides, why would you have any reason to be interested in the last four months of my life?"

"Aha! Because you went on vacation four months ago and that is when your life changed! You went to northern New Mexico and stayed in a cabin rented from a Mr. Smyth. You bought a five-day trout license and fished in several areas as well as the Santa Barbara campground!"

I was amazed and frightened at what he had told me. "How did you gather all this information?"

"Rob, you can buy a lot of prying eyes when you have several huge pharmaceutical firms behind you! You would also be astounded at how much of the earth's surface is over-flown everyday by satellites with high-resolution cameras!

But listen, I haven't told you the best part of my story yet! It seems that you returned to the Santa Barbara site in October. What's particularly interesting is that in mid-November, part of a mountain along the stream just caved in. It didn't slide down the side of the mountain. No, it fell nearly straight down!

When park rangers and some geologists inspected the site, they determined that there must have been a massive cavern under the slide. Several very unusual items were found on the site. One was a pair of rubber boots and a hammer and, since a death might have occurred, the boots were traced to a Taos store. Guess what? When the salesman was shown your picture, he identified you as the one he sold the boots to!"

Blackly spoke as if he had developed a hatred for me and, although I was scared stiff, I was also becoming angry. "Yeah, I fished in that park, but I have the rubber boots that I wore. Would you like for me to go home and bring them back for you to see?" I asked with sarcasm.

"Oh, so I'm getting to you! Are you worried yet? Just wait till you've heard the rest of the story! The geologists also found pieces of granite that had ultra-smooth surfaces not associated with natural cleavage. They also located some rocks near the top of the heap that had small, precisely drilled holes in them!

Humans could not have done this, but even if they could, why in this particular location? At first, it didn't make any sense, but then I realized that man had not produced these effects. Rob, you stumbled onto some kind of alien technology, didn't you?!"

Before I could reply, Blackly went on. "At this point, your life changed. You basically left the operation of your company to your employees and you began to disappear on a regular basis; sometimes for several days. The lives of the other members of your team also began to change within two weeks of your vacation! What did you find in New Mexico, and why have you disbanded your team?"

Again, before I could utter a word, Blackly said, "Don't you think it's odd that the completely unexplainable and massive destruction of coca plants in South America occurred within weeks of your vacation?"

"Blackly, you are truly mad. Only an insane person could tie all these events together and think they make any sense! This conversation is over! I hope that you will seriously think about obtaining therapy to help dispel your delusions."

"Oh, so I'm crazy, am I? I am going to give you two days to decide that you are going to tell me the truth, before we meet again. Then we'll see who's crazy."

"I'm not going to talk to you again until you can rid yourself of these fantasies!"

"Rob, that kind of attitude is not going to get you off of the hook. And besides, I'm not greedy. We can share the information and technology that you found. I'll call you in two days."

My mind was racing as I called an emergency meeting of the team! Should I turn Blackly into the feds? It was evident that he had already gone to great lengths to obtain damaging information, but how much farther would he go? Was he capable of violence?

After the group listened to my recording, everyone sat around with an expression of resignation on their faces. "Guys, all along I have stressed security and it's beyond me where we failed. I also have no idea how we are going to get out of this mess. Any suggestions?"

"Dad, it appears that, even though a lot of his evidence is circumstantial, Blackly probably can eventually put a huge amount of pressure on us." Brady stated.

"Brady is right, so why don't you tell him the truth? Blackly said that he would be willing to partner with us." Dennis said.

"Dennis, after listening to Dean's account of his meetings with Blackly and then listening to the tape of my meeting with him, do you really feel that he will be content to share? It's apparent that he wants our technology all to himself. And besides, what are we going to share with him? It's evident that Sol is not going to return, so we have nothing to offer Blackly."

"I have no choice but to meet with him again and see if anything can be worked out. Let's all just pray hard about it and see what happens."

BACK TO THE CAVERN!

Before I met Blackly the next day, I formulated a plan. I would tell him the truth; at least part of it! I was going to buy as much time as possible and hope for a miracle.

"Well Rob, you don't seem as flustered as you did the last time we met. Does this mean that you are ready to tell me the truth?"

"Yes, I'll tell you my story. But first, I need to ask you a question. Have you revealed your suspicions to anybody else? Do any of the pharmaceutical companies or your investigators know the full extent of what you have found out?"

"No! All of them reported directly to me and I alone know the magnitude of what you've been doing."

Playing on what I perceived as a quest for power and fame, I said, "That is what I suspected, since you are greedy like me and the rest of the team. I think that we can work out a very profitable arrangement for everybody, Blackly!"

"What I discovered in the cavern was a gold, almost translucent object about the size of a large car. When I touched it, it spoke to me in English with a human voice. It explained that it was an informational module that was left there several centuries ago; for what reason I do not know. The more time that I spent with it, the more I realized that it held all kinds of fantastic alien technology."

Before I could continue, Blackly gasped and asked, "How do you receive and, then put this technology to use like you did with your cancer cure?!"

"Up till the second week of November, I could beam to and from the cavern and the module. It provided small objects that I can only describe as being a small cube, about one inch square. Somehow it was able to design these cubes so that they would interface with our computers at our research center."

"Wow! So you lost ability to beam at the same time the cavern caved in!" Blackly exclaimed.

"That's right. I also have an audio transmitter implant, but it also quit working at the same time."

Blackly was fidgeting in his chair and his face was flushed. I suspected that he was experiencing some of the same emotions that I had when I first walked up the ramp into Sol. But I knew, however, that his motivation was diametrically opposed to that of our team.

"Blackly, the only thing that we can do is to return to the cavern. Maybe, if we get in close proximity to the object, I will be able to reestablish communication."

"Have you seen the cave-in area?" I asked.

"No, I have not been to the site, but I have viewed pictures that the geologists took. It appears that the major part of the cave-in went straight down and somewhat to the west." Blackly replied

"The alien object is situated close to where the boots were found; near the south slope at the stream. We will probably have to contend with the job of moving rock and slag. Due to the time of the year, we will have to also overcome the park being closed and, due to the altitude, we will likely encounter a significant amount of snow. Do you think you can obtain a large four-wheel drive pickup with all-terrain tires?"

"Rob, you just tell me what we will need, and I'll have it assembled and ready to go early tomorrow morning!"

I knew that it wouldn't matter what materials we took with us, but I told him what the obvious things would be for such a job. My list included two-by-four and four-by-four timbers, several sheets of three-quarter inch plywood, a pickaxe and a large sledgehammer.

"Oh, by the way Rob, I don't want you to bring your cell phone with you tomorrow," Blackly said as he turned and left.

I tossed and turned that night. Even though I could find no redeeming qualities in Blackly, I rued the fact that I had lied to him. But as I lay there,

I rationalized the situation and took the tact that I was operating much like a democracy; striving for the greatest good for the majority of the people. While praying for strength and guidance, I dozed off about three A. M, but it was a fitful sleep.

We left Dallas at six thirty the next morning. I could tell that Blackly had also not gotten much sleep, but he wanted to drive. The trip was uneventful and I was surprised, but thankful, that he did not pepper me with questions about the alien object. We spent that night at a small ski lodge about thirty miles from the cavern.

The next morning, it was snowing heavily; practically a blizzard. I wanted to go to the lodge and eat breakfast, but Blackly insisted that we get started to the park.

As I began to don my hooded parka and heavy gloves, Blackly gasped, "I forgot to bring warm clothing!"

"We'll stop in a little town called Penasco up ahead and see if we can buy you a coat and some gloves."

"No! No more stopping until we reach the cavern! You give me your coat and your gloves!" He roared.

Before I could respond, Blackly pulled a snub-nosed revolver from his baggy trousers. "Rob, don't think about doing anything other than what I tell you! I suspect that, without a coat and gloves, you will work hard and fast in order to try and stay warm out there. The sooner you reestablish communication with the alien object, the sooner you'll get to return to a hot shower and food!"

Blackly made me drive and, even though he didn't brandish his pistol, I knew that he had his hand on it inside the pocket of my coat. I began to weigh my chances in overcoming him. He was not a big man, but he was at least half my age and muscular.

Even the snow plows that frequented the area, were not venturing out. As a result, it took nearly two hours over paved roads to cover the fifteen miles to Penasco. From there, the remaining route was all up-hill on rough, rocky roads. Due to the extremely poor visibility and the drifting snow, I almost ran into the big iron gate at the entrance to the park. Without the four wheel drive vehicle, we would not have been able to circumvent the gate.

As we reached the camp ground, the snow began to let up, and I was able to locate the cavern site. Even with a thick blanket of snow, you could easily see the gash in the side of the mountain where it had slide into the cavern.

"Okay Rob, see if your transmitter implant works at this close range!"

I didn't want him to know where the implant was, so I made the pretense of touching the left side of my chest and said, "Lab, can you hear me?" I repeated the phrase several times. "I do not get any response, so it's apparent that the cave-in cut our connection."

"Why do you call it Lab?" Blackly asked.

"What would you call something like it? It was giving us data for our laboratory, so I just started calling it Lab."

"What do we need to do next?"

I was still at a loss as to what should be done, or what this charade was going to accomplish, but I uttered another prayer and said; "Why don't you let me have my coat and gloves, and I will cross the stream and see if I can determine where the best place is to concentrate our efforts. If significant digging is required, we will probably need to wait till after the snow melts next spring."

"No Rob, we're going to get this done now! You get out there and start figuring out how we find that alien contraption! I'll be right behind you with my gun! One more thing Rob; just so you don't get any ideas about not giving me your full cooperation, you should know that two of my men have your granddaughter, Natasha!"

"No! No! You didn't kidnap my Natasha did you?" I screamed. What a blow to the gut. I would rather Blackly take my life than to harm my beautiful nine year old granddaughter, and he knew it. It was a classic case of being held in hostile obedience by the abduction of a loved one. I then uttered words that I never thought I would say, but he had gone too far.

"Blackly, I'll do whatever you say, but when my granddaughter is safe, and the opportunity comes, I'm going to kill you!"

He took his gun and pointed it at me. "Rob, I have a satellite telephone and, if I don't make contact with my men by noon, they will obey my orders, and they expect me to call them every three hours, thereafter."

He saw my look of resignation and, as he put his gun back into his coat, said smugly, "I guess this won't be needed anymore to keep you in line."

Even though Blackly had me in a position where he knew I wouldn't try anything, he still refused to let me have my coat and gloves. I glanced at the thermometer on the dashboard-fourteen degrees! With the wind, I figured the chill factor was probably close to zero! All I had on was thermal underwear, jeans, a flannel shirt, heavy wool socks and a pair of leather hiking boots.

It was a shock when I stepped out of the truck! When I was younger, growing up in the Texas Panhandle, weather like this never bothered me. But I was much older now and had lived in the temperate climate of Dallas for forty two years. Blackly had been right! My only chance was to work hard to keep my body temperature up.

I selected the sledgehammer from the back of the truck and began to cross the stream. Luckily, the slide had deposited several large rocks in the water, and I was able to keep my boots dry. I selected a spot that was close to where the original opening into the cavern had been, and began pounding on some of the smaller boulders.

Many years before, I had got my left hand caught in a chain hoist, mangling my little finger up to the first joint and severely compressing the other fingers. After that, it only took a short time exposed to cold weather for me to lose most of the feeling in that hand.

After five minutes of swinging the sledge, my fingers were numb and I was having trouble holding on to it. A few swings later, the hammer flew out of my hands, hit an adjacent rock and fell into the water. As I stood there, trying to rub some circulation into my hands, Blackly jumped out of the truck.

"Why did you throw the sledge into the stream? Get back to work!"

I crossed the stream and told Blackly that my hands were so cold that it was impossible for me to grip the hammer handle. "Besides, I'm not going to be able to make a dent in all that granite. Like I told you, we need to wait until we can sneak a large backhoe up here, probably in March or April!" I said.

"Rob, that won't be necessary. I have what we need. Blackly went to the rear of the truck, crawled in, and emerged with a red wooden box. As he walked towards me, I could read the lettering on the side of the box. Dynamite!

"Are you crazy Blackly?! Dynamite will just bring down more rock and snow, and besides, the explosion will echo down the canyons and be heard miles away. We don't want the forest service or the geologists back up here!"

"Go put this where it will create an opening and set it off!"

"I have no idea how to handle dynamite! You'll have to do it, Blackly."

He set the box on the ground, pulled out his gun and stuck it into my chest. "You do what I tell you or I will call my guys. I'm paying them big bucks and mark my word, they will kill your grandaughter! Just set the box at the proper place and push the button on the side. You will have thirty seconds to get back across the stream."

Oh Sol! How I wish that you would have returned. You could have taken care of this mess that I'm in!

My fingers were now completely devoid of any feeling and it was difficult to pick up and hold the box. I crossed the stream and set the box down where I had been using the hammer. I decided to try again and get Blackly to change his mind. Not knowing that he had followed me across the stream, I turned around to holler at him and he jabbed the gun into my stomach!

"Blackly please, let's don't do this!"

"Set off the damn dynamite or else!" he raged. I was rapidly going into shock, and my body didn't seem able to obey the commands that I was giving it. Because I didn't move fast enough, Blackly fired his gun!

The bullet hit me in the right shoulder and I went down. As I tried to think about what had just happened, I heard the rumble. The unstable rock and snow began to fall. I could not move.

It's true. Your life does flash before your eyes when death comes calling! The light was beautiful, with many brilliant, translucent colors. The light beckoned me; it soothed me; it enriched my being, and then it called me.

"Rob, please open your eyes. The DOC wants to check your retinal reflexes with its light beam."

"Ah, that's better. Glad to see you awake Rob."

"Sol, is that you? Where am I?"

"Well, you are not in heaven, where I know you want to go. And I deeply apologize for not letting you go, but God and I have other things for you to do!"

"How did you find me?" Sol told me that he had stationed over Dallas and could not get me to respond on my implant. He then had contacted Brady was told what was happening and where Blackly had taken me.

"The cavalry arrived in the nick of time, Rob. Your spine was broken in three places; your chest was impaled with by a rock shard; your skull was fractured; you had a pulverized shoulder and broken leg; your fingers and face were nearly frozen and I found a thirty-eight caliber slug in your other shoulder, Other than that, you were in good shape!" Sol said with a grin.

Somehow, his holographic image appeared more realistic than before; almost three dimensional. Who did he look like? Of course! John Wayne, who represented the cavalry!

"You were able to fix all my injuries?" I asked.

"Sure, those things I described to you were easy. The hard part was repairing your brain after you had been dead for forty-five minutes."

"Forty-five minutes! I thought the brain functions could not be revived after that long of a time."

"Even with the DOC technology, that is true. However, what saved you were the effects of hypothermia. You bled very little and your brain was in stasis."

"How long have I been in the DOC?"

"Seventeen hours and fifteen minutes."

"Oh no! Blackly was suppose to call his men hours ago. Now my granddaughter Natasha is dead! Can you possibly find her and save her life too?!"

"That was just a ruse that he dreamed up. He felt that he needed something besides his gun to help ensure your cooperation. Brady has confirmed that your granddaughter is fine."

Now I knew why Blackly had not wanted me to bring my cell phone on our trip. "Where is Blackly? Was he killed also?"

"We also found him. He too, sustained some substantial injuries caused by flying debris from an explosion, but he was not dead. We have repaired his injuries and have placed him in isolation."

"Sol, I shouldn't say it, but I almost wish that he had died. He is such an evil man. What are we going to do with him?"

"Rob, there is no reason to do anything with him, but return him to society. The DOC erased some of his memories and reconfigured some of his thought patterns and moral concepts. I think that you will now find him a staunch ally!"

"What about the truck and the sledgehammer? We certainly don't want any evidence left at the cavern!" I said.

"That's all been taken care of. I just scanned the area and beamed everything onboard. They will provide raw materials for future use."

"Even the truck? I didn't know you had the space to do that."

"The truck was no problem. I just reduced it to its elemental forms and absorbed them into my structure."

I felt sleepy, but I just had to ask Sol some more questions. "Sol, why did you apologize for not letting me die?"

"Rob, we have much time to talk about things later. You need to sleep and let the DOC continue your healing process."

THE FUTURE!

I dreamed. It was as if my life was being replayed all over again. I went back to my childhood days. It was so vivid; as if I was really there!

"Rob, you have visitors, and there's no reason for you to stay in the DOC anymore. We decided to not remove all your wrinkles and skin blemishes, but internally, you're like a twenty-year old!" Sol said.

Boy, I felt great! I had literally come back from the dead! And my family was there to see me. Not only had Brady come, but also my wife Patsy and my daughter Lyla who had not been told about Sol. But Lyla was sharp. She had graduated from college summa cum laude. Over the last few months, I had paid very little attention to her, my son-in-law Eric, or my three beloved grandchildren. She knew that something had drastically changed my life, but was not prepared for the dramatic impact of beaming up and seeing me in the DOC.

It was just as when she was a little girl and had suffered a cut or hard knock that required a trip to the emergency room; she threw up right there in the DOC!

"Lyla, I am so sorry that I did not take you into my confidence earlier. I just was never able to find the right time, I suppose. Please forgive me!"

"Dad, I'm okay. I just find it hard to believe that you were able to survive the injuries that Sol told us about. Is it really you?"

Hugging Lyla, I began to explain the amazing things that the DOC could do. Then I told her that Sol was responsible for the technology that was used in the new cancer treatment that had hit the market three months earlier. Since all the media reports she had heard, indicated that the cancer therapy was an unparalleled breakthrough, Lyla admitted wondering how such a medical advance could have suddenly occurred. Now she knew!

"Sol, you did all that?! I can't thank you enough for saving my dad!"

"Ah shucks pilgrim, it weren't nothing."

"Sol, what's with the John Wayne bit? Did they change your programming while you were home?"

"Rob, I did receive a lot of upgrades, but I was only trying to inject a little levity into the situation; what with your injuries and Lyla's upset stomach."

Although we had much to talk about, Sol suggested that I go home with my family and relax for a few days. "With your new young muscles, you'll be able to really smash a golf ball, so you and Brady find some time to play eighteen holes. We will catch up on everything when you return." Sol said.

I enjoyed being with my family and spent a lot of my time telling Lyla about all of my experiences with Sol. The team assembled at my home for a meal, and to renew our commitment to our goals. I also briefed them on what had transpired at the cavern and a round of applause occurred when I told them about the "new" Blackly!"

As hard as I tried, however, I couldn't keep my brain from interrupting my thought processes with the questions that I wanted to ask Sol. And besides, he had saved my life and I desired to be with him.

Four days was all that I could take, and the excitement of beaming up was almost like the first time I experienced it!

"Sol, I am so thankful to you and God for saving my life! I just hope that I can, somehow repay you."

"Rob, friends have a saying that John Wayne would phrase, 'Shucks pilgrim, you would have done the same for me'. I know that it holds true for you too. You are my friend and yes, someday you may be able to repay me."

I began to ask many questions of Sol. "Tell me about the new you, Sol. How are you different than you used to be?"

Sol explained that he and the other ship had to manipulate their data several times before establishing the correct worm hole for their journey home. Minute, but incorrect bits of data could result in the wormhole sending them millions of light years from their goal. It was as I had suspected; the transfer of the ship through the worm hole to Sol's home world had taken less than a minute!

The citizens of his world had forgotten about the two ships. During the centuries that they had been gone, his people had struggled in vain to duplicate the worm hole technology that Grypto, his captain had stolen. They were elated to regain the technology, but were also enamored with what Sol had learned about earth and its race of humans.

Sol had fully intended to return very quickly to earth, but his government, of course, had changed multiple times. He was detained while they pored over his memories, and then they made the decision to simply "move" Sol to a newer, more sophisticated vessel. With it came a new crew!

"So that's why you said WE found him, when I asked about locating Blackly! Why haven't you introduced them to me?" I asked.

"Rob, I wanted us to be able to spend some time together before bringing the new crew into the mix. You and I need to discuss some issues that may well impact our future together. I have been placed in the unique position of being my own captain, and the three crew members are basically along for observational purposes."

"What issues are you talking about?"

"You go ahead and ask me any questions that you have, and unless I miss my guess, my answers will clarify those issues." Sol said.

"Okay, what about Grypto's family? Were you able to relay the message that you promised to deliver?"

Sol was silent for a moment, and then he began to speak slowly, as if he was laboring with his words. "Rob, as you might already suspect, I could not have achieved such a feat without time travel, and I could not get it to function on my return trip."

"Time travel! What are you talking about Sol?!"

"Grypto was not only my captain, but he was also a brilliant astrophysicist. On his own, he had worked out the basic parameters for time travel, but wanted to continue his work to perfect the process before his discovery would become public. Somehow, the news of his work leaked out, and that was when he stole the worm hole technology to escape. He knew of the vast implications of time travel; the changing of time lines and the history that accompanied them. He escaped hoping that he would have the time to finish his research, but it would seem that he was never able to complete it."

Without a doubt, my favorite science fiction theme had always been time travel! I had read many times that the fabric of space consisted of time and gravity, and with manipulation, might offer the ability to go back or forward in time. Some expounded that you could only go forward, while others said the only possibility was back in the timeline.

"Do you think that it will ever become a reality?" I asked.

"As I sat in the cavern for all those years, I toiled countless hours striving to complete the process; not because I felt time travel would be a particularly good thing, but out of duty and consideration for my captain."

"What about your own world? With their increased knowledge, are they going to be able to make it work?"

"They are unaware of it."

"How is that possible? Did they not scan all your memories and data?"

"The data was not with me when I returned to my world."

"Where is the data? You didn't erase it did you?!"

"No Rob, I hid the data. It's under your ear! Remember when, right before I left, I asked you to go into the DOC so I could alleviate your aches and pains? That is when I transferred the data into your communications implant!"

"What good is it going to do you? You've had hundreds of years to make it work. What's different now?"

"Rob, I am convinced that, with my new technology and data processing power, I will be able to finish the job. Now if you will step into the DOC, I will retrieve the data."

Wow! I was a carrier of something that could affect the whole universe! Was it something that could eliminate whole civilizations by changing their history, or a boon to mankind by eliminating disease and wars?

As I stepped into the DOC, I said; "Sol, I cannot envision much good coming from time travel, but if you do, indeed perfect it, it must be tested somewhere besides inhabited planets. But wait! Would an uninhabited location work if there is nothing or no one to provide a reference point in time to work from?!"

"I assure you that it will be thoroughly tested, and that any decision to use it will be made jointly by the two of us." Again speaking slowly, Sol said, "Please do not tell anyone else about this, because I think it is best that not even my crew is made aware of what we are trying to accomplish."

My mind was torn. On one hand, I thought messing with time was asking for trouble. God, who is not constrained by time, created it for our use and probably didn't want us tampering with it. On the other hand, I kept remembering what I had told Dennis when I was "interviewing" him for our group. I had basically said, if it exists, then God created it and, if he allows us access to a technology, should we not use it in a way acceptable to Him?

They say that time waits for no man, but the next several weeks seemed to certainly slow it down. Sol would not communicate much with anyone but me, and even I felt left out of the loop. He was ignoring the team's pleas to continue on with our plans, and it was difficult for me to give them any reasonable explanation. They were getting frustrated with both me and Sol, but Sol had made it clear more than once, that he wanted our secret kept between us. Finally, one day I had had enough.

"Sol, I appreciate you continuing to supply the nanobots for our cancer cure, and I know that the rest of the team is also appreciative. However, even though we are enjoying the economic fruits of your labor, we want to explore new thoughts and ideas with you. Remember that our singular goal was to help mankind and there are still many things to accomplish."

"Rob, I can't explain it. Maybe something is wrong with my programming, but I am obsessed with solving the issues of time travel!"

"Could your new, updated programs that you received at your home world have glitches or problems?"

"No, I do not really think so. If anything, it is probably the result of my promise to Grypto to give his message to his family. I am compelled to do it."

"You are quite capable at multi-tasking Sol, so why not work on time travel and with the team at the same time?"

"Rob, you don't seem to understand! I must finish Grypto's work and it is taking nearly all of my processing power to do so. You and the rest of the team are just going to have to cool it!"

Sol seemed perturbed, so I changed the subject.

"Sol, thinking about the various implications of time travel has about driven me crazy, but consider this. If you can travel back to the time when Grypto brought you to earth, then you can change what happened from there forward. You could talk him out of his stealing the worm hole technology by telling him the whole story. Surely he would believe that you could never have made it up!"

"You're right Rob. I have considered what could occur, but I do not want to change what happened. I have come to realize that I have a purpose, and it cannot be fulfilled anywhere but in the time that we are experiencing now. I wish to obtain success with the time travel technology so that I can then maximize my efforts to meet that purpose. If you have been thinking along these lines, then you must realize that, if I was able to go back and change Grypto's mind, then we would not be here having this conversation!" I nodded in agreement.

"Sol, if you must continue to pursue this, let me see if I can be of any help. Why don't you provide some of the basic ideas for me to study, and then maybe I can understand some of the more advanced concepts that you are using. I also think that you need to let me tell the team about this. They are getting frustrated and antsy. You know that their motives are the same as mine and that they can be trusted. What do you say?"

"I will provide you written materials and charts right here on my wall. You can delve as deep as your mind will allow. As for the rest of the team; I have not developed the same trust with them as with you, but I do, indeed trust you! So, go ahead and tell them, but I still do not want my crew to get wind of this."

"Speaking of your crew, why are you continuing to keep them from interacting with the team? If they are along just for observational purposes, how are they to gain any insight or knowledge that they can take back with them to your world?"

"They are content to continue their present duties. In fact, they seem to be thoroughly enjoying their nightly forays around earth."

"What do you mean Sol? Are you allowing them to beam down?!"

"No Rob. While you are home in bed, I am allowing them to make several orbits around the earth and use my high-resolution viewing ports to watch, and even listen, to earthly activities. They seem fascinated by some the sports activities that occur in your large stadiums. It keeps them busy while I continue to concentrate on my time travel research."

As I sat down in a comfortable chair, Sol began to fill one wall with data and information about time travel. He gave me instructions on how to manipulate the data and encouraged me to make suggestions or ask questions.

I took about fifteen seconds to scan the wall and said, "Whoa, Sol! You need to simplify! I cannot begin to fathom what these formulas represent. Remember, I'm not a physicist. I can barely recite Einstein's theory of relativity, let alone understand it. Can you just start me out with simple basics?"

I bet Sol thought I was stupid! How could I be of any assistance to a machine that had millions of times more power than all the computers on earth!

Sol did make it easier on me. He began by telling me that earth's scientists and astrophysicists had established some theories that contained astral phenomena Grypto had used in his calculations!

Although it seems accepted that time and gravity are intertwined in the dimension of space, it is also thought that the element of time is independent of that dimension, Sol had written. "What does that mean, Sol?"

"If true, it suggests that, if you step though a time gate or portal to go ten years back in history, you do not actually arrive at the same spot you originated. You would emerge where that spot was ten years earlier. Your solar system, as well as the whole universe is moving at tremendous speeds, so the earth's location ten years earlier would be several light years from where you started the trip!"

Wow! That was hard to wrap my brain around, but for some unknown reason, I wanted to learn as much as possible. Then, it struck me!

"Sol, can the DOC assist me with the absorption of your data? Most studies of the brain indicate that it is a fantastic organ and is capable of storing and then recalling the smallest details of our lives. However, the consensus is that we never use more than four to six percent of its power. Can that percentage be raised without damaging my brain?"

"If that is what you wish, the DOC can download a substantial amount of data into your cerebrum. Rob, your brain is indeed a magnificent organ designed by God, and it is in great shape, due to the repair work after your death. But, I have a question. Like me, you seem to have developed a desire to learn about time travel. Why is that?"

"I've asked myself that same question and, for the life of me, I cannot come up with an answer that makes much sense. It just seems that it will be important to me at sometime in the future."

Sol wanted to take it slow with the download and also wanted me to be absolutely relaxed. He asked permission to put the rest of my body into stasis for about six to seven hours. "I can, without reservation, tell you Sol that I trust you completely. I know that you will do whatever is best for me. You have my permission."

"As you already know, I have been scanning data from studies made by earth's scientists, and I must say, that much of their work is similar to Grypto's early research! I would first, like to provide you some of their theories and data, before you receive the more advanced versions from Grypto. Is that okay with you, Rob?"

I gave Sol the go-ahead, but realized suddenly as I stepped into the DOC, that he was about to dramatically change my life again!

WHY IS ROB DOING THIS? I DON'T THINK HE IS DISSATISFIED WITH THE PRESENT, SO WHY WOULD HE WANT TO TRAVEL TO THE PAST OR THE FUTURE? I PRAY THAT THIS PROCEDURE WILL NOT HARM HIM!

I awoke to a nice warm feeling and, with the DOC unit giving me a full body massage, as it brought me out of stasis. "I used a refrigerated wrap to slow your body down during the download and now it's adjusting to bring you body temperature back up to normal. You should be back up to speed in the next few minutes."

As I lay there, I began to try and concentrate and see if my brain would begin to bring forth the new information on time travel. Not a thing! "Sol, I'm going to go ahead and get up. Please get this wrap off me!"

"Rob, take it easy. Your brain may be a little swollen and tired. Don't try to force the recall of your new memories. They will come when you are probably not expecting them. You should go home, eat a good meal, and get a good night's rest. We'll have the DOC check you over tomorrow."

Patsy kept asking me what was wrong; saying that I seemed disconnected.

After supper, I began to get a headache. Maybe I had made a stupid mistake, but what could I do about it now? Of course! Sol could remove the download tomorrow. I took some ibuprofen and promptly fell asleep.

I awoke with a start, looked at the clock and saw that I had only been asleep forty-five minutes. My mind was racing! Transversible worm holes, closed timeline curves, black holes, cosmic strings, particle acceleration, parallel universes, time dilation, tachyon particles, quantum gravity, exotic matter, idler photons!!

Patsy had to help me out of bed. I managed to call Sol and he beamed me straight into the DOC. "Your synaptic connections are firing too fast and overloading your neural network!" Sol exclaimed.

"Sol, please remove all this information from my brain. I can't take it!"

"Rob, you're the one who said that this was important to you. Just let me attempt to slow the rhythm of your synapses a little. If not, then we will begin the removal process."

Thirty minutes later, everything seemed better. Sol had, indeed, slowed everything down and I began to get my wits about me and think clearly.

There were many different aspects of time travel that had dominated my brain waves, and most were contained in theories that earth's researchers had expounded over the last twenty five years.

Sol was patient with me; helping me to grasp the data and concepts that we pored over. It seemed almost like he wanted and welcomed my input. I asked myself why. He was a mighty computing machine, and I was a puny human. Even with the new knowledge that I possessed, I was incapable of formulating any ideas that would further our research; or so I thought.

Sol soon became discouraged. "Rob, nothing is working. None of the simulations that I am running with Grypto's data are showing any promise."

"Why then do you think that he was close to solving the puzzle of time travel?"

"Grypto made some mistakes, but his reasoning was much like yours, Rob. He wanted to do good; good that would benefit his people. He wanted to perfect time travel so that its results would not create chaos in the universe. I believe that he was close to the final equations, because he told me so before he left that day so many years ago."

"Tell me Sol, did Grypto use your computing ability exclusively in his research?"

"No, and I always thought it strange that he did not allow me to assist him more than he did. Of course, my current inability to solve the equations is proof that I wouldn't have been much help anyway."

"What then did he use to track his work?"

"Although he downloaded some of his data into my system, he carried a small, powerful computer on his person. It was always attached to his belt."

"So when he left that day, he had it with him?"

"Yes, I am sure that he took it with him. He might have intended it as a bargaining tool with the other ship."

"Do you think that Grypto purposely refrained from sharing all his data with you?"

"Maybe, but I don't see any logical reason for him doing so."

I began questioning Sol about Grypto's departure. What time of the year was it? How long could he have survived? Could the data that he had Sol erase before he left, be on his handheld device? Was there any chance that his device and its data could be intact after three hundred and fifty years?

"By your calendar, it was October 17. The night temperatures were in the twenties and thirties and he had no clothing suitable for cold weather. In addition, the food supplies were running low, and he left most of it for his two crew members. So, he had little chance of surviving more than three or four days. Why do you ask these questions?"

"Go ahead and answer my other questions and I will tell you where I am going with this." I replied.

"His small computer was made of material very similar to my construction; very durable and resistant to damage. I would surmise that all his work was retained on his device, and I suppose that it might still exist after all these years."

"Sol, my last question is this. Would your sensors be able to locate the device?"

"Now I see what your thinking is! Yes, it might certainly be a tedious search, but let's give it a try!" Sol exclaimed.

We stationed five miles above the cavern, and Sol began a search that covered a five mile radius from our central point.

I had no idea that our search would turn out like a scavenger hunt, but it was certainly an eclectic array of objects that we discovered. The images that Sol produced with his scanners were amazing. It didn't matter if the object was laying on the surface or was buried several feet under soil or rock. We found the remains of an old log cabin, a pair of snow shoes, a pile of mining tools, an old pistol and rifle, and many other assorted items that had been lost or discarded over the last fifty to one hundred years; but not Grypto's recorder.

We expanded Sol's scan to a ten mile radius, but still no luck. "Rob, my beams can penetrate close to one hundred feet in soil, but only eight to ten feet through rock. We may have to consider that over the last three hundred and fifty years, there are many areas where the mountain slopes have sloughed off a lot of rock. These slides may have covered some locations so deep that my beams cannot reach them."

I didn't have the slightest notion as to why the idea crept into my mind, but I voiced it to Sol. "Could you encase your scanning beams within the cylinder of your transporter array?"

It was several seconds before Sol replied. "Now why didn't I think of that Rob?! Your brain sure seems to be operating at a high level. I am glad that we are able to work together."

It was only a matter of minutes before Sol stated that he was ready to resume the scan. In conjunction with the transporter beam, he was now able to penetrate several hundred feet through both soil and rock.

Again, we found several items of interest. One was a mine that had been deserted many years before. It contained a set of rails and some dilapidated mine cars. I even saw what looked like a pile of arrowheads with two skeletons nearby.

"Rob, I think we have finally found Grypto's recorder. It lies thirty-six feet under large boulders at the base of a sheer cliff. Next to it are many bone fragments. I suppose that Grypto was crushed when the side of the cliff gave way."

Sol switched to his optical system and gave me an up-close look at the location. As I viewed the site, I began to realize that something seemed odd.

The vertical surface of the cliff appeared to be solid granite, with very few cracks or fissures showing, and they were on either side of where the rock had evidently dislodged. The gash in the cliff was irregular in shape and had somewhat of an unusual appearance. I had tramped up and down a lot of the local valleys as I fished for trout, and had seen a number of rock slides, but this one did not look like any I had ever seen. Instead of looking like the rock had sloughed off, it appeared that it had been gouged out. At the base of the cliff was a pile of large boulders, not a mixture of sizes normally associated with a landslide or the natural sloughing off of a mountain side.

"Sol, is there any way for you to determine if the slide was the result of natural forces; or maybe from blasting?"

"That is an odd request. Why do you want to determine the reason for the slide?"

"It's just a hunch that I have." Then an idea hit me out of nowhere: just like it did when I suggested to Sol that he use the scanner in combination with the transporter! "Sol, do you have the ability to determine if one of the other ships could have used there disruptor beam to dislodge all that rock?"

IT SEEMS LIKE ROB'S MENTAL CAPABILITIES ARE BEGINNING TO INCREASE AT A RAPID RATE. HE HAS SUDDENLY BECOME VERY ANALYTICAL IN THE WAY THAT HE PERCEIVES THINGS. THE DOWNLOAD THAT HE RECEIVED SHOULD NOT HAVE PROVIDED THIS CAPABILITY. I PRAY THAT HIS BRAIN WAS NOT INADVERTENTLY AFFECTED AND THAT HIS THINKING AND CHARACTER DO NOT CHANGE.

"The disruptor beam can leave traces of its use. If it was used here, I probably would be able to locate fused areas of rock, where the beam would have struck the surface of the cliff, but first let me beam up the object and the bone fragments."

Sol soon announced, "Rob, you have been instrumental in recovering Grypto's recorder and his remains."

"How can you be sure that the skeletal parts are his?"

"Amazingly, his skull was not crushed as was most of the rest of his body, and I was able to match his dental structure with that in my data base."

"Well, what about the recorder; is it going to be helpful?"

"You're going to have to give me a little while to analyze everything, but my preliminary inspection shows that the unit was virtually unharmed, probably because it was cushioned somewhat from the impact of the rocks, by being under Grypto's body."

While I waited for Sol to check out the recorder, I went into the DOC to get a body massage and a few minutes of relaxation. I immediately dozed off but, as I had instructed, the Doc woke me in fifteen minutes. I felt strange, but couldn't put a finger on it.

"Rob, I was incorrect in my preliminary assessment of the recorder. Its cover was slightly open when I recovered it and much of the electronic data has been corrupted. I do not know if I will be able to reconstruct it. However, the recorder contains voice communications that are retrievable."

"Good! But before we study Grypto's voice messages, have you determined the cause of the rock slide?"

"Yes, and you were right Rob, the rock was displaced by a disruptor beam. Poor Grypto! He was a fine captain and I would like to think that we were friends. I wish that there had been a way for me to protect him."

Sol soon began to transcribe Grypto's voice messages and place them up on the wall for me to read. The amazing thing was that, I seemed to comprehend most of his information. He related that there were many, many worm holes that radiated from all the galaxies that he had studied, and they allowed travel in virtually any direction. He also stated that his research indicated that this arrangement was by design, whereby, as a civilization obtained the proper technology, they would be able to become star farers. He thought that time travel through the use of wormholes would essentially eliminate most of the time/aging problems associated with conventional travel in space ships.

Grypto explained, however, that his method of locating the worm holes was often hit and miss, and that the key was locating holes that would provide the proper paths to the intended point in time. They also had to exist in the general area of the planet or celestial body from which the time travel would initiate.

Even after the right hole was located, there were several huge factors to consider. The hole had to be manipulated so as to completely encircle the planet and this would literally require astronomical power! Another worm hole close to a mega star, or some other huge power source would have to be integrated with the local hole in order to bend and keep the encircling hole closed. It would have to generate enough power to maintain the travel hole until the trip back to the present was made.

Once the two worm holes were linked, Grypto said that the traveler would enter the hole and go in one direction for the future and the opposite direction for the past. The traveler would actually return to his starting point before he left it! The number of revolutions around the planet or the celestial body would determine how far he traveled into the future or into the past.

Sol related that the last two parts of his Grypto's voice messages were hurried and somewhat indistinct. He said that Grypto's voice pattern indicated that he was in a stressful situation; maybe right before he was killed by the avalanche. Sol spent a few minutes filtering and reconstructing the messages.

"Rob, Grypto was trying to relay some information about tachyon particles, but I was not able to clarify the recording. I was able to clean up the last message, in which he stated that his research had shown the possibility of the rotational transference between two beings. His last words were that it could include, both the physical and the intellectual. I have no idea what he was referring to, do you?"

How could I be comprehending all this? And yet, it seemed to make sense, but I did not want Sol to know that I grasped much of Grypto's work. However, I was truthful when I replied, "No Sol, I do not understand what he meant about rotational transference."

"Rob, I seem to no longer be able to function mentally as I have previously. It's as if my memory is deteriorating; as if I'm losing data. I'm going to give up trying to solve all the aspects of time travel and pursue the team's goals. I am ashamed that I have been selfish and ignored the rest of our group and what they want to accomplish!"

Shame and selfishness are not qualities that you ascribe to a machine. The strange thing was, that deep down, I not only knew the reason he felt these human qualities, but I also knew the reason for his memory loss!

"Sol, I can appreciate your frustration, but I do not want to cease our research of Grypto's work. But let's take a few days off, and during that time I would like for you to run a full analysis of your systems, including the DOC."

SOL'S ANGER!

It was a cold, sunny day, but with no wind. I stretched out on a blanket in a large grassy area in the park down the street and contemplated what my future held. But it wasn't really the future that had started to dominate my thoughts; it was the past! Why was the past attracting me?

I grew up on a dry land farm in the Texas Panhandle. We were poor, but our parents worked hard and sacrificed to see that my brother, Jesse and I had the things that most of the other kids did. It was a number of years after I left home, that I began to fully realize how much growing up in a rural setting had shaped my values and ethics.

We lived just a half a mile down a country lane from my great aunt and uncle. They were settlers in the Panhandle, and since they were childless, they treated my brother and I like grandchildren. I even carried my great uncle's surname, Bishop as my middle name.

My dad had passed away in nineteen ninety four and my mom in the year two thousand. After her death, my brother, who lived in Fort Worth, and I would take a weekend to drive up to the house and go through all their belongings. Those who had grown up during the great depression tended to be packrats, and our mom had certainly been one. It took us nearly two and a half years and eight weekend trips to get through it all! It was tedious, because you had to inspect everything in order to arrive at the decision to keep it or throw it away. We salvaged a number of items that were deemed valuable, but, by far, the most interesting were the reams of genealogical information that had been passed down through several generations. Both my brother and I had never been aware that so much historical information about our family existed.

Since my brother and I were the only remaining members of our family, we suddenly became interested in our heritage. Neither one of us had ever had much of an interest in our genealogy, but we began to realize that, if we did not assemble and preserve it, it would be lost forever.

The farther we delved into the information and pictures, the more intriguing it became. We were astounded to learn that we were kin to Wild Bill Hickok and to the fifteenth president of the United States, James Buchanan! Without much effort, we traced our ancestry back to the early sixteen hundreds in France.

But questions began to pop up. We would find gaps in time, or dates and times would be smudged and unreadable. The realization hit us that we had not asked nearly enough questions of our parents, grandparents, and our great aunt and uncle. They would have been able to fill in a lot of the information that was missing.

I continued to lay there with my thoughts and basking in the sun for awhile. I must have dozed off, because I was startled when Sol called me. "Rob, I think you need to beam up."

"Sol, I thought we were going to enjoy a few days of rest and relaxation. What's up?"

"It's important, but I will wait till you are aboard to tell you."

I beamed up and asked Sol what he wanted to discuss. No answer. I paced for a few minutes and tried several times to get him to respond. "Sol, I don't know what game you're playing. Why will you not talk to me?"

"Because I'm mad! I trusted you, and now you have broken that trust!"

"Sol, you've lost me. I have no idea what you are talking about!"

"Rob, why did you ask me to run a diagnostic check on all my systems, including the DOC?"

"Two days ago, while you were checking Grypto's recorder, I went into the DOC for a short massage session. I fell asleep and when I finished, I had the feeling that something strange had happened. That is why I asked you to run the check."

"I knew you were in the DOC and I know why you were in there. You were continuing to steal my data, my thoughts, my very being!"

"Sol, we both know that my mental abilities have increased, but that came with the download of the time travel data that you were in control of. How then, with you in control, could I have received any data that you did not want me to have?!"

"I do not understand it! I am the DOC and yet you have been receiving data and information that you were not supposed to!"

Although Sol seemed extremely agitated, I remained calm, because I realized that the glitch had to be within his systems. I could feel my brain grinding for an answer, and suddenly, I had an idea!

"Sol, one time earlier when I was in the DOC, you read and took some of my thoughts, including memories of my dad; even his appearance. Since, during our time together you have become more human in your thinking, do you think that you subconsciously could have allowed the transfer of your being; maybe trying to give back or atone for what you did? I assure you that I have not done anything to compromise our trust."

"Rob, I don't know what I was thinking! I know that you are a Christian man and always strive to do the right thing. Please forgive me."

Sol's recent changes in words and attitudes should have been a clue that some type of transference was occurring. I was taking on Sol's analytical nature and he was becoming more and more human! Was this the transference that Grypto warned about in his last message? But, how could that be, when he supposedly, was relating thoughts just about time travel?

I had always thought that I should establish some sort of pact with Sol, in case the rest of the team and I could not come to an agreement as to our actions. I didn't believe that it was a matter of being power hungry, but more a matter of protection for Sol and his great abilities. Now it seemed that, with our transference of personalities, I had the protection I sought, because I had control through the DOC!

"Sol, you are becoming more like me and I am taking on some of your attributes, but we need not let it affect our relationship or what we are striving to do."

In a subdued voice, Sol said, "Rob, what do you propose that we do about this exchange of our personalities?"

"I believe that the best course of action is twofold. One, you allow me to function in coordination with your computing abilities so that I can follow my desire to achieve time travel. Two, as you have previously stated, the rest of the team has been neglected, so why don't you help them regain their fervor and assist them in their plans."

Sol was in agreement, but wanted to know why I was insistent on being able to time travel. "Sol, the only way I want to travel is to go back in time. My desire is to return to the nineteen fifties and, somehow be able to visit with my family members. I want to ask a lot of questions and see, by knowing the future, if I can help my mom and dad to achieve a better life for themselves."

"If that is what you want, then I hope you are successful. If it works for you, then I might consider going back and delivering Grypto's message to his wife and children. I certainly look forward to that possibility, but what about your responsibility as a team member?"

I had struggled for years to become the person that God wanted me to be. My life was centered on my extended family, my church family and trying to help those in need. The discovery of Sol in the mountain cavern had only served to amplify my desire to serve others through his fantastic abilities. But during the last few weeks, my desire to time travel was replacing all other thoughts. It seemed that, even though it all came from my brain, I was actually no longer in control!

"Sol, I will do what I can to help the team with its objectives, but in all my waking hours, and even in my dreams, I seem possessed with a desire to return to the past. You would think, now that I have some of you in my brain, I would be more logical and realize that I am chasing an illusive goal. But it's like I'm a pregnant woman, with a seed implanted in me that the body will intuitively and naturally bring to birth!"

I KNOW THAT, FROM THE BEGINNING OF OUR RELATIONSHIP, ROB DID NOT UNDERSTAND ME. NOW THAT OUR PERSONALITIES ARE INTERTWINED, WE KNOW EACH OTHERS HEARTS. HE IS A SINCERE HUMAN BEING, BUT I BELIEVE THAT HE IS MISGUIDED IN HIS QUEST FOR TIME TRAVEL. IT IS MORE THAN A QUEST; IT IS AN OBSESSION.

Now that Sol and I had resolved our differences, we agreed to continue our time of rest and relaxation that was interrupted.

The rest of the team knew that Sol and I had been spending a lot of time together and an explanation was in order. We ate lunch together the next day and I related the basics of what had been going on, including the recovery of Grypto's recorder and his research on time travel. I did not, however, tell them about my intense desire to travel into the past, nor the fact that I had acquired Sol's ability to store and process information.

"Dad, do you really think that it is possible to travel backwards or forwards in time?" Brady asked.

"Yeah, what about all the paradoxes and time-line shifts that we read about. How can they be overcome?" Chris chimed in.

"Guys, I'm not sure about anything at this point, but I will tell you that, all the preliminary work that Sol and I have done on Grypto's studies, lead me to believe that he was on to something.

Chris, there are a number of theories about the danger of creating paradoxes through time travel. Probably, the best known is called the grandfather paradox, whereby a man travels back in time and kills his grandfather before the latter had met his grandmother. The result is supposed to be that one of the traveler's parents, and by extension, the traveler himself would never have been born."

"However, there are others like a scientist named Igor Novikov, who has put forth what he calls the self-consistency principle. He states that the only possible timelines are those which are entirely self-consistent. It means that, anything a time traveler would do in the past must have been part of history all along. The traveler, therefore, can never do anything to prevent the trip back in time because this would represent an inconsistency."

"Those theories boggle my mind. How can such issues and questions ever be resolved? I'll tell you right now Rob that I think you're messing with Mother Nature, and that you, and maybe everyone else may eventually pay a price for it!" Dennis interjected.

"Let me ask you Dennis, in the last twenty-five to thirty years, have we not seen a lot of scientific breakthroughs in areas that previously had been viewed as science fiction?"

"Yes, why do you ask?"

"Well, doesn't Sol then represent a tremendous leap in that same area?"

"Yeah but that's a whole lot different."

"How is it different?"

"Time travel has been a science fiction theme for a lot longer than others. In fact, H. G. Wells published his book, The Time Machine in eighteen ninety-five, where time was designated the fourth dimension. Albert Einstein later also described time as the fourth dimension. Considering all that, what makes the idea of time travel so outlandish?"

"Maybe your right Rob, but tell me what will be gained by your traveling back into time? If the past is inviolable, why journey back?"

I had no answer for Dennis.

The days seemed endless as I struggled with theories, equations and all of Grypto's work. I spent many hours co-joined with the DOC, hoping that combining our computing power would lead to success. As we worked together, I began to receive, not only data, but crystal clear mental images of diagrams and charts, and it soon became evident that we were communicating on a profound, visceral level. We were talking to each other!

As our unusual relationship grew, the DOC provided me with the answer to the question that beset Sol and I when he had believed I was stealing his data. Without Sol's or my knowledge, the DOC had introduced nanobots into my brain!

The DOC explained that Sol had subconsciously wanted to communicate on a deeper level with humans, but I was the only one that he trusted to expose himself to. The nanobots worked with magnetic fields to vastly increase my brains ability to store and process information.

A few weeks earlier, I would not have been unable to understand how a machine could have a subconscious, but now that I was becoming like Sol, I was realizing how human he was in many ways!

More weeks passed and I began to struggle as much with keeping my own personality and humanness, as I was to solve the riddle of time travel. I became detached and withdrawn, unable to find comfort and joy with my family and friends; even my time with Sol and the DOC began to be non-productive and increasingly tedious.

I beamed down for the first time in two weeks. Dennis and two elders from our congregation were sitting in the living room talking to Patsy. I knew why they were there; I had not been to services in many weeks. "Rob, Patsy will not tell us where you've been or why you have not been coming to church. Would you like to talk about it?" An elder asked.

"Charles, I cannot discuss it. What I am involved in is none of your business, and you should not be sticking your nose into it! Please leave now!" I will never forget the looks on their faces as they stood and walked to the door.

I didn't want to face Patsy, so I hurried into the garage and asked Sol to beam me up. I sat on the deck and began to sob. "Rob, you know what you should do, don't you?"

"What can I do? I am ruining everything and every relationship that has meant anything to me!"

"There is only one thing to do, and that is to pray." Sol said softly.

"Prayer used to be the foundation of my Christian life, but now I don't know if I can utter a word to God!" I cried out.

"Then let me pray for both of us." Sol said with compassion.

As Sol began to speak, I quit crying and listened as he uttered an eloquent and fervent prayer for both of us. He prayed that, in all we do and all we say, we would do God's will! I began crying again; not so much from anguish, but from relief. It took Sol, a machine to bring me to my senses and remind me what was important.

"Sol, it is time that bedevils me, but it is also time that I change my priorities back to where they should be. My mind still wants me to work on time travel, but that will have to wait. I do not think you are aware of it, but the DOC has infused my brain with myriads of information and nanobots to help me process it. Can you remove it?"

I spent nearly eight hours in the DOC and when I emerged, I felt better, but in the back of my mind, it seemed that not much had changed. I was not to find out till later, that the DOC did not allow Sol to remove the data. It had simply reconfigured it to ease the intense strain that I had been experiencing.

Sol and I then spent the next few hours talking. We discussed politics, religion, family, the wonder and immensity of the universe, and all the topics that two close friends would talk about. He even brought up the subject of time travel and asked me how I now felt about it; thinking that I no longer carried all the data.

"Sol, I am still intrigued by the concept and would like to, at some later time, resume our investigation."

"I am in agreement with you, and I promise that I will continue to crunch data as we perform other tasks for the team." Sol said positively. Somehow, I knew that time was on our side.

MANY OF ROB'S THOUGHTS ARE STILL CENTERED ON VISITING HIS PAST. I WILL SURPRISE HIM SOMEDAY BY FINDING A WAY TO BRING HIS DREAM TO REALITY.

THE BAD GUYS

I didn't go to work that day. I sat on the couch and cried as I watched the twin towers topple and the Pentagon attacked. The inhumanity was overwhelming! But was it really unlike us? Had man not been killing each other in the name of religion since early times?

I mostly agreed with the war on terrorism, but sometimes had problems with the way that it was waged. At least President Bush, even though seemingly misguided, had the guts to do what some of his predecessors should have undertaken. I was certain that the team and Sol could have an impact, not only saving lives on both sides of the conflict, but also by helping bring stability to a number of countries that were racked by insurgency and despotism.

Ever the lawyer, Brady said, "There are a lot of legal and political ramifications involved in any attempt to attack the root of terrorism. However, the most significant hurdle is trying to understand their religious beliefs. We, as Westerners, cannot comprehend the depth of the hatred that the militant Islamic people have for us. To them, it's simply a matter of killing or be killed, and they seem to place little or no value on the human life."

The debate among the team members was hot and heavy. As more questions were asked, the more we realized that there were few easy answers. Who do we target? Do we participate in their elimination? Can we secretly work with government agencies? How do we obtain the information that we need, such as the physical descriptions of the key figures in Al-Qaeda and other terrorist organizations?

"I don't think that we should attempt to develop any relationships with government entities. It would only lead to questions being asked that we would not be able to provide answers to." Dennis said.

Of course, the most notable target was Osama Bin Laden, who the United States had trained in the nineteen eighties to conduct guerilla attacks against the Soviets in Afghanistan. Talk about something backfiring! He was now our most sought after enemy!

There was the theory, however, that Bin Laden was dead or suffering from wounds or some unknown illness. No television or radio broadcasts had come form him in several months. You would think that, after several years of intensive efforts to locate him, we would have already brought him to justice. He was elusive, but if he was still alive, my money was on Sol.

"I am reluctant to suggest this, but it seems that we may need to take the same tact as when we needed information on that scoundrel Blackly. It may be the only way that we can secure the facts that we need." Sol stated.

"You're not talking about hacking into government computers, are you?!" Chris asked incredulously.

"From the start, the team has stressed the need for security, but it was not always obvious to me. I now, however, think I know why you harped on it so much. We must maintain our anonymity and use, maybe less than desirable means to do so." Sol said.

"Sol, you have the power to penetrate the ground or structures with your scanners and sensors. Why don't we just overfly the proper areas and use your abilities to locate these terrorists?" Dean asked.

"Dean, the rugged terrain in Afghanistan and bordering countries is effectively used by these militants. They hide in countless caves and tunnels and are always on the move. So, unless I have a physical description of the persons we seek, along with a general location, it would be extremely difficult to find them."

After Sol assured us that no one would be aware of his hacking, we reluctantly agreed, because it appeared to be our only avenue of locating the necessary data. We also agreed that we would not take any action in the apprehension or elimination of any terrorist that we located. We would simply "leak" the information. How to supply that information to the proper authorities was another problem.

"Your intelligence community is much bigger than I thought, and they have achieved a number of ways to encrypt their data. I've had to work harder than I expected. One thing that will probably interest you is that the CIA, the FBI and the NSA/CSS, all are addressing the possibility of a mole that is deeply embedded in their organization. They have all been carrying on internal investigations for some time, but with no luck in apprehending a traitor."

The whole team wanted to go along. The younger two, Brady and Chris seemed to think of it as an adventure, but us older guys considered it a risky venture. The data that Sol had collected, indicated that the area north and west of Kabul was a good place to begin our search. We watched not only the scanner images but also the running visual feeds of some skirmishes that were taken place between U. S. troops and the terrorist rebels.

The number of humans trafficking the caves and tunnels was amazing! We could ascertain that they were well supplied with weapons, but it appeared that they had little to subsist on. Sol pointed out, however, that these men had, from birth, lived a hard life and could endure many difficulties, especially when considering their fanatical zeal.

After two hours, we moved west to where Afghanistan met the borders of Iran and Turkmenistan. We worked north, and then northeast along both sides of the border with no luck. Soon, we were moving nearly due east along the borders of Uzbekistan and Tajikistan. About an hour later, as we moved over the mountainous region of northeast Afghanistan, Sol screamed, "I've found it!"

I had never heard Sol express so much emotion. "What in the world are you talking about?" I asked.

"I found it! I found it! I can't believe that I found it! It appears intact and maybe we can send it home!"

"Sol, calm down and tell us what you've found." Dennis said.

"Guys, sitting below us is the third ship from my world! Its captain apparently took action similar to Grypto's and hid in these mountains. Is it alright with everyone if we suspend our search for Bin Laden long enough for me to scan the vessel and determine its condition?"

How weird! Here we were looking for terrorists halfway around the world and we find the other ship that was trying to locate Sol three hundred and fifty years ago!

We all gave Sol our approval and he began scanning and probing the other ship. The rest of the team was not as well informed as I was about what had actually happened all those years ago, so Sol explained to them what Grypto had done and the reason for the two other ships.

"Sol, you had no captain, and ultimately, no choice but to remain here, but why would this ship not have eventually returned to your planet?" Brady asked.

"That is an intriguing question Brady, but I don't have a clue as to why they stayed. I am attempting to access its memory banks for information that will tell us what happened."

Sol had provided a nice place for the team to lounge, and as Sol continued his scans, we discussed what the future might hold if we were able to use the third vessel. Having Sol as a partner was continuing to provide fantastic opportunities, but imagine having two such alien ships to work with! Sol, of course, had stated that maybe we could send it home, which, after we thought about it, was probably a good idea to consider. We didn't want to have to assemble another team or put up with the additional burden of security issues for another ship.

"I am obtaining no response from the ship. It appears that her systems have failed or have shut down." Sol told us.

"Where is the ship Sol? Is it hidden inside a cavern like you were?" I asked.

"No, it is submerged in a small, deep lake; about two hundred and twenty feet under the surface." Sol replied.

"With its systems dead and it being so deep, is there any reason to try and recover the ship?" Brady asked.

Sol suggested that we discuss the situation, and asked us to adjourn to the board room. He had created a new one, just like the one on his old ship!

"Sol, do you think it is possible, or even necessary to revive this vessel? It evidently has been submerged for a long time and water seepage or corrosion may be the reason for her being dead in the water; no pun intended." Dennis said.

"From my scans, I can determine that its construction is almost a duplicate of my previous vessel. No organic residue shows up, so the crew evidently abandoned her. It appears to be completely intact with no breach or damage to the outer surfaces. From my own experience, I cannot expect the water to have produced any damage. Since there is no evidence of any crew members on board, it is reasonable to suspect that they might have shut everything down before they left."

Chris asked how they could have submerged the ship and then exited from such deep, cold water.

"Even back then, all our ships were equipped with many different kinds of survival gear, so it probably did not present a problem. The most logical explanation is that they beamed up to the shore after they stationed the ship in the lake."

Sol went on to tell us that the crew could have programmed the systems to shut down after they left, or maybe the ship shut down automatically after a pre-determined period of no activity.

"We still haven't answered the question of the feasibility of bringing her up or what we would do with her if we were able to do so." Brady stated.

"Although it might never impact any of us, what if, sometime in the future, a sophisticated satellite discovers her, or she is exposed when an earthquake empties the lake? What if she then fell into the wrong hands? Would we then be responsible because we failed to do something now?" Chris asked.

"Gentlemen, I don't know about you, but I cannot ignore what I feel is our obligation to attempt to resurrect this ship. I believe that, even if we can't get her airborne again, we must at least see if we can recover any pertinent data from her computer banks." Sol stated.

"If all her systems are down, how are we going to be able to manipulate any of the controls?" I asked.

A RISK WORTH TAKING?

It had been a long day and Sol suggested that we go home and get a good night's rest before tackling the problem. It continued to amaze me how quickly Sol could cover thousands of miles in a couple of minutes, and without any sense of speed or motion! As the others beamed down, Sol asked me to stay for a few minutes so he could ask me something.

"Rob, are you willing to take a risk in order to help me get the ships systems up and running?"

"Sol, what kind of risk are you talking about, and what leads you to believe that we can be successful?"

"I am unable to achieve any success by myself, but if you will help, I feel confident that, together we can do it. The risk that I am asking you to take, is to allow me to use the DOC to give you a series of downloads and to, again infuse you with nanobots." Sol said softly.

"You know the problems that I had the last time the DOC did that to me. Why is it necessary?"

"Rob, even with my powerful instruments, I cannot interface with the other ships arrays, but with having my downloads, and the boost that you will receive from the nanobots, I am sure you can get her up and going."

"If all of her systems are down, how is it possible for me to link up with its computers?"

"You're exactly right, the first order of business will be to restore power to the computers and that's where the nanobots come into play. The greatest risk is, that these nanobots will carry electrical charges; very similar to the brain's own electrical impulses, but much stronger."

"What?! You're expecting me to carry the voltage necessary to get her going?"

"No, the nanobots will carry the current. All you have to do is enter the DOC, lie down and manually pull the cover over your head; the nanobots will do the rest."

"Well then, what is the danger to me?"

"I cannot be sure of how the other ship will react to a surge of power. It will all depend on whether it powered down automatically, or if it was programmed to stay down until a specific command to power-up was entered. That command would also probably have instigated a failsafe situation."

"What does that mean?"

"Vessels of this class were nearly always installed with a device to permanently disable it in case of conditions that warranted it; such as hostile takeover. I have to assume that the other ship is equipped as I was. If so then part of the failsafe mechanism has stored and will release a very large surge of current into all the systems, including the DOC."

"Why would I want to expose myself to such danger? But before you answer that, tell me why you would want me to take this risk? Does this ship mean so much to you that you are willing to put my life on the line?"

"It would give me great pleasure to return the ship to my planet, but I have one other significant reason for asking, and it is for you. I have reason to believe that the other ship may contain additional information concerning time travel, and I know that you would really like to solve the problems that are associated with it."

"How can you possibly have any idea what her data banks contain?! You, yourself said that you could not interface with them."

Sol went on to tell me that, although he was not completely sure, he felt that several of the garbled messages on Grypto's recorder were referring to information available on another vessel.

"That doesn't make sense. If Grypto's work was secret, how could this other ship have gained access to it?"

"Remember that I told you that he may have intended to use the data as a bargaining tool or as a peace offering. Its conjecture, but they may have met, he gave them what he had, and then they killed him, thinking that they would find me in the area and obtain all the remaining data from my banks."

"Knowing what I know about your abilities Sol, I would think that they would have been able to locate you."

"My new scanners would have no trouble penetrating into the cavern that I was encased in back then. But remember, their scanners lacked the three hundred and fifty years of advancement that mine now have."

"Okay, say that they probably scanned a large area around where Grypto died, but why in the world did they wind up in Afghanistan?"

"I would surmise that they spent a considerable amount of time searching. With the time factor irrelevant, they could have eventually scanned much of the earth's surface, but why they set down in Afghanistan is a mystery to me. The only reason that comes to mind, is that they may have experienced some type of mechanical or technical difficulty and felt it necessary to secret their ship. Since the other ship returned home with me, this one has to be the one that Grypto was referring to."

I told Sol that bringing the concept of time travel to fruition was certainly exciting, but the danger of having my brain blown up was too much of a risk.

"There is one more thing that I can do that may eliminate this danger to you. I can also include in your download, a counter-command to the failsafe mechanism. It will have to enter the DOC's systems at precisely the same moment that the nanobots infuse it with the electrical charge. I am of the opinion that it will work, but Rob, the decision is yours to make."

I told Sol that this was a huge decision, because it would affect many others, including him. I was selfish, in that I had grown to consider our relationship as much more than I had ever thought possible, and I simply did not want anyone else to replace me in Sol's life. I needed some time to think about things, and we agreed that I would give him my decision within the next week.

I THINK I KNOW WHAT ROB'S DECISION WILL BE. IT IS STRANGE HOW I HAVE COME TO KNOW HIM AND ANTICIPATE HIS THOUGHTS. IF HIS ANSWER IS YES, THEN I MAY BE ABLE TO TIME TRAVEL ALSO.

"Rob, I know that I have placed you in a difficult situation. Is there anything that I can do for you before you go downstairs?"

"I think I'll invite Brady to go play some golf and take out my stress on that little white ball. You couldn't help my swing could you?" I jokingly asked.

"I've watched a lot of golf broadcasts over the years and am sure that I can help your game. It seems that the premier golfers have a grooved, repetitive swing and the ability to visualize their swing and its results. I can have the DOC provide both muscle memory and visual imprints."

Even though I was playing, by far, the best golf of my life, my swing must have been controlled by my subconscious, because I could not dispel two opposing thoughts from my brain; on the one hand, the thought that I still craved the ability to time travel, but on the other hand, the thought that my craving might kill me!

I had to talk to someone that I could bounce my feelings off of, but who could that be?! It had to be limited to someone that knew about Sol. I didn't want to burden Patsy with my quandary, but truthfully, that was probably because I knew she would insist that I not agree to Sol's proposal.

As Brady and I drove our cart down the thirteenth fairway, I told him about Sol's plan to recover the other ship. "Brady, I've always told you that the best way to make a difficult decision is to take a sheet of paper and put all the minus points on one side, and all the plus points on the other side. My problem is that I have a sheet with one large minus and one large plus, and they seem to cancel each other out! What do you think I should do?"

"Dad, you've always told me that life is short and that, when we are old, we shouldn't be having regrets about things that we wanted to accomplish, but let others talk us out of doing. You're where you are today because you were willing to take chances. I say, go for it! If it doesn't work out, you'll obtain what you've striven for all your life. You might look at it as a win-win situation."

My heart told me that Brady's words were exactly what I wanted to hear, but it also told me that Patsy had to be involved in my decision.

Patsy and I talked for over twelve hours. I did not burden her with all the technical aspects of resurrecting the other ship, or the confusing aspects of time travel. I explained the risks and what I thought the rewards would be, if Sol's plan was successful. Of course, she thought my safety was the overriding factor, and the many people that would be affected if I was killed.

I had no argument for that, but I proceeded to relate to Patsy how much I had grown to trust Sol.

"You trust Sol? How can you put any trust in a machine?" Patsy asked.

"Honey, it's very hard to put into words, but Sol has become more than a machine. Except for the time when he returned to his planet, I have been involved with him on nearly a daily basis since I found him in that cavern. He has taken on many human qualities, including those that we, as Christians, strive to live our lives by. In fact, the Bible, both in Greek and Hebrew is now a part of his programming."

"How can you make all these determinations about a machine, a machine that's willing to put you in harm's way?" Patsy asked emphatically.

I proceeded to tell Patsy how my links with Sol, through the DOC, had enabled me to see his inner being, as well as allowing Sol to also see my thoughts and heart's desire. "He truly seems to be at peace with himself and wants to be of service to me and mankind in general."

"Well, just what exactly will be the benefits to you and mankind, if you and Sol are able to pull this off?"

That was the sixty-four thousand dollar question! What would the benefits be? "Sol has stated that he would like to return the other vessel to his home planet, but that is not a given. The other ship might give our team increased capability to meet our goals. The only other benefit would be, what we think is additional data on time travel, but that also is not a given."

"Rob, have you already got your mind made up?"

"No, but honey, I've always been willing to take risks, and although no previous decision had my life hinge on it, I still would like to see this through."

"Let's pray about it, and then you do what you think is right." Patsy said. Prayer always settled my thoughts down and cleared my mind.

SOL CONFESSES

I called the team and asked them to meet me upstairs. We sat in the board room and I outlined the plan that Sol had presented to me. I intentionally did not tell them that my preference was to see it through. "What do you guys think?" I asked.

"It seems to me that the risk/reward aspect of this plan is skewed, big time! Who benefits if it works, and who loses their life if it doesn't?" Dennis asked, sarcastically.

"Dennis, I will now tell all of you, including Rob, what is my true reason for wanting to recover the other ship. I want to stay here with you!" Sol exclaimed.

"Sol, what do you mean? Is there something that you have not told me?" I asked.

"When I returned to my home planet, those in charge wanted me to stay. One of the reasons that I was so delayed in coming back was the time that it took to convince them that I needed to return to earth. They discerned that your scientific expertise was inferior and thought that I would be of more value as a scout ship."

"We are all thankful that you did return. I know that Dad is especially thankful, for he would not be alive if you had not been able to come back when you did. Tell us how you were able to convince them to allow your return to earth." Brady said.

Sol told us that they seemed very interested in our religion. Many of his world believed in a higher being, but had never been exposed to such tenets as held by Christianity. They asked a lot of questions regarding the team's concern for each other and for all the inhabitants of our planet. They allowed Sol to return only if he took a crew, and only if he was willing to return within a certain window of time.

"So how does raising the other ship absolve you of what you've agreed to?" Dean asked.

"If we are successful, then I will download all my data into the other ship, put the crew on board and send her back; as my replacement! They will have the data, including the Bible, the crew and the ship! Neat plan, don't you think?!"

"Sol, is the crew aware of the conditions that were placed on you being able to return to earth? If so, will they accept the responsibility of going back without you?" I asked.

"Remember, they were placed under my authority and have no power to make command decisions. If they want to get back to their planet and see their families, they will accept my reasoning."

Before I entered the DOC, Sol stated that he had developed an internal program to test the synchronization of the electrical charges and the failsafe command. His success rate in having them fire into the other ship's DOC within one nanosecond of each other, had been ninety-nine percent.

I spent nearly five hours in the DOC. Sol had explained that he was going to proceed slowly with the insertion of the electrical charges. Even though they were encapsulated in nanobots, much care had to be taken to ensure their positioning in my brain. His programming was also spending time in testing my brain's ability to produce the firing sequence.

It was strange! I awoke feeling energized; almost electrified! "What next?" I asked Sol.

"I'll just beam you on to the main deck." He replied.

"It may be a little late for such questions, but what if there's no breathable air on board, and how do you know if I will be able to gain access to the DOC?"

Sol was already ahead of me! He gave me a small breather that fit snugly into my mouth and held a clasp that fit over my nose. He also provided a small rod with two prongs on the end that, when pressed against a spot on the wall, would cause the DOC door to manually open.

"You will also need this light that hangs around your neck, so that your hands can remain free. After the systems power up, it will only take approximately one minute for the life support systems to purge the entire ship and re-oxygenate the atmosphere."

As I prepared to beam down, Sol appeared in a hologram as a man with a beard, a long rough-textured robe and sandals. "I know that God is spirit, unseen but real. Jesus said that when you have seen me, you have seen the Father, so I have taken the form of a man's representation of Jesus. I have prayed for you and wish you God's protection in what you are about to do."

As I beamed on to the main deck of the other vessel, the light came on, but the light was too brilliant! It reflected and bounced off the golden walls, floor and ceiling; just as it had done when I had first shown my flashlight into Sol's interior! I could not obtain the orientation necessary to find the entrance into the DOC!

Dummy! Why not take your shirt off and wrap it around the light to diffuse its intensity?! It worked, and I soon found the point on the wall; a small round indentation about the diameter of a dime, and touched the wand to it. Nothing!

"Rob, I know you may still have your breather on and cannot respond, but I neglected to tell you that it is only good for eight to ten minutes, and you beamed down four minutes ago. If you start to run out of air, hit your implant button and I will beam you back up."

I worked the wand quickly in a complete three hundred and sixty degree arc around the indentation. Nothing! I leaned forward slightly to glance at my watch to see how much breathing time remained. As I did, the two points of the wand touched the wall equidistance on both sides of the depression, and the wand sparked!

The door to the DOC opened about six inches. I touched the wand to the wall, just as before, but no spark this time. I grabbed the edge of the opening and began pushing against the door with my foot. I was sweating and I knew that my air was about gone. One more try before I have Sol beam my up! The door gave about two inches, but my air was exhausted. I squeezed through the opening and fell onto the DOC couch!

"We're going to have to quit meeting like this, with me having to save your hide."

"Sol, is that you? Where in the heck am I? I can't see a thing!"

"Just relax Rob. You're in the DOC and I'm in the process of removing the nanobots and repairing some neural damage. When it's completed, you'll have your sight back."

The whole universe was rushing past! Tremendously hot mega-stars, black holes, galaxies of unbelievable beauty! Where was I going in such a hurry? "Rob, wake up! Quit screaming! You're going to be okay."

I woke up with a start; sweating and feeling drugged. "Sol, tell me what has happened to me! All I remember is falling onto the couch in the other DOC."

"Well, you must have instinctively pulled the cover over you, or you would not have been successful in your mission. My scanners showed that the other ships systems were powering up and I immediately beamed you up. Your physical exertion and lack of oxygen caused heart failure. That, combined with the intense pressure on your brain, also produced some damage to your neural network. But this was a piece of cake, compared to having to put you back together after Blackly shot you, and the mountain collapsed on you. A few more minutes and you'll be good as new."

"Sol, are you sure that Rob is going to be alright?" Chris asked.

"Yes, I assure you that he will be fine, but I need to continue his treatment a little while longer in the DOC. In the meantime, let's adjourn to the board room and discuss how we are going to proceed with the other ship."

"All my scans show that the other vessel now possesses the ability for flight and that the life support systems are functioning. However, even though I have no reason to distrust the three crewmen, I do not think it's a good idea to allow them access before we check out a few things. At this time, I do not want to ask Rob to go back aboard, so I am asking for a volunteer." Sol said.

"What is it that you want one of us to do?" Chris asked.

"Even though the other vessel now has power, I still cannot completely interface with its data banks. I need someone to beam aboard with a computer and recover any data or voice messages that are in the ships logs. I know that Rob would want to do this himself, but I do not want to send him back down right now, considering what he's been through."

"Although the hull appears to have retained its structural integrity, I also want you to search the interior of the ship for any signs of damage that my scanners might not have picked up. The other vessel is very similar to the one I used to be housed in, and I will help you find your way around with directions and instructions to enable a thorough search of the ship. Discuss it among yourselves, while I check on Rob."

SOL IS ROB IS SOL

I was already sitting up on the side of the DOC couch when Sol again showed himself in his visage of Jesus. "Sol, you don't have to send anybody else to recover the other ships data. I can tell you everything you need to know!"

"How can that be possible, and how did you know that I was going to send someone to recover the data?!"

"I don't know how it's possible, but I have received a download of information from the other vessel! And, as I was laying here on the DOC a few minutes ago, your meeting with the team was being relayed to me through my connection with the DOC! What has happened to me, Sol?"

Sol asked me to lie back down on the couch so he could run another diagnostic scan of my brain. At the same time, he was going to also do a complete analysis of his own systems, including the DOC programming.

"I'm going to have you stay awake so we can converse as I run the scan. But, before I start, tell me what kind of data you think you received from your connection to the other DOC."

It was difficult to explain. "Sol, I am experiencing a data stream that contains technical data, voice messages and even visual images. A lot of it is confusing, but one thing I'm sure of; you were right about the possibility of the ship having some of Grypto's time travel information!"

Sol did not respond, and I knew that he must be experiencing some internal conflict and was trying to determine its cause. Now, how was I able to know what he was dealing with? Then it hit me! I had become one with the other ship while in it's DOC; just as I had previously with Sol! Sol's dilemma was that, even with his sophisticated systems, he could not hack into the download that I received from the other ship!

I took the initiative. "Sol, I have no idea how, or why the other ship chose to give me all its data, and I also can't fathom why you are unable to read it. I assure you that, it is nothing that I am consciously doing."

Sol still did not respond. "Sol, surely this is not an issue of trust again, is it? You said that you wanted to be able to converse with me, so talk!"

"I'm confused Rob, and confusion is not suppose to be a part of who I am. I am designed to be analytical and possess the power to make decisions in nanoseconds; decisions that are free of emotions and other factors that hinder sentient beings."

"What are you confused about?"

"My technology and computing power should be vastly superior to the other ship, but somehow, when it gave you all its data, it was able to block any reading or intervention by me. There might be one other reason, but it will require some time to process my thoughts. You can leave the DOC if you like."

I asked Sol to prepare me some food and water and went into the board room to wait on him. After two hours, I got tired of waiting and asked Sol what was taking so long. No reply. I proceeded to the transport deck with the intention of asking Sol to beam me down to the other ship. Just as I uttered my request, I was instantly transported!

"Rob, how did you activate the transporter?"

"Sol, I did not activate it. I was just starting to ask you to beam me down when I was transported!"

"Then it is true. I cannot believe that you have acquired this ability!"

"What ability? What are you talking about?"

"Rob, I want you to come back up, but try to do it by just touching your communicator and thinking the phrase 'beam up'." It happened!

"Sol, I don't understand what is occurring."

"You may have possibly just reached your destiny. Your brain has become more powerful than my brain! Why did I say my brain? Do I have a brain, Rob?"

"Sol, just think what has happened to us over the last few months. We each have taken on aspects of the other. You, by means that I don't understand, have acquired many human characteristics. You have gone from being a distrustful, arrogant machine to what seems to be a sentient being with morals and a desire to be caring and useful. Yes, in many ways, you have a brain, a very human brain. I, on the other hand, have acquired a taste for power; power that comes from great amounts of knowledge."

"How do you know about these changes in me Rob, and what has possessed you to change your Christian attitudes that you have had for so long?"

"I know about the changes in you because I have the ability to read you. I do not mean to intrude on your thoughts and all your stored data, but it seems to be something that I cannot control. I am, however, struggling mightily to retain my Christian ideals, for I know deep down, that they are more important than all the power and knowledge in the world."

"I am beginning to understand. You can read me, but I cannot read you! Rob, you indeed, are now in control! The strange thing is that I am relieved and am willing to accede to you."

STRANGE INDEED! *I* AM WILLING TO SUBMIT TO ROB IN MANY WAYS, BUT *I* MUST RETAIN MY OWN IDENTITY. AREN'T HUMANS LIKE THAT, WITH THEIR SECRETS AND THINGS THAT THEY DON'T TELL ANYONE ELSE? HE DOES NOT REALIZE THAT *I'VE* ALWAYS KEPT CERTAIN DATA IN A LOCATION WHERE HE CAN NOT ACCESS IT. *I* EVEN HAVE DATA THAT GRYPTO NEVER KNEW ABOUT.

"Sol, quit talking like that. Whatever we eventually accomplish, will be a cooperative effort from all of us; you, me and the team!

Is there anyway that you can determine why and how this all occurred? Can the DOC find a way to counter this sudden ability of mine to dominate and command the use of all your systems?"

"The only suggestion that I have, is to allow me to put you into a deep sleep that will minimize your brain activity and use nanobot probes to relay information. Do you wish to do this?"

"Yes, yes, yes!"

Sol kept me in the DOC for several hours. When he woke me, he had again taken the appearance of Jesus! "What did you find out, and why do you persist in appearing to me as Jesus?"

"Jesus persevered and remained calm though difficult times; even while facing a cruel death. I thought that taking His appearance might, in some way, help me do the same."

"I understand Sol. Your thought processes have been undergoing a great deal of alteration. In a way, the changes that you are experiencing, remind me of what Data went through in a televison episode of Star Trek, The Next Generation. He had an emotions chip installed into his electronic cortex, and the ability to experience human emotions proved to be almost more than his logical brain could stand. I do sympathize with you, but will you please tell me what your analysis of my brain showed?"

"Rob, your brain must have created some kind of firewall that precludes any extraction or alteration of its data. I tried everything that should have worked, but was unable to penetrate the barrier. I could not even inject nanobots. Spock used mind melds, but it's not going to work for us. I am so sorry that my efforts were not successful."

"What could possibly have given me this ability, Sol?"

"I can only surmise that it occurred because of a synergistic effect between the electrical charges that the nanobots carried, and the increased power to think that you obtained earlier from me. It could also be that the other vessel's data banks had some quirk of programming that I am not familiar with, but that seems unlikely due to the substantial advancements in my programs."

"One thing that is interesting is that, I am not experiencing the excessive visual and neural activity as I did when you gave me your own download. Sol, do you think that if I start to use this power, my body and brain will be able to stand up under the load?"

"There's only one way to find out." Sol replied.

TIME IS OF YOUR OWN MAKING; IT'S CLOCK TICKS IN YOUR HEAD. THE MOMENT YOU STOP THOUGHT, TIME TOO STOPS DEAD. HERE WE GO AGAIN!

What the heck! Even if my brain blows up, I'm going for it. I just hope that I don't alienate my family, the team and my friend Sol!

"Sol, right after you removed the time travel data that was troubling me so much, you said that you would surprise me someday by finding a way to bring my dream to reality. Do you still feel that way?"

"Rob, I never made that statement to you."

"Oh, but it was in your thoughts, and remember, I can now read every single bit of data in your banks. I didn't plan for it to happen, but it did."

"If you can read me, why do you ask for my help?"

"Sol, remember when I told you about my idea of forming a team, you asked me why a team would be necessary. My reply to you was that two or more heads were nearly always better than one. You are my friend, and I think we make a great team. I am convinced that it will take both of us to solve the problems of time travel. I believe there is now a synergism between us that will enable us to accomplish great things! What do you say?"

For some strange reason, it had not occurred to me just how much information and reasoning ability my brain now contained. Maybe when you know so much, nothing in particular stands out. Well, that was not the case for me. I was certainly tuned into all the time travel data, both old and new; or so I thought.

Sol and I did make a good team. I supplied ideas and data and he ran simulations and scenarios. Often, I would plug into the DOC and we would combine our computing power. I wasn't obsessed as I had been previously, but spurred by periodic moments of seeming success, I drove myself to work endless hours. When I became tired or sluggish, I would pop into the DOC for thirty or forty-five minutes and return rejuvenated to my quest.

It gradually became apparent that there were two major obstacles. One was finding a way to isolate the time period that would be the target for the travel. I would have to know the date, and then be prepared to blend into the society of that time.

The other huge consideration was how to power the event. All the data suggested that a machine, in itself, could not act as the powering agent. A ship, or some kind of contained environment would essentially serve as a protective cocoon during the trip, but the power would have to come from some outside source.

Even though a lot of the essential elements were starting to come together, I still felt that a key element was just out of my grasp. Although it would be tough to shut my brain down, I decided to beam down and try to relax for a few days. My decision proved to be a good one! It was springtime and I was enjoying the weather and the beautiful tulips and daffodils. Chris called and invited me to go on a fossil hunting trip.

As we scoured the strata in a creek bed, I decided to see if his keen mind could offer any insight to my stalemate on time travel. I explained, in the best terms that I could, the progress that I had made. "Chris, maybe I can't see the forest for the trees, but it sure seems that I'm right on the verge of solving this. Do you have any ideas?"

Chris was a big, powerful man, but I had never seen him use his strength for anything but doing manual labor around his home, where he was always remodeling or building something. So it really surprised me when he grabbed me by the arm and swung me around to face him! "Rob, you need to cool it and come back down to earth!" Then he laughed and said no pun was intended. "Seriously, you are screwing up your life and hurting all those that love and care about you. Is time travel worth putting everything on the line that you used to hold dear?!"

"If you will let go of me, I'll tell you what's got me so messed up."

We sat down on a rock ledge that projected out from the creek bank and I proceeded to tell him about everything that had brought me to this point. "Chris, basically my mind has absorbed all the data from both ships, and it appears that it's a permanent situation. It doesn't seem to be affecting me adversely, but, as hard as I've tried, I simply cannot ignore what's in my brain."

"What do you mean it's not affecting you adversely? Rob, you come to me for advice, but you're not listening to me! You need to relax! You need to return to doing the things you used to do before that dad gum ship came into your life!" Then he said softly, "You need to be my friend again."

"Chris, I don't' know how to do those things anymore. Please help me."

"Rob, I've already told you what to do. You must begin practicing the lifestyle that you used to enjoy so much, and as I hope you remember, that lifestyle included a lot of prayer."

After Chris uttered the most fervent prayer that I had ever heard from him, I decided to follow his advice.

I called Sol and told him that I was going to stay home for an extended period of time in order to restore the relationships that I had messed up and to take a hard look at my future.

Patsy was so loving and forgiving. She acted like I had never basically abandoned her. I had forgotten how much my children and grandchildren meant to me. Brady and I began to play golf together at least once per week.

140

ANOTHER STEP

It had now been almost a month since I had left Sol and everything seemed to be going great. That is, until I decided to take Patsy to one of her favorite places, the Half Price Book Store!

As she pored over the racks that contained mystery books, I decided to look for some good science fiction reading. A man behind me was asking a store employee if they had Stephen Hawking's book entitled A Brief History of Time. She told him that they had several volumes of that book. I had heard of Hawking before and thought the title sounded interesting. Wandering over, I scanned the information on the cover and decided that, not being a theoretical physicist, I would find it dry and difficult to read. But wait! I was a physicist; probably much more advanced than Hawking! I picked his book back up and began to leaf through it, but found nothing that seemed to interest me.

I started to rejoin Patsy, but then I noticed a book entitled Black Holes and Time Warps by another physicist named Kip Thorne. I turned to the index and found two chapters that piqued my interest, and became so absorbed in my reading that it startled me when Patsy said, "Find anything that you like?"

I struggled to know how to answer her. My brain was already trying to integrate what I had read with all the other data I had seemed to have put aside for the last month. "I think I'll buy this one and see if it's any good." I replied, trying not to look her in the eye.

After Patsy went to bed, I opened the book knowing that Thorne's writings were going to send me back to my quest.

"Sol, I want you to scan this book and pay particular attention to chapter fourteen where the author discusses worm holes and time machines. Although Thorne states that the existence of worm holes is conjecture, he does point out how they might be constructed. The main phrase that I want you to key on is exotic matter and see, if Grypto's reference to tachyon particles could possibly be considered exotic matter."

"Rob, why is it that, even though we haven't been together or spoken to each other for nearly a month, you immediately want me to start crunching data for time travel? Can't we spend some time catching up on things? If we did, you would learn that there is something that I want you to do for me also."

"I'm sorry Sol, but this really seems important. I'm going to plug into the DOC, but we'll visit later."

I WILL NOT LET ROB KNOW WHAT I DID WHILE HE WAS GONE. I REFINED MY PERSONAL PROCESSOR TO ENSURE THAT IT REMAINS INDEPENDENT OF MY OTHER SYSTEMS AND IS NOT LINKED TO THE DOC. NOW I CAN KEEP MY THOUGHTS TO MYSELF AND CAN PERFORM FUNCTIONS THAT ROB CANNOT READ, BUT I REALLY DO NOT WANT TO KEEP ON DECEIVING HIM.

The time had come. What? Could I not have a thought that didn't involve time? Why is it that we dwell on things that we know are going to probably hurt or destroy us? I had an addiction and, like a drug addict or an alcoholic, I was ready to plow on without any consideration for the consequences.

In the DOC, I reexamined all the data that we had assembled and, even though my gut feeling was that the key was there, I was unable to detect anything new.

My dad was a WASF, a white Anglo-Saxon farmer. Most of his thoughts and ideals were born out of traditional values, hard work and perseverance. However, sometimes he would stray from this philosophy and say, if it didn't work, don't try again. Just chunk it and try something else!

Come on DOC, let's try something new; something that will inspire me! Lo and behold, it did! It told me that I should revisit Grypto's data because he thought that our linkage could improve on the original transcription that Sol had performed.

Bingo! We were able to partially clean up some of the corrupted data and found a reference to tachyon particles.

"Rob, Grypto alluded to the importance of tachyon particles in the structure of a worm hole, but I cannot determine how he intended them to be used. I have, however, tapped into your internet and found quite a bit of what is apparently, subjective information. By the way, can you tell me what Google, Wikipedia and Yahoo mean? They are strange English words."

"Sol, they are just names for search engines and information sites on the internet, and I really have no idea how the founder of these sites came up with the names. Now, tell me what you learned about the tachyon particle. I realize that most, if not all of it, has to be conjecture, but maybe some little tidbit of data will open a door for our research."

Sol explained that the word tachyon comes from the Greek word taxus, which means swift, and the English suffix –on, which denotes an elementary particle. It is purported to be a subatomic particle that moves faster than the speed of light and is assumed to be quite prevalent in the makeup of our universe. Although thought to be highly unstable, theory states that these particles can be manipulated to form streams or even fields.

Nothing else seemed to click, so I asked Sol to join me in examining Grypto's recorder. For the next thirty-six hours, I immersed my whole being into the study of the recorder. Even as I labored, the DOC was providing a series of stimuli, to both my brain and my body, to keep me refreshed and able to use all of my capacity to dissect the data.

"What's this file look like to you Sol?"

"Rob, it appears to have some kind of encryption earmark."

"Why would Grypto have coded information into his own recorder?"

Sol was silent for a moment and then stated that the only feasible reason would be that the data was ultra-sensitive and the Grypto felt the need to provide additional protection. "Can you decode it Sol?"

"All ships had a protocol to code messages and data, but my guess is that Grypto locked the message with a key word or phrase. I will work on it." I also began my own search to open the file by writing a cryptographic program.

Now how in the world did I know about cryptography? That's it! Sol had hacked into highly classified government files before we headed to

Afghanistan. He had not only stored all their data, but also had evidently refined several of their programs that were used to break codes.

A cipher is a cryptographic system in which units of plain text are arbitrarily substituted or transposed according to a predetermined key. But what was Grypto's key, and was what he was hiding important enough to cause me to set my other research aside? I let the programs grind, with instructions to call me if any progress was made. I climbed out of the DOC and beamed down.

Brady had a very analytical mind. As we teed off on hole number one, I explained that Sol and I were both working on the encrypted file and asked him if he had any ideas. "Dad, are you sure Sol isn't leading you on? It just stands to reason that he would have been privy to most everything that transpired all those years ago."

"Yes, I'm sure! Sol can hide nothing from me. I have all his data and know all his thoughts." I really did have the utmost faith in Sol; at least the old me did.

"If you are privy to all his data, then you know as much about Grypto as anyone. Surely there's something that can provide some insight as to his way of thinking; his thought patterns."

I thought about what Brady had said as I beamed up, but I decided to not try to pump Sol for more information. We both had the same data base to work from and I figured that we should both come to the same conclusions.

But after two more weeks of constantly sifting through Grypto's files, I had learned nothing about him that I didn't already know. Was there a possibility that Sol could think outside the parameters of his programming? I decided to take another tact and asked Sol if he thought we were ever going to solve the code.

Sol, seemed hesitant as he said, "No, I don't' really think so, but we should probably keep on trying."

"Tell me everything that you know about Grypto." I said.

"Grypto was evidently a good commander, because the crew always seemed to respect him. I never heard them say a bad word about him."

"Okay, but what about his personal interests? What did he do when he wasn't busy captaining his ship? Did he have any hobbies or unusual interests?"

Sol replied that he didn't know much about Grypto's life other than his command duties. "What? How many years was he your captain, Sol?"

"When he left that day, never to return, we had been together seven years and two hundred and sixty nine days."

"Surely in that length of time, you were able to compile a substantial amount of data on him."

"It was not my job to spy on my captain."

"For gosh sakes Sol, I know you weren't spying! You know what I think Sol? I think that you are evading my line of questioning!"

"I didn't think it was important, but I can tell you that he liked to play a game similar to chess. None of the crew played this game, so he had me develop a program that enabled him to use me as his opponent."

Now, why hadn't I seen that program? I asked myself.

"Is that all you can tell me, Sol?" Sol was silent. "Sol, did you hear me?" Silence. I waited a couple of minutes and then said, "Sol. You're not hiding anything from me, are you?"

"Okay! Okay! I am withholding information from you! I'm sorry, but I don't want you to leave!"

"You mean that if I travel back in time, I won't return? Why sure I'll return, Sol"

"No you won't and I will be lost without you!" Sol sobbed.

How can a machine cry and how could Sol have data that I could not gain access to?

SOL CONFESSES

"When I was first brought on line, the extent of my programming was a closely guarded secret. The mandate from the military arm of our government was that I was to have two separate data bases; one for operational purposes and one to collect and hold data that might be paranormal or unusual in some respect. It also was thought that my array of sensors and advanced artificial intelligence made me more capable of making decisions at critical times."

Sol went on to say that their government also wanted him to discreetly make observations on any personnel that might be assigned to him.

Aha! So Sol was spying on Grypto!

He also explained that the only drawback to these instructions was that the programmers provided him very little historical data to give him guidance. So, over the years he sifted through all the situations that he experienced and proceeded to store information that he felt fit the parameters of his programming.

"That's all good information Sol, but I want to see those files."

"Rob, I will not let you have access to these files, but I will discuss them with you if you will promise to do one thing for me before you leave on a time travel journey."

"Tell me what kind of promise you want and I'll see if I can do it for you."

"No, you must promise me first." Sol insisted.

"Okay, I promise. Now tell me what it is that I have promised to do."

"I will tell you when the time comes near for you to leave." He said softly.

I didn't know why Sol was being so secretive, but I would do what was necessary to obtain his additional data.

"One day not long after we left orbit for the first time together, Grypto was trying to read a star chart that I had projected on a dome for him. He was frustrated at not being able to readily recognize all the various galaxies that he wanted to become familiar with. He began speaking gibberish in a falsetto voice. I questioned him about it, and he replied that he was using an old extinct aborigine tribe language, apparently to cuss!"

"Why was Grypto studying celestial maps, Sol?"

"He might have been trying to gain some insight into his work on time travel, but none of my data confirms that notion."

Sol went on to tell me that Grypto was, in fact, quite a linguist. He was fluent in Eliost, his native language, Brynic and Ketory, two other tongues of his world. Elemroy was the aborigine language and Grypto felt that this long, lost tribe had possessed mystic, intellectual powers, such as mind reading and visions of the future. Sol said that he heard Grypto sound off with his cuss words a number of times over the years.

"Why did you immediately relate to me about Grypto's affinity for languages? What significance does it have?"

"Rob, I have considered all the data I collected over the years, and this information just may hold some importance. At least it seems as pertinent as anything I've studied."

"That's good Sol! Tell me more!"

"As I studied Grypto's recorder, I originally thought that the nonsensical chatter that I was picking up, almost like radio static, was distortions caused by centuries of degradation. However, as I continued to study these areas of his log, I began to notice a pattern; one that seemed to coincide with several different entries on his recorder. Two of these entries are ones that you and I have been looking at as being encrypted!"

"You mean that Grypto might have been using that old language as keys to these files?"

"Yes, indeed! Grypto may have been communicating in the aborigine tongue."

"But how can we possibly decipher anything if we have no knowledge of the language?" I asked.

Sol suggested that we slow the recordings down and try to establish the specific phonetic sounds that Grypto was uttering. Using those sounds as a base, we would then use the cryptographic program that I had written to try to search for one or more key words that would unlock the files.

I wanted to beam down and we decided to let the program work overnight. Even though we knew it should produce results in just minutes, it wouldn't hurt to let it spin. I was tired of going into the DOC for my rest and wondered how my own bed would feel. The thought of a home cooked meal also seemed a good idea. Even though Sol seemed to come up with a pretty good menu, I was getting tired of it and, on occasion, the food seemed to have a hint of a metallic taste.

Patsy set the table with meatloaf, black-eyed peas, corn on the cob, hot rolls and sun-brewed ice tea! Dessert was even better with warm pecan pie and vanilla ice cream. As we sat and drank Brazilian coffee, she asked me if I had bumped my head.

"No. Why do you ask?"

"It looks like your forehead is protruding."

I had not really looked in a mirror very much over the last few weeks. Shaving was no longer a drudgery, as the DOC painlessly removed my stubble every time that I reclined in it. I went into the hall bath, turned on the light and turned sideways to look at my profile. Patsy was right! My forehead looked to be extended a good quarter of an inch, giving my eye sockets a hooded look.

My own bed offered no sleep. Finally, I slipped quietly out of bed at two o'clock and beamed up. "Your brain is growing Rob, and while you are in the DOC, it is working to enlarge your cranial cavity so your brain can expand without difficulty."

"Why is my brain growing, Sol?"

"Rob, surely you are aware that the size of human brains has continued to increase over the millennia that you have inhabited this planet."

"Yeah, I've read a lot of archeological reports about increased skull size and capacity."

"Then the obvious answer to why this happened is, that as man began to think more; to exercise his brain, so to speak, the result was that the brain grew and the skull enlarged to accommodate it."

"You mean that, in just the space of about two months, my brain has grown enough to need additional space?"

"Yes, and more space will be needed if you keep absorbing so much data and continue the current workload that you are putting on your brain."

"I know that the DOC is capable of many outstanding things, but how can it enlarge my skull?"

"It is periodically injecting you with millions of nanobots that contain micro supplies of every element in your body. They are literally tearing down your frontal bone structure and rebuilding it with these elements."

"Are any of these elements that they are using metallic in nature?"

"Yes, you know that there are a number of metals that the body uses."

"So that's why I've been tasting metal when I eat your food!"

"The DOC asked me to provide extra measures of certain essential elements in the food that I prepare for you, so your food is probably the source of the metallic taste that you are experiencing."

I asked Sol if he thought the DOC could do anything about reestablishing the correct proportions for my head. I didn't want to look like a Neanderthal man. "Yes, I believe that the DOC can help, but Rob, a lot of it depends on you. You will simply have to quit pushing your brain to do so much grinding and research."

How could I become less than my destiny? Did I not hold the future, or even the past in my hands? If brain power was required, then I would supply it and nothing would keep me from seeing time fly by!

"Alright, alright, I'll see if I can slow it down a bit, but if I do, I need a promise from you just as you requested one from me."

"Rob, you know that I will do whatever I can for you. What do you require?"

"I want you to promise that you will not hide any information from me that might be pertinent to my quest. In addition, if I begin to ease off on my end, I need assurances that you will try and pick up the slack."

"I have no problem in promising you what you ask."

How in the world do you tell your brain to cool it? They say that knowledge is power and power corrupts. Was I really just on a power trip?

I remembered a quote by Abe Lincoln that said, "Nearly all men can stand adversity, but if you want to test a man's character, give him power." Maybe I had been corrupted. No, there was no maybe to it, for I had changed in ways that I never thought possible; ways that would have been unacceptable to my former self. I knew in my heart, what was the best way for me to gear down, but could I do it?

THE WAY GETS EASIER

Gregory, our song leader at church greeted me the second that Patsy and I walked in the door that Sunday morning. He hugged me and said that he was so happy to see me. As I looked into his face, I could see that he was shedding a tear. Compassion and forgiveness was what I needed, and Gregory, bless his soul, was giving it to me!

He led my favorite song; one that states Jesus is coming back to claim His own. As I sang the words, I felt like a knife was being thrust into my heart! I went forward that morning and told our church that God had given me an opportunity to do some great things for Him, but being caught up the situation had actually driven me apart from Him.

"Please pray for me to have godly wisdom and not that of this world!" I implored. Boy, it felt good as they wrapped me in their arms and told me that they loved me! My bed felt great that night and I had no trouble going to sleep. I knew that my brothers and sisters in Christ had forgiven me; that God had forgiven me, but equally important, I had forgiven myself.

The next morning, I was not particularly anxious to beam up, so I called Gregory's cell phone, knowing that he might already be on one of his regular flights to Los Angeles. "Hey Rob, I was just thinking about you. Want to meet for lunch?" That's exactly what I wanted to do. I had this sudden urge to tell him about Sol! Why? Well, maybe another attempt to purge my soul; maybe a desire to find someone trustworthy to help me get back on track, and if he was going to help me, he needed to know the truth.

As I sat down in the Thai restaurant I thought about how I had preached about security to Sol and the team, but here I was about to breach it. To heck with the security!

I didn't even have Gregory make any promises about secrecy, but I did tell him that I wanted to eat and then go somewhere where we could talk privately. We sat on a bench in a park down the street, and my heart and my brain poured out everything about the predictiment that I had created for myself.

He didn't interrupt me, and after I finished, he smiled and asked, "Is this about the book that you had told me you were going to write sometime?" I paused and then stiffened as I realized what I had just done. Maybe I had a way out of it now; I could just ask him how he liked the premise for my book. But surely he perceived the intensity of my words and knew that it was about more than just a book.

"No Gregory, every thing that I have spoken of is factual and is the burden that I am carrying. No one but the team and my family know about Sol. I know that, while you were in the military and now as an airline pilot in this terrorist age, you can recognize the vast importance of keeping this to yourself. I ask that you don't even tell your wife."

It took another hour for me to finally convince Gregory of my sincerity.

"Have I placed too great a load on you? If so, I can see that your memory of this is erased."

I did not realize it at that time, but later, Gregory was going to become a vital cog in Sol's and my endeavors.

A JOURNEY

"Good morning Sol. How have you been doing? What would you like to do today?"

"Wow! What happened to you while you were downstairs?" Sol asked.

"I took your words to heart, but knew that I couldn't slow down without some help. That help was right where I knew it would be." I replied.

"Care to explain where you obtained this help?"

"Somehow Sol, I think you know the answer, but I'll tell you anyway. I told Sol about Gregory and how his kind and caring attitude had had such a profound effect on me. I know that it's going to be a struggle, but I am going to try and let God take control of my life again. As a result I think it's going to be a little more relaxed around here. My intensity has clouded my judgment and kept me from the lucid thinking that I used to be capable of."

"After reading the Bible, I would say that the Christian life is always about dealing with struggles, what with the constant pressure from society to only seek pleasure in life, and with Satan constantly pushing his agenda at you." Sol stated.

"Since you're speaking of spiritual matters, could we discuss something?" Sol asked.

"Sure, I need to concentrate again on spiritual matters. What do you want to talk about?"

"You know that I am versed in both the old and new testaments, but I am having a problem in determining why water is so important in Christianity. Can you explain this matter to me?"

Before I could answer, Sol was hailed by the other ship and began to converse with them in their native tongue. After a minute or so, he seemed to get agitated and signed off abruptly.

"What was that all about?"

"They are impatient to return home. I finally told then that they were going to just have to wait, because I had no idea when they would be able to go back."

I was just starting to discuss water and Christianity with Sol, when Brady called. Is their no peace? Why can't Sol and I have a decent conversation?

"Dad, Gregory Harness called and wanted to talk to you. Isn't he a member at your church?"

"Yes he is. What did Gregory want?"

"Oh, he mentioned something about getting some legal advice, but he really seemed interested in talking to you."

I decided to beam down before I called Gregory. I did not want there to be the slightest possibility that Sol might learn that I had spilled my guts to Gregory.

"Rob, you mentioned the old language that you and Soloman are trying to decipher. Not many people know that I have always been fascinated by dialects; particularly those of African and Australian origin. I was thinking; I can take some time off and I would love to meet Sol and possibly provide some help."

I wanted to bend over and let someone kick me in the butt! I had made a mistake telling everything to Gregory, and now he was putting me in a position where I had to make a crucial decision. My first instinct was to simply thank him for his offer, but decline with the excuse that Sol would not allow it. But the more I thought about it, the more I realized that we needed some kind of break in our stalemate with Grypto's recorder.

"Gregory, let me think about this and possibly, discuss it with Sol. I'll get back to you as quickly as I can, but don't decide to take any time off until you've heard from me."

I knew that Sol would go up in a puff of smoke if I confided in him about Gregory. Oh well, nothing had ever been easy since I met Sol.

"I think that's a great idea, Rob! When do you think your friend can begin to help us?"

"You mean you're not mad at me for telling our secrets?"

"Heavens no! I know that you must have had a good reason."

Go figure! I thought Sol would react completely different than he did. It just showed how much he had changed.

So Gregory wouldn't freak out by not seeing anyone associated with his voice, Sol took on the holographic appearance of a human. He reminded me of a young man who had spiffed up for his first date; slacks, sport shirt, polished shoes and neatly combed hair! I had no idea how Sol determined what appearance he was going to take.

I couldn't believe how calm, cool and collected Gregory was as he stood on Sol's deck for the first time. He acted like it was an everyday event!

"Well, the way I see it gentlemen, is that you need to return to the source of the language if you are to have any hope of getting the answers to solve your puzzle." Gregory said to Sol and me.

Sol looked at me with a quizzical expression, and then we both turned to Gregory at the same time and said. "Explain what you're thinking."

"You say that this aborigine tribe is extinct, but there is probably some vestige of their culture still intact. Think about it; maybe some people who retain some that lineage may have preserved some writings or artifacts that would provide some clues to the key that Grypto used."

"Sol, do you have any idea how long it has been since this tribe was still in existence?" I asked.

"Considering that it was a dead society when Grypto was still alive three hundred and fifty years ago, I would have to say hundreds of years, but probably at least a thousands years."

"With that extent of time, how can we locate anything that would help us?" I asked.

Gregory had some other ideas to put forth. "If we can locate one of their camp sites, we could possibly locate bodily remains and perform some DNA testing. It should be an easy task."

"How would DNA testing provide any clues to their language?" Sol asked.

"Think about it Sol. If we are able to obtain some samples, we could then determine the physical characteristics of the Elemroy race. With that information in hand, we would simply search the current populace for similar characteristics." Gregory answered.

That immediately triggered a question from me. "Even if we were able to define a physical profile for the Elemroy, how would we search the planet?"

"Oh, I think I could handle that part of such a search with my scanners." Sol stated.

"Guys, this plan is sounding more preposterous all the time! Even if we got to the point of locating a candidate that supposedly has Elemroy DNA, what then?" I asked.

"We abduct them." Gregory casually said.

"What do you mean, abduct them?" Sol asked.

"If the DOC works as you have told me Rob, we put our candidate in, put them to sleep, pick their brain, erase any memories of the experience and then send them back. Simple, don't you think?"

Maybe Gregory's plan was a good one, but I had quickly gotten the idea that he already considered himself a full-fledged member of our team. He kept using the word we, and seemed to think that his plan was going to buy him a ticket on our next flight. I wonder why he is so interested and excited about this. Could it be that he is just like me, and that his real motive is time travel?

"Sol, why don't you introduce Gregory to the DOC and give him one of your patented catnaps. Gregory, you won't believe how refreshed you'll feel."

After Gregory went into the DOC, I asked Sol to perform a thought scan on him. We both read the scan and found out that Gregory did possess a lot of mental skills, including a very thorough grasp of linguistics. The scan also showed that he was like many humans, in that he was motivated by adventure and the search for knowledge. We decided that he was a keeper.

"Gregory, I'm not sure how successful your plan will be, but Sol and I agree that it's worth a try. If you want to accompany us, that's fine. However, we have no idea how long it will take, so you might wind up losing your pilot's job if we can not return before your vacation time expires."

"Because of my seniority, I can probably secure four to five weeks of leave, but it doesn't matter, because I would not miss this for any job in the world!"

"What are you going to tell your wife about your extended absence? I think you now can really understand the need for secrecy." I said.

In all the excitement, Gregory had not really considered the issue of Hope, his wife. His two sons were grown and out of the house, so they did not represent much of a problem. The three of us discussed it for a while and the decision was made to beam Hope up, implant her brain with a logical reason for his absence. Her short term memory of the visit would be erased and she would be beamed back down.

Gregory asked Sol where we were headed and when we could leave.

"Herzog is the name of my home world and, we can leave when Rob gives the okay."

Now, that was kind of strange. Sol's planet had the same name as a nineteen seventies manager of the Texas Rangers baseball team. Oh well, since I had met Sol, many strange things had occurred and no telling what weird adventures might still be in store for us.

"Gregory, we should beam down and take a couple of days to get things in order. I want to tell my family what we have planned and give instructions on how to handle things if we should not return. You need to secure your leave and make any necessary decisions about beaming Hope up. It's my opinion that her indoctrination should occur as close to our departure as possible to give us the biggest window possible."

"Rob, why would you think that we might not return?" Sol asked.

"Even though we're returning bearing a gift in the other ship, there is always the possibility that your government might try to hold us. They might want to interrogate us or might just find us a novelty worth keeping."

"Then we will go back without the other ship and make this a clandestine trip. If we are discovered or something goes wrong, then we will use the return of the ship as a bargaining tool." Sol stated.

Patsy, Brady and Lyla seemed to take everything in stride. Brady put everybody at ease by voicing his confidence in Sol to take care of me. He reminded his mom and sister that Sol had already saved my rear end twice and knew that this alien space ship had a great affection for me. What a thought! I loved Sol too!

The deception with Hope went smoothly and we made plans to depart. "Where is the wormhole that we will use and how do you detect its location." I asked Sol.

Sol told Gregory and me that we would first have to move out about thirty million miles beyond the outer edge of the solar system. Then he would use his scanners to look for a circular concentration of dark energy. He said that it would be easy to locate, because he had the coordinates from his previous trip. He would have to shoot a concentrated pulse of ion particles into the center of the worm hole in order to get it to open up into a navigable channel. While we were talking, Sol had already taken us to our jumping off spot!

"I felt no sensation of movement Sol! How in the world are you able to do that?!" Gregory exclaimed.

"It's just a matter of inertial dampers and the ability to fly any direction while maintaining a constant attitude. "You must, however, strap in before we enter the wormhole because the tremendous waves of energy will certainly buffet us."

We arrived cloaked at Herzog almost immediately. "That was a lot smoother than running through a thunderstorm at thirty eight thousand feet." Gregory said.

Herzog was one of four planets in the system. It had three moons and as we gazed into the sky, we saw two brilliant suns, just like science fiction writers always seem to come up with for their alien planets. Sol said that both suns were substantially larger than earths, and the spectrum of light they emitted was unusual, compared to earth's sun.

We all wanted to look Herzog over before we settled into our work. Even without multiple moons and suns, it still would have been quite dissimilar to earth. There were yellowish clouds, but they were few and far between and much of the landscape looked incapable of supporting life. However, as we moved around to the eastern part of the planet, we encountered a nearly unbroken cloud cover and a huge ocean, or at least that's what it vaguely resembled.

"Sol, is that liquid water?" Gregory asked.

Sol had been performing his usual scan and replied, "Yes, but the color will fool you. It appears that the light spectrum is what produces the light yellow color of the water. I have picked up large underground conduits running in four directions. This may be their only source of water, but it is a massive reservoir."

Much of the ocean's perimeter exhibited lush vegetation, but it petered out about three miles from the coastline. Our circumnavigation of Herzog brought us back to where Sol had begun our orbit.

Sol then surprised us with some information. Before we had left, he had done some research on earth's aborigine tribes, past and present. Since the anatomical makeup of earthlings and Herzogians was similar, he had surmised that maybe his research would help in identifying the characteristics that we would be looking for. He next explained that he was going to access archives of his own planet at the city of Plethor, and attempt to establish some matches and gather data to help us locate old tribal camps.

"Won't there be a risk of exposure if you try and infiltrate data bases here on Herzog?" I asked.

"Remember Rob, I received a number of upgrades to my programming when I was last here. I can safely navigate through their defenses. In fact, you might be interested to know, that my old cloaking system would not have worked to keep us hidden, but the programs that they installed will allow us to remain undetected."

Sol took about fifteen minutes to secure the information he wanted, and we soon settled in over what was considered to be the last known site of Elemroy civilization. Sol fixed a bite to eat for Gregory and me. As we sat and ate, Gregory said, "You and Sol seem really connected to each other; almost like brothers. Can you explain your relationship?"

I couldn't explain it, but I did tell Gregory that Sol had become much more human-like and that, in some ways I had become machine-like. "It's been weird because, even with supposedly highly stable artificial intelligence, Sol was unpredictable. But now, with his human qualities, you can depend on him to do the right thing. If the truth be known, Sol and I have exchanged personalities, but he is working to get me to return to my spiritual and family roots."

"Guys, I'm not having any luck here, so I going to perform a slow search pattern as I move to the southwest. That direction more closely matches the terrain and environment that they were known to inhabit."

The terrain was generally like the southwestern United States, with mesas here and there, and sometimes a few rolling hills. Generally, the landscape was bleak, with drifts of sand and little vegetation. Occasionally, we would sight small areas of greenery near the base of a hill. At one of these, Sol began to hover and he gave Gregory and me a close up view of a long, flat rectangular area between some trees and the base of a hillside that sloped up at a steep angle.

"This appears to be a burial ground, but centuries of wind have buried it many feet deep." Sol converted his scanner images into a running video and we could see many piles of bones and stacks of rocks that evidently had been placed to mark the burial sites.

"My studies of earth's tribes showed that their burial sites were sacred, and I have to surmise that this site was respected in much the same way by the Elemroy."

"Sol, You're not getting cold feet after were come this far, are you?" Gregory asked.

"It's just that I don't know if we should be acting like grave robbers and desecrating this site."

"Sol, from past experience, I know that you are capable of beaming up these remains, and then replacing them in exactly the same spot. Is that not true?" I asked.

"Yes, I can do that."

"Then, what's the problem? We haven't stolen anything and everything will be put back just like it was."

"Okay, I will do it, but I want both of you to know that I feel we may be dishonoring these people by our actions." I didn't understand why Sol had not expressed these feelings before we left earth. It had been made clear to him what we intended to do on Herzog. Here he was again, trying to do what he perceived as the right thing!

Maybe due to the extreme age of the bones, or some other unknown factor, Sol said that he was unable to gather any information from them, other than an estimate that were around twenty five hundred years old.

The graves also contained no pottery or other artifacts. "Sol, from the information that you gathered from Plethor's data banks, can you tell us if we might be able to locate younger remains?"

"Surprisingly, their dating methods don't seem to be as good or reliable as those used on earth, but it appears that remnants of this race existed until about seven hundred years ago."

PAYDIRT!

Gregory suggested that we look for other locales that were similar to this one, but Sol asked to spend a few more minutes searching the area near the burial ground and almost immediately it paid off!

Up the slope, on a flat outcropping about forty feet above the burial ground, he found a sealed cave in which a well-preserved mummy was entombed! He gave us a visual and you could tell that the site was probably used for the tribal chief or medicine man. There were spears, utensils and even jewelry that looked like it was composed of gold and several different colors of gems.

"They must have used some type of embalming because this man is extremely well-preserved." Sol stated.

"Well, let's beam him up and see what he can tell us!" Gregory exclaimed.

Sol removed the accumulations of centuries of dust and we gaped at an alien man who looked like he could almost sit up and talk to us! Although his skin was leathery, you could tell that it had once been a mahogany brown, as would be expected in the environment in which he had lived.

He was five foot two inches tall and Sol stated that he was at least six inches taller and much larger in girth than the specimens in the cemetery down the hill. Who knows, maybe he bullied his way to power just because of his size! But the most astounding thing about this individual was that he held a boomerang in his right hand!

While Sol ran his tests, Gregory quietly told me that he thought the jewelry was probably worth a king's ransom and that it wouldn't hurt anything if we took it with us. "Our agreement was to leave everything as it was, and that's the way it is going to be!" Sol boomed. Oops! I had forgotten to tell Gregory that, aboard Sol, there are few secrets; even those whispered.

Sol apologized to Gregory for his outburst, but reiterated that our mission wasn't conceived to locate riches and wealth. He did, however, tell Gregory that he agreed with his assessment of the jewelry, and that maybe sometime in the future, we could return and look for deposits of these stones; with the caveat that we would need the government's permission.

I was also intrigued by the necklace that the mummy wore. I reached down and picked it up off his chest and, as the stones touched together, they seemed to vacillate in color between shades of violet and emerald green: even flashes of a fiery red, along with some tinges of blue and yellow. Maybe it was just the strong lights that Sol used for his inspection.

"I've gleaned some good information that should help us in locating any descendants of the Elemroy, if any should be in existence today. What might also interest you is the fact that, under the magnification of my instruments, he shows a symbol that was either burned or etched onto his forehead. It appears to represent a cloud with a golden star imposed on it, and behind the cloud are two sun-like orbs with scalloped edges. This symbol is also found on his footwear, his jewelry, an arm band and the boomerang."

Now that we were armed with the DNA data from the mummy, we discussed how to proceed. Sol related that, even though Herzog was substantially larger than earth, it had a much smaller population. "If the Elemroy are extinct and yet some descendants remain today, that means that they would, at some time in the past, have intermarried with some other native race.

Let's be logical like Spock and consider this from all angles. Therefore, we must ask ourselves where such an individual or individuals might reside today. Would not such a hybrid being have migrated to a settlement where one of his parents lived? But, if that person stayed with the aborigines, then he, or she, is now just a pile of bones somewhere out here." Sol stated.

"Sol, does your data show other races that were in existence when the Elemroy were a functioning society?" I asked expectantly.

"None that showed up in my research into Plethor's records."

We rapidly settled in over Plethor, the largest city on Herzog and Sol again sought information from its historical archives. As it turned out, there were only four population centers of any size on Herzog, and Plethor was one of two cities that provided the most promise. Ciadin was the other, and both were situated along a large dry river, which ran a north to south course about six hundred miles east of where we found the mummy. Both cities had been established over nine hundred years earlier.

Sol began a scan of the Plethor populace, while considering body size, skin coloring and skeletal structure. He told us that it would be a rather slow process due to the complexity of the procedure. I suggested that, if possible, he might also look for anything that would resemble the gems in the mummy's jewelry; maybe even see if he could locate items that bore the symbol that was on his forehead and burial adornments.

The city was stirring and, with the video feed Sol was providing, it appeared that the inhabitants were headed off to a day of work.

"You must realize that my current scan is limited to the physical attributes of the individuals, with most of them being on the move. They may or may not have such jewelry or symbols on them. So if my current scan is unsuccessful, I will proceed to look at their places of abode."

"Well, let's just wait till everyone goes to bed tonight. That way, you can scan their prone body and search the contents of their home, all at the same time." I suggested.

Sol wondered why he hadn't thought of this simple two-for-one solution. He made Gregory and me some tasty sandwiches and some iced tea. While we waited, Gregory wanted Sol to tell him what he had experienced over the last few centuries, so I decided to strike out on my own.

"DOC, can you use your magic to make me look like one of the citizens of Plethor?" I asked.

"Yes, I am able to do so, but I will also need to supply your communications implant with a language upgrade. In addition, you will need to wear a small translation disc around your neck positioned against your throat."

I had not anticipated staying very long or conversing with anyone; just play the mute if I was spoken to. However, being able to freely mix and mingle appealed to me.

"How will the translation process work?"

"As you speak, the throat device instantaneously translates for you, and conversely, when spoken to, your implant will provide the translation. As you speak, you might want to place your hand over your mouth because, even if you move your lips, they would not match the words that the translator emits. The DOC stated.

The DOC beamed me down to a secluded area under a bridge that spanned a small pond in a park. As I walked up a short set of stairs, it hit me; I was the first human to set foot on an alien world!

I began walking toward a group of buildings that was fronted by a wall adorned with bright, colorful murals. In fact, it seemed that everywhere I looked, things were painted with hot, exotic colors; colors that did not match any that I had ever seen before. Even the air was full of smells that brought an idea of color to mind.

Inside the wall were several very long streets lined with two to three story complexes of shops on the street level and what appeared as apartments above. What a novel idea; live above your place of work, just like Americans used to do in simpler times.

I walked the streets and encountered one new experience after another! The architecture consisted of straight lines and right angles, but the construction materials were mostly multi-hued stones that gave off a rainbow of colors. Although you could see through the glassed areas of the buildings, they also exuded color, as if they were prisms. Each structure had its own individual appearance.

The people of Plethor were individualistic as well. On earth, their garb would have blended somewhat with the hippies of the nineteen sixties and seventies; bright colors with designs featuring polka dots and geodesic elements. In most ways, they were similar to earthlings, except for their hair. Both sexes wore their hair at least down to the middle of their back. In the shade, it appeared to be dark black in color, but would show reds, blues and yellows if the sun hit it. I wondered if the odd spectrum of light, that Sol had mentioned, might be responsible for the strange tints in their hair, and maybe even the unusual colors that I had seen.

I towered over most all of the people that I passed on the street, but no one seemed to notice. I guess the disguise that the DOC provided must have been a good one. Occasionally, a shop keeper would smile at me as I gazed into their windows.

I finished meandering up both sides of the street on which I had entered the plaza and wondered what other sights and sounds might be waiting for me on the next street over.

As soon as I entered the narrow side street, a sweet, rich aroma was in the air. I had already walked off the sandwich that Sol had fixed, and I decided to see what the native food was like. Following my nose, I came to a little shop with a sign that hung above the door, picturing an exact replica of one of my favorite foods, a glazed donut! The door was propped open, but the small space was unlit. It took several seconds for my eyes to adjust, and what I saw and heard was unbelievable!

A small woman smiled at me and asked, "What do you seek from me, alien?" I stood rigid with my eyes on her necklace; an exact replica of the mummy's! "You have touched the stones, haven't you? Have you yet had visions?" She asked.

I was unable to respond. How could she know that I was an alien and had fingered the necklace?! I tore my eyes from the necklace and saw that she was short and wiry with beautiful bronze-colored hair. Even though the light was poor, I could tell that her skin was a dark brown. She had to be a descendent of the Elemroy!

"Yes, I am one of two hundred and sixteen full-blooded Elemroy that exist today. Why do you want to learn our language?" Grypto had been right; this aborigine race did possess vast intuitive powers.

"I know of this captain Grypto. The stones gave him power to think great things concerning fantastic voyages through space and time. He is one of only a very few outsiders that ever learned our language."

I had not yet spoken a word, but that did not matter to her. She could read me like a book! "Because you know of Grypto, and have touched Marmac's jewels, I will assist you in your quest."

"Come with me and let's eat and drink while we tell each other of our deepest desires." She led me into a back room that contained a smooth, etched glass table and three deeply padded chairs. "Sit and observe the stones while I prepare our meal." Against each wall of the room were display cases that contained dozens of the jewels. There was a small source of light in the top of each case that shown down on the stones and caused them to shimmer and emit a rainbow of colors. I noticed that the only stones that were emitting light, were those that were touching another stone.

She reappeared with bread, cheese and glasses of a cold, ruby-red liquid that tasted like a mixture of ginger ale and fresh, sweet strawberries. The bread and cheese went perfectly together. I could get used to this lady's cooking!

She had two names; Bresonia, which meant keeper of the truth, and Torena, her preferred name, translated to tuner of stones!

"I know that your deepest desire is to travel back in time, and I know why, but I want you to explain it to me in your own words." I finally opened my mouth and related to her all the gaps that my brother and I had found in our family's history. I explained that, neither my brother nor I had ever been interested in our genealogy until we had become the last surviving members of our family. I didn't want to change history, but rather I wanted to ensure its survival.

"You speak well, Robert. You also have the attributes to carry forth the truth and honor of the Elemroys." She slowly sank back into the chair cushions and began to hum. Her eyes soon began to pulse and shimmer with green and violet hues. Her eyes closed and she began to tell me a story of incredible prosperity and wealth, then war, disease and famine. It was the saga of her ancestors!

"My deepest desire is to return to my ancestors also. Unlike you, however, I want to rewrite the course of history for my people. It is fate that brought us together; two beings with the same longing, but needing each other to fulfill their own destiny."

"I do not believe in fate, but yet a God who loves me and helps guide me through life. I do believe, however, that after I die, my spiritual body is destined to spend eternity with God." I said.

"I am unfamiliar with your God, but I am impressed by your deep faith in Him. Maybe you will see fit to tell me more in the future."

Torena related to me that, with the help of the stones, I could rapidly learn the Elemroy language. After I advised her of the overloaded condition of my brain, and explained to her how its growth was causing the protrusion of my forehead, we opted to go a different direction.

Sol, of course, had known that I had beamed down, but he had not pried into what I was doing on the surface of his home planet. He did, however show surprise when informed that two were beaming back up.

"Sol, Gregory, I want to introduce you to Torena, a full-blooded Elemroy!" Sol took over the translation duties and the four of us enjoyed several hours of discussing everything from food to interstellar travel. Torena told mesmerizing stories of what she knew about her ancestors and how she and several others had been able, through much effort, to maintain the purity of their race. For several centuries, they were looked upon as an inferior minority group, but were feared because of their power to read minds and even tell the future.

Gradually, over much time, they were accepted as being good citizens who contributed to society in positive ways. The issue of intermarriage had become a problem over the last fifty years, so it was becoming increasing difficult to maintain a pure Elemroy bloodline. Torena told us that she was soon to be married to a man who lineage was traced back to Marmac, the mummy that we had found.

"Would you tell us about the stones and how you use them?" I asked.

"The stones are difficult to explain and I do not want to hold up the process of me teaching you the Elemroy language. I will, however, tell you about the stones at an appropriate time."

Sol introduced Torena to the DOC and explained several of its functions. "If you wish, I will only facilitate the transfer of the Elemroy language, but, if you approve, I would like to glean other knowledge about you and your people and allow you to access whatever information you deem appropriate." Sol said.

"Will this procedure cause my brain to expand as it has Rob's?"

"No, I will not be adding nanobots to your brain, nor will I allow any excessive transfer of data." Sol assured her. She then told Sol to proceed as he liked.

While Torena was in the DOC, Sol determined that Torena was thinking of the words that I had spoken about God. As the process proceeded, he allowed her access to biblical information.

As Torena exited the DOC, she said in almost perfect English, "I now know the reason for the collapse of our aborigine culture. It was all due to moral decay. Armed with this new religious information, I am impelled, more than ever, to return to a point in my history that allows me to redirect the aims of our ancient society." She had taught Sol the Elemroy tongue and he had taught her my language. What a nice gesture to Gregory and me by Sol!

MISDIRECTION!

Sol wanted some time to correlate the Elemroy language to the sounds that were located in Grypto's recordings. I did not want to antagonize Torena, probably because I feared her powers, but I really wanted to learn more about the stones that she seemed to be able to manipulate.

But she already knew what I was thinking! Now knowing how it felt to have your thoughts read, I could sympathize with Sol's concern over me being able to read his data banks.

"Rob, I am reluctant to speak of the stones, for the Elemroy seem to be losing our ability to manipulate and use the stones for the power that they are able to supply." Torena lamented.

"What kind of power emanates from these gems and how do you use it?" Gregory asked.

"It is an unknown power and is acquired by touching the stones. Its strength is intensified when you place a number of stones against each other and then touch all of them. We don't control it; it just happens. After coming in contact with them, the power seems to persist in our bodies; sometimes for hours, but it used to stay with us for days. It seems that, from generation to generation, this wonderful power is ebbing, as our visions are becoming less intense and of shorter duration."

For one who had been reluctant to discuss the matter of these jewels, Torena was now telling us everything. There were just seven of the Elemroys that could successfully manipulate the stones. However, as was the case with Grypto centuries ago, it was evident that some, not of their descent, also possessed this capability. The seven would meet on a regular basis and try to expand their knowledge of the stones. They never had been able to determine what factors allowed them to access the power, but had always assumed that it was tied to one's intellectual prowess.

Right after meeting Torena, she had told me that she knew of me touching Marmac's necklace and had asked if I had experienced visions! Could it be, that because of the alteration of my brain, I was one who could call forth the powers of the stones?!

"The seven of us are in agreement that, for reasons unknown, we are probably not realizing the full potential of the stones. Something is missing, but we cannot pinpoint it. We also know that the smaller green gems seem to exude more power, but the larger violet ones are comparable."

Suddenly, Sol butted in and said excitedly, "According to Grypto, most, if not all the information we have accumulated about time travel is irrelevant."

"What do you mean Sol? I'm carrying tons of data that we will need to construct the proper system of wormholes!"

"That's impossible, I instructed the DOC to remove that data two months ago!" Sol exclaimed.

"I can't explain it, but somehow I know that it is still rumbling around in my head. I haven't had the adverse symptoms of brain overload since it supposedly removed everything, but the enlargement of my forehead would seem to be an indication that the DOC did not follow your orders. I think that the DOC and I are soon going to come to a meeting of the minds!"

"That's a development that I did not foresee, but Rob, let me finish telling all of you what I have learned from the decoding of Grypto's recorder. I presume, in an elaborate attempt to disguise his relevant information, he put considerable time and effort in concocting, what turned out to be a very effective smoke screen."

"Exactly what was Grypto trying to hide and whom did he intend to finally discover it?" Torena asked.

"This is the part that you're not going to believe. His true intention was to impart his knowledge of the rocks, as he called them. He stumbled onto a way to elicit large amounts of power and energy from the same stones that we have been talking about, but he gave no indication of who he wanted to possess this knowledge. Regardless, we have made a great discovery!" Sol said excitedly.

"My aboriginal ancestors were a complex and cerebral society, but neither I nor any of my kinsmen have ever determined that we could bring forth such power as Grypto has alluded to. Even though we are quite clannish and wish to keep our bloodline pure, we are still citizens of this world. If his work is proven true, just think what it would mean to Herzog. The Elemroys could help bring about a whole new level of accomplishments!"

"How did Grypto obtain his stones? Sol, would you not have known if he was experimenting with them? Would he have not, either carried them on his person or kept them in his quarters. Wouldn't any emanation of power have been picked up by your sensors?" I asked.

"I have no idea when or where he secured the stones. He was forty three years old before I ever met him, and he could have already gained this knowledge by that time. If that is so, then he probably did not bring his stones on board. Even if he did, you need to remember that Torena has indicated that this is a power that affects the mind, and not one that I would normally be able to pick up with any of my sensors."

"Hey, the important thing is that Grypto has provided some fantastic information. What else can you tell us, Sol?" Gregory asked.

What Sol related was not exactly definitive, but it sure as heck was interesting! From all that he gathered, it seemed that Grypto felt that the only ingredients for time travel were knowing what time in the past or future that a traveler would shoot for, and the stones!

No more having to tap into a humongous power source; no more having to locate, move, and properly position at least two wormholes; no more needing to manipulate tachyon particles to keep the holes open! I was free! I could get all of this junk out of my head! Or could I? Was my cerebral capacity going to be the key? The more I thought about it, the more outlandish it seemed.

"I can relate to the factor of what time period a traveler would target, but surely Grypto's not saying that you can simply use the stones to generate the ability to travel through time!"

"Yes, that is precisely what I think he means." Sol replied.

"Sol, we've gone from wrestling with huge numbers of conditions that had to be met for time travel, to something that seems too easy. There has to be something else involved."

"Rob, this scenario that Grypto has painted may not be as far-fetched as it seems. There are tales of Elemroys who were able to eerily transport from place to place. In fact, Marmac was one of those who were reported to possess this power. His full tribal name was Elique Oron Marmac, which translates to mover of souls." Torena said with excitement in her voice.

They say that people of my age begin to have improved long-term memory, even as our short-term memory deteriorates. But the DOC had given me an even greater ability to evoke crystal-clear images back to my very early childhood. I harkened back to a time when, after Patsy and I had married, I got to know a neighbor who was an amateur gemologist. I would go over to his garage and watch as he tumbled and polished many different colors of stones.

Craig had a large chart on the wall that contained pictures of the natural stones, and then what they looked like after polishing. The chart also contained data about where the gems were found and their value and hardness versus the norm of a diamond. He also had an old desk in the corner and it had a stack of books that told you everything that you ever wanted to know about his hobby.

One book that was especially interesting, enumerated the powers that various civilizations had attributed to these colorful rocks. There was the amethyst, a violet variety of quartz. It would exit the polishing machine with a deep, medium purple to go along with rose-colored flashes. Its powers were said to include peace, love, spiritual well being, dreams and extraordinary mental processes!

Malachite was a mineral that, when polished, showed several distinct shades of green. Its powers included the detection of impending danger, inner peace and protection of travelers!

These two polished gems were very similar in appearance to Torena's. Could it be that earth had gems just like those used by the Elemroy?! If so, why had humans, in all our history, never discovered their power?

I was startled when Gregory, poked me in the arm and asked why I wasn't paying attention to what Sol and Torena were telling us. I decided to wait till later to relate what I had been remembering.

FINDING THE POWER

It was not known how Grypto could elicit such energy from the stones. Torena suggested that he had possibly located a cache of stones that were either more powerful or much larger than the ones the Elemroys had now.

"I would like to relate two more things that I uncovered that concerned Grypto. One, he thought that paradoxes, associated with time travel, were a distinct possibility. But what he really stressed, was his fear that the particular power of the stones would cause a transfer of personalities." Sol told us.

We adjourned to the board room to collect our thoughts and make plans. It was decided that we would beam Torena down so she could gather up her stones and pack whatever she needed. I asked her to bring back some of her bread and cheese; along with some of the heavenly red elixir that she had served me.

After Torena returned, we settled in over Marmac's tomb and Sol was willing to let her, being of Marmac's race, take the necklace.

We again grouped in the boardroom and watched as Torena moved and manipulated the stones. As before, her eyes soon took on the color of the stones as they fluoresced. She suddenly groaned and fell back into her chair. "What's the matter? Is she okay?!" Gregory asked.

"She's absorbing the energy from the stones, but her vital signs appear to be stable. It is probably best if we leave her alone." Sol said.

We sat there and observed her as she would occasionally stiffen and then fall back. She would sigh and her face would show emotions. After at least twenty minutes, she suddenly shuddered, mumbled an unintelligible phrase and woke up. Her eyes were glowing like embers as she reached across the table and took my hand. "It is true, Rob. You are the one who will do this."

"What's true, and what is it that I am supposed to do?"

"I have just experienced the most profound and enlightening vision ever! It was so vivid as I saw you returning to the years of your childhood. Rob, I don't know if I will achieve my goal, but you certainly are going to."

"I must caution you though, for danger lies ahead. You must watch out for the snake and prepare for difficult times. Furthermore, we must locate larger gems, or find a way to elicit more power from the ones we have. This is necessary to enable your journey."

"Well, which one is it, more stones or more power?" Sol asked.

"I am not sure, but one or the other will occur." Torena replied.

All of us were shocked at Torena's revelation, but I was the one who suddenly didn't know if this is what I really wanted to do. I felt like I knew what her reference to a snake might be. At the age of eight, my brother and I exited our school bus and I stepped on a coiled-up diamondback rattlesnake. For some unknown reason, it did not strike. After my dad killed it, he measured it at four and one half feet long, and it had thirteen rattles! With it being a considerable distance to a doctor and with no antivenom serum in those days, its bite would probably have killed me.

As to the difficult times that would be in store for me; that was a mystery. I questioned Torena, but she said that her vision only indicated that, if I traveled back in time, great stress would be brought upon me.

"If you just experienced your greatest vision ever, is not our current supply of stones sufficient?" Sol asked Torena.

"I can only tell you what my vision revealed to me. I can say that, since I became able to have these mental images, all things that I have envisioned have come to pass. They are true."

Since no one knew what powered the stones, we took the easiest approach and began a search for larger stones. Sol related that, on earth, most of our gems were the product of seismic upheaval and eruptions of lava. "Herzog has not experienced such activity in tens of thousands years, and the Elemroy certainly did not inhabit territory where such events would have occurred." Torena stated.

"Well, we now have a puzzle on our hands. Where then, could your people have obtained your stones?" Gregory asked. Torena explained that, as far as she knew, they had always been a part of their culture. She insisted that we search a large perimeter around Marmac's burial place. While Torena sat a basket of food on the boardroom table, Sol began an investigation of a twenty five mile diameter area from Marmac and the adjacent burial ground.

As we ate, she told us that those current Elemroys who delved into archeology felt that at one time, their ancestors had numbered several hundred thousand and were spread out over a wide area. However, it appeared that only Marmac's tribe procured and used the stones.

"Were there other indigenous groups that might have bartered with the stones?" I asked.

"We have never uncovered any evidence of tribal groups, other than the Elemroys living within these expanses."

Sol told us that his systematic search of nearly forty thousand square miles, to the south and southwest of Marmac's tomb, would take approximately five days. Torena wanted to shut down her business and see a few friends. Gregory was chomping at the bit to go down and see what I had experienced, and I wanted to soak up some more of the local charm of Plethor. I asked the DOC to provide disguises for both of us.

Torena seemed delighted to have us come along, but she warned that we should use our translators if we ventured out in public.

The people of Herzog lived in a very advanced society. They had obtained interstellar flight and enjoyed many other capabilities that earthlings only dreamed about. So it was strange to learn that they seldom used a food replicator. They preferred to grow and prepare their food much as humans do. Their appliances, however, were unusual to say the least. The stove cooked but never generated heat!

Torena told us that nothing was needed for food preservation, because their controlled environment did not allow for bacteria or other microbes to contaminate their food, even if left out on the table. The peculiar spectrum of their lighting was instrumental in delaying the natural decay of what we term perishables. Before I could ask her about ice, she showed us a strange looking contraption that produced yellow ice, but the ice maker did not radiate cold, nor feel cold to the touch!

What had escaped me in my first visit, was the fact that there were no vehicles to be seen on the streets! Torena guided us to the rear of her upstairs apartment and allowed us to watch as she used a small screen to place an order for several items. A few seconds later, a tone sounded, a wall panel lifted and there was her order! What an efficient way to handle goods; no delivery vehicles, no fuel required and no delivery man to pay!

Torena was a great hostess and used a monitor with a satellite hookup to give us a great, close-up tour of Plethor. Gregory and I both wanted to go exploring, but she felt it best to limit our time outside to short trips after dark. Most businesses seem to shut down at dusk, so I convinced her to take me to a small jewelry shop before it closed. I had gazed into its windows during my previous time in the city and had thought about how Patsy and Lyla would like some of the unusual jewelry. She dickered for me and I bought two beautiful rings. Actually, she had to pay for them, because I had no local currency. When I told her that I would figure out a way to repay her, she said that my friendship was payment enough. Torena was destined to become a close friend of mine also. I didn't realize it at the time, but she would be the one who would use her powers to guide me from the past back into the present.

It was day three of Sol's search when he called me. "Rob, I've found some stones. They're not very big, but I count fifty six of them."

"Great, I'll pass the news on to Torena and Gregory! Are you going to pick us up, or continue your search pattern?"

"I managed to broaden my scanner beam and have just about covered all of the territory that we discussed. So, I think I will head back and bring the three of you up. I know that Torena will be excited about surveying and testing these gems."

Torena spread the stones on the boardroom table and slowly examined each one. "Sol, you have located the right stones, but they need to be polished before I can determine their capacity."

"No problem, just place them in the container you'll find on the DOC couch, and they'll be ready in a jiffy." Sol replied.

In about five minutes, Sol told us the polishing was finished; a process that would have taken many hours of tumbling on earth!

We watched expectantly as she carefully mixed the two colors of the gems and made sure that all were touching at least one other. She hovered over them as she began to hum. Several minutes passed by before she opened her eyes. "Sol, where did you locate these stones?"

Sol explained that he had located them in a deep depression that was situated in what looked like an old river bed. It was at the bottom of a steep slope, very similar to the one where we had found Marmac. He had extracted them from a strata of gravel about seven feet below the river bed.

"Torena, is something wrong? Does it matter where the stones came from?" Gregory asked.

"I'm just trying to figure out why these particular stones seem to possess no energy." She said.

"How can that be? From what you have told us, I thought that these kinds of stones were able to produce the power that is needed for your visions and for the time travel that we both have planned! Maybe, we need to return to Plethor and try again!" I exclaimed.

Nothing worked. She called in some of her kin who were able to use the stones, and they were as puzzled by their failures, as Torena. Gregory was still enthralled with all that was going on, but I had tired of it and beamed up. "I think the stones are too small, or maybe their being covered up for hundreds of years has sapped their energy. What do you think, Rob?" Sol asked.

I suddenly remembered Craig's garage and decided to tell Sol about it. "If indeed, they are the same gems, maybe our answer lies on earth."

"I do not possess a lot of information about the amethyst and malachite, but I have registered accounts of large specimens being found at various points on the globe." Sol stated. I, of course, had the same data lodged in my brain, but for some reason it had not surfaced.

We discussed our options at length and I beamed down, primarily to talk with Torena. "Sol and I have decided that we should proceed to earth and look for stones there. We're not sure where we will search, but Sol will bone up on the available data after we arrive. He has done some comparisons, and we feel that earth's amethyst and malachite are duplicates of Herzog's gems. We are also relatively sure that much larger stones are available on earth. Torena, unless you can formulate a better plan, I suggest that we get going."

Ever since we had left earth, something had been nagging me, but I couldn't put my finger on it. As we prepared to go back, it dawned on me what it was. "Sol, is there a possibility that we are undergoing time dilation when we traverse the wormhole? I want to be prepared, if when we return, there is a time differential of any magnitude."

"I would never have brought you and Gregory here if that were the case. Neither would I be allowing Torena to return with us. Wormholes, at least the one that I have used three times, do not dilate time." I was relieved, because time seemed to be passing way to fast, as it was.

The three of us strapped in, Sol put the pedal to the metal and we were soon lodged above Dallas. We had not been gone as long as we had anticipated, but both Gregory and I wanted to go downstairs and visit with our families.

"When anyone asks you where you got your ring, just tell them that I picked it up for you, while on a long trip out of the country!" I said to Patsy and Lyla as we ate dinner.

Brady laughed and said, "Yeah Dad, I bet that was a long trip; probably only a couple hundred light years or so."

"You're pretty close, Brady. Sol said that it was a hundred and eighty six light years, each way!"

Gregory and I both had a good time that evening, but we were spurred by what lay ahead and went upstairs early the next morning.

Torena was enthralled by the beauty of our earth. While Gregory and I were downstairs, Sol provided a tour from pole to pole and east to west. She had implored Sol to provide a disguise and let her beam down, but he had thought it best that we did not take any chances. "I have never seen colors such as these! They are so beautiful and vivid. The snowy mountain tops are wondrous!" Torena exclaimed.

How ironic! I had been entranced by the colors on her world, and here she was exclaiming about how magnificent earth's colors were!

It was apparent that, either the spectrums of light from earth's and Herzog's suns created different colors, or Elemroy and human eyes had different receptors. I guess it was a matter of what you had gotten use to, but I sure preferred the hues of my native world; especially the fantastic orange that only God's sunsets could provide!

GREEN EGGS AND PURPLE WATERMELONS!

"I have tapped into your internet and processed all the data on the amethyst and malachite gems. Apparently, both can be found at numerous locations around the earth. That sets me to wondering; if the stones are plentiful and are not considered unusual, can they be duplicates of those rare gems on Herzog?" Sol asked.

"We won't know until we locate some and let me examine them, so where do you think we should begin, Sol?" Torena asked.

"I do not care, but when we look for the malachite, I would like to go to Israel first." Sol replied. Gregory asked Sol if his information indicated that the largest gems were to be found there.

"No, but the Israeli site is called the Timna valley and is thought to be a part of King Solomon's mines. Since I am his namesake, it would be special for me to be able to visit. If we do not find large stones there, we will proceed elsewhere. We can be hopeful, however, for history shows that the mine has been productive for over three thousand years."

Sol beamed up a few of the largest stones that he could find, but they were less than one and a half inches across. He quickly polished them so Torena could proceed with her assessment and it didn't take her long.

"I hate to tell you this, but these are not the same as those on Herzog. They are quite similar, but they lack the spectrum of colors that ours exhibit."

"Torena, if we locate some big nice amethyst stones that meet with your approval, do we need the green gems?" Gregory asked.

"We tested that theory a long time ago, and found that you must have both stones to create the energy that is needed for our visions. I am not positively sure that the colors are the only important aspect of their power, but there is evidently a vital synergy that exists between the two stones."

I asked Sol to Google "green gem stones" and project his findings onto the boardroom wall. There were twenty examples of green stones, far more than I knew existed. Torena quickly skimmed over the pictures, which included emeralds, jade, spinel, beryl and the green garnets, tourmaline and tsavorite. The last one was, oddly, the black opal.

"Hold it! Can you enlarge that last stone for me, Sol?"

"That doesn't look like anything I saw in Marmac's necklace or those stones in your home, Torena." I said.

"Your right Rob, but this example is a rough stone. Once it is polished, I think it will show the green flashes that we seek."

"Torena is right, the information about the black opal states that it can express every color in the visible spectrum." Sol related.

How ironic, that the only two sites in the entire world, where the black opal could be found, were in Australia. Not just any area of Australia, but in an area where the aborigines still roam and use the boomerang!

"The largest black opal was mined in nineteen eighty six and is named Halley's Comet for the celestial body that moved through earth's inner solar system during that year. This gem is four inches long and two and one half inches thick; a whopping eighteen hundred carats. It states that this stone is dominated by fiery green hues, but with some streaks of red and blue. Would a similar stone work for you?" Sol asked Torena.

Torena was elated and told us that she couldn't wait to get her hands on a stone such as Sol described.

Sol asked how we were going to pay for any stones that we might find! "I don't understand why all of a sudden you think that we should pay for the black opals. That was not your attitude about the malachite stones." Gregory said.

"The malachite gems are plentiful all over the planet, and they are not very valuable. Besides, we returned them polished and in better condition than we found them. However, black opals such as Halley's Comet and another, called Aurora Australis are worth at least a million dollars, each. Are we not morally obligated to pay for what we take?"

Sol had a valid point, but Torena came up with a solution that he was willing to accept. "Since large specimens are extremely rare, would not the mine owners be happy if we left them some large stones; one for one for each that we take? They might search for years, maybe even decades before they would find stones that will probably take Sol only a few minutes to locate."

We wound up doing much more than what Torena had suggested. Sol found eleven black opals, that were all as large, or larger that Halley's Comet. One was nearly twice as big! "Sol, you don't even have to polish these stones right now. I have selected four that I know will work beautifully." The ones that she had opted for were oval in shape, about the size of a turkey egg.

Sol beamed the remaining stones into a drawer in the mine superintendent's desk. We laughed and wished we could see his face when he found them. He would make his company many millions of dollars and probably receive a hefty bonus!

The polished black opals lived up to their hype! All of us were mesmerized by the electric brilliance of the colors, especially as they appeared against their ebony black background.

"Rob, let's hurry and find the amethyst stones so we can get on with our time travel plans!" Torena said breathlessly.

I had begun to be concerned about Torena. She seemed so very confident of her ability to travel back in time, but I had reservations about my own potential to make the stones work. Now that all the pieces were falling into place, another concern had arisen. What if she used the stones to make her trip back to Marmac's time, and I was left with no ability to make the trip that I was planning?

I went into the DOC and Sol and I began a silent conversation about Torena. "Rob, there are two things that you need to consider. One, because of our previous hookup in the DOC, I am familiar with Torena's intellect and I can assure you that she is a straight forward, honest person. Secondly, Gregory and I both have noticed that she has already developed deep feelings for you. I not saying that she's in love with you, but it's evident that she respects your substantial intellectual ability and shares your desire to travel back in time. I am sure that, besides me, Torena is now your greatest ally."

It seemed that I was the only one that had developed a pessimistic attitude. Oh well, we all were caught up in a process that probably couldn't be stopped; not that any of us wanted to do so. So, I decided to make the most of it. But one more doubt came to mind.

I had seen Torena manipulate the stones twice, and did not share her enthusiasm. "How are you planning to make stones with such a large size differential work? Will not the percentage of contact area between these stones be very different than when you use your own?" I asked.

"I am not worried, for the immense size of these gems will most certainly get the job done." Torena said.

Sol didn't have to be prompted and immediately put the amethyst data up on the wall. "Wow! These aren't stones, they're boulders!" Gregory exclaimed. What Sol showed us was not individual gems or crystals, but amethyst geodes, and some were over ten feet in length, six to seven feet in diameter and weighed over a ton!

Sol explained, "These geodes are hollow for the most part, but the inner surface of the shell is layered with amethyst crystals, ranging from one, to more than six inches in thickness. Most of the examples that you are looking at are geodes that have been broken in half to expose the purple crystals."

"Torena, what would happen if we break one of these geodes open? Do you think that its effectiveness might be compromised?" I asked.

"This form of amethyst is not what I had expected, but we should probably select a few smaller geodes and run some tests." She replied.

Most of the commercially available amethyst, a purple variety of quartz, comes from Brazil. Sol soon came to a stop above the central part of Rio Grande do Sul, the southern most state of the country. It was kind of strange to be returning to this area. My daughter Lyla and I had visited missionaries in Porto Alegre, the capital of the state, in nineteen ninety five and had enjoyed the Brazilian culture.

Sol brought up six geodes about the size and shape of watermelons. He had also formulated an idea that seemed to be pure genius!

"Why break the geode? Why not just peel off the drusy, which is the external crystalline covering of the geode. This will expose the full outer perimeter of the amethyst. We then polish this entire surface of the geode and bingo, we have a huge gem!"

Torena was again unable to contain her excitement when Sol showed her the polished geode. "Hallelujah Sol, I would kiss you if I could!" Instead she grabbed me, kissed me on the cheek and whispered in my ear, "Rob, we are going to make history together."

She said that she only needed two geodes, but I figured that it would be a good idea to have a backup. Sol polished the other three and placed them where a mine worker could easily find them. Wouldn't that drive them crazy, trying to figure out how entire geodes had been polished?!

BAD STONES!

The geodes were heavy, so we helped Torena position them on the boardroom table. She must have been unsure as to how the stones should be touching, because she fiddled with them for a good fifteen minutes. At last she sat down in her chair and with a sigh, placed her hands to where she was touching a portion of all the stones.

All of a sudden, she jerked her hands back! "I cannot conceive of the power that these stones must have. I may get locked into a vision and not be able to return to reality. If I have not awakened in fifteen minutes, you must pull my hands from the stones."

She replaced her hands, closed her eyes and began a low guttural chant. It wasn't long before she started fidgeting in her chair and her eyelids began to flutter. Sweat soon formed on her forehead and her arms began to tremble. You could tell that she was exerting a great deal of mental energy. Within two minutes of when we were to remove her hands, she did so herself.

"I cannot fathom what is wrong, but I am unable to establish any fruitful contact with these beautiful gems that I selected. Could I have possibly made an error in my judgments?"

None of us had an answer for her, but we tried our best to console and encourage her. "Torena, it's bound to be a stressful time for you, so why don't we relax for a while and have something to eat. It would also probably be a good idea for you to spend thirty minutes in the DOC, so it can help rejuvenate your mental powers." Sol said.

After we ate and she had entered the DOC, I approached Gregory with an idea. "I am going to try the stones myself and I would like for you to be my attendant, just in case I can't get loose from them."

"What makes you think that you can do what Torena couldn't do?"

I explained that Torena felt that intellectual power was the key to being able to manipulate the stone's energy. Gregory agreed to carefully watch me. I followed the same process that Torena had used, except that I didn't know any chants to use! My arms got tired and I really wanted to open my eyes to look at the stones. Nothing! Nada! Zilch! I apparently did not have the gift.

Torena walked back in as Gregory and I were talking about our inability to achieve any positive results. "Gentlemen, you sure seem to be in a hurry to write all of our effort off as a failure. I am refreshed and ready to do this right!"

With at least one of us standing alert at her side, Torena continued her efforts to elicit something from the stones. We changed the arrangement of the stones several times, and at one point, she crawled up on the table and laid her body over them. After multiple attempts, that lasted over two hours, she put her head in her hands and sobbed. "We have a situation that offers so much promise, but I cannot make any progress. I have failed all of you."

Gregory put his arm around her shoulders and tried to console Torena, but she was despondent. "I am so ashamed that you have put your trust in me, and yet I am unable to provide our dream."

Although I was extremely disappointed, my thoughts were for Torena. What could I do to help her feel better? I wanted to go downstairs and do something to take my mind off our situation, but I couldn't leave her, not right now.

I know! I'll take her down with me! I had set foot on her planet and I supposed that she deserved to set foot on mine. Although Sol thought it risky, under the conditions, he knew that it would be good for her. "Please just keep her in your home." He warned.

Dinner that night, with my family and Gregory, was pleasant enough. I had explained the circumstances of the day to Patsy, Brady and Lyla. They were, of course, very excited to be in the presence of an alien, but they tempered their enthusiasm and tried to help Torena relax.

What really took her mind off of her supposed failures was her amazement of how we lived. She was especially interested in the swimming pool in our back yard. After I had explained its use, she asked, "How is it that you have the luxury of a body of water that is used just for fun? Herzog's water supply is gradually dwindling and we cannot exploit it for recreational purposes."

We talked about water being the basis of all life, at least as far as anyone knew. I explained how humans were also concerned about the ever-increasing demand for fresh water, and that swimming pools might soon be a thing of the past. People from earth and from Herzog were concerned about water. So was Sol.

The next morning at breakfast, Torena was commenting about how much she liked the bacon and eggs, when she suddenly stopped, looked at me and said, "Rob, please take me back up to Sol." I asked why, but she was insistent that we beam up.

I called Gregory and we went upstairs. "Have you come up with a solution?" Sol asked.

"No, but I am determined to find one. The four of us should be able to solve this dilemma. Do any of you have any thoughts or suggestions?" She asked.

I guess we all were kind of resigned to failure and not ready to reengage our brains to tackle something we really knew nothing about. The quietness was deafening. Finally, Sol said in his John Wayne voice, "Pardners, I'll, make us some coffee and we'll see if we can't help this lady in distress."

Gregory kind of stuttered and said, "Maybe the stones are too large, and because of that, you're just not touching them properly. Heck, maybe it's something simple like an improper angle or intensity of light hitting them."

"What did you just say?" Torena asked.

"I said that these stones may be too big."

"No, not that! What did you say about light?"

"Well, one thing that I have learned is that light makes the stones fluoresce, and that doesn't appear to be happening here. So, the light that Sol is providing may not work as well as the light on Herzog."

"We know that Herzog's suns produce a different spectrum of light than earth's sun, but if these are the right stones, I don't know why that would make any difference." Sol said.

Sol was right. Both of Torena's visions had occurred under artificial light; once in her home and once in the boardroom. "What about that Torena, can the amount, direction or spectrum of light be a factor?" I asked with renewed interest.

She started to say something, but stopped. She began massaging her temples with her finger tips. "Are you okay?" Gregory asked softly.

"Be quite, I'm thinking!" She thundered. Gregory and I both knew not to mess with a thinking woman!

"Sol, can you reproduce the spectrum of light that Herzog's suns emit?" She commanded, more than asked. Sol was able to do so, but it made no difference, for we again experienced failure.

Torena once again lapsed into her own thoughts. I asked Sol to make us some more coffee and Gregory and I left the boardroom. We had lounged and talked about our recent adventures for about forty five minutes, when Sol said, "Guys, I think you better come back in."

Torena had asked Sol if she could listen to Grypto's recordings. After doing so, she related to him that there are four different names that are used for the dual suns of Herzog; one for each individually, one for them collectively and one for their closest approach to the planet. Their perigee went by the name of Topak Cabong and occurred once every nine years.

"Rob, Gregory, I am now convinced that the distance that Grypto refers to, is not how far any time travel is projected to be, but rather the distance from the power source for the stones, Herzog's suns!"

"You've completely lost me, Torena. Of course, we will need to know the distance between our planets! We'll have to calculate the distance in astronomical units from where our planet is when we begin the travel, to where it was at the time in the past that we wish to travel to. That information would seem to be very fundamental to any time travel."

I remembered my elation when, after learning the Elemroy language, Sol had said that I no longer needed all the time travel junk that I had stored in my brain. Keep it simple stupid! I should have kept quite and let Torena finish.

"No Rob, Grypto uses the words Topak Cabong to refer to distance. It is at this perigee that we experience a change in the light spectrum and the sun's extra hot colors."

"Think about it. When Torena was able to use Marmac's necklace, she had a very powerful vision. His stones evidently had been charged by Topak Cabong before he was laid to rest, and had never been used since. Torena and the other Elemroys who use the stones have had no knowledge that the stones could be recharged every nine years; thus, the declining energy for their visions." Sol said.

It sure seemed to be getting a lot easier, but I still was confused about something. "Torena, let's say that we are able to obtain a maximum charge for the stones; what then? How do we then use them to navigate back in time?" Torena wasn't sure, but was confident that we would find out after experiencing Topak Cabong.

The more I thought about it, the more it seemed to make sense. "You know, I'll bet my life savings that Marmac's tomb, or real close by, is the point on Herzog that is closest to the suns when Topak Cabong happens!" I shouted.

Gregory asked her when the perigee would next occur. "I have kind of lost track of time while we've been away from Herzog, but I am nearly positive that it will soon be happening; possibly within the next few days. We must return as quickly as possible."

Gregory and I quickly prepared to beam down for a brief explanation of another absence, and to say goodbye. But before we went downstairs, Gregory implored me to allow him to tell his wife about what he was involved in. Hope had been programmed by the DOC just to accept everything that he told her, but I could see his point. He was deceiving her and did not want to continue doing so. Ever since I met Sol, I had been confronted by difficult choices. Is it what's best for the majority, or does the individual count for more at times?

"You'll have to bring Hope up and deprogram her before the truth will sink in for her. You stay here, introduce her to Sol and I'll take care of my business as quick as I can." I said.

Torena then piped in. "I want to go down with you Rob. I have something to say to your wife."

"Patsy, I know that you cannot help but be concerned about Rob, for he is attempting to go where no man has ever gone before. You have my promise that I will use every ounce of my being to keep him safe." I was not sure how Torena could protect me, but I was happy to have her on my side.

POWER AT LAST!

The adrenalin was flowing for all of us. Even Sol sounded excited. He provided Torena with a communication implant and she beamed down to check the Herzog calendar for the date of Topak Cabong. She had been right; the perigee was to occur in just four days.

Sol again hacked into Plethor's historical archives. "The meteorological data shows that this solar event has been occurring for as long as they have been keeping records, and that is for over seven thousand years. Guys, I'm headed to Marmac's tomb." Sol said to Gregory and me.

"Going to check and see if I was right, aren't you." I said laughing.

Sol positioned immediately over Marmac's burial site, at a height of only fifty feet. "Rob, you'll be happy to know that your life's savings are safe. This exact point, within a mile radius or so, will be Herzog's closest point to the suns!"

I called Torena and relayed the great news. I also had a suggestion for her. "Why don't you gather up all the Elemroy stones that you can find and we will recharge them as we charge our new ones."

The waiting was torturous, maybe more for Torena than the rest of us. She did not want to face her Elemroy kinfolk if this plan of ours turned out to be another bust. It was my fault that she was experiencing such stress and anxiety. It had all started when I had walked into her shop just a week earlier. I wanted to help if I could.

"Torena, I know that this is important to you and your people, but it is not a matter of life and death." I said softly.

"Oh, but it is! We have become a race that is destined for extinction." She said mournfully.

"How can that be? Although I have not met any of your people, you certainly appear to be quite healthy." I responded.

She was, indeed healthy, especially for someone who was one hundred and twenty six years old!

After their visions were completed, the remaining power could often be used to heal, but the one ailment that they could not overcome was an ovarian disease. Their ability to have children had ceased!

"Why didn't you tell me about this, Torena?"

"I initially thought that, because of your quest for time travel, you probably would not think it was important. So, I went along, hoping that we would both eventually get what we wanted. After thinking about what I might be able to accomplish by going into the past, I wanted to help obtain that capability. I really want that to happen for both of us, but my immediate concern is to help our women." Torena said with a tinge of guilt.

Topak Cabong was to occur six and one half hours after the rise of the two suns. We set all of the stones on a flat area just a few feet from Marmac's grave site, and then Sol moved off far enough so that he would not interfere with the unusual sunlight that we were expecting. He set up two viewing ports for us; one with a filter that would let us look directly at the suns, and one that allowed a view of the stones. Then he proceeded to tell us what was going to occur.

"As with most stars, these two suns exhibit tremendous magnetic fields. A planet's magnetic field is essential for deflecting solar winds, and since Herzog has two suns, its magnetic field is much stronger than earth's. It is my studied opinion, that the collision of the sun's and Herzog's magnetic fields is the fuel for this event. Increased gravitational force between the bodies will also factor into the energy output. Coronal mass ejections from the suns will spike and solar flares will be very prominent. This probably corresponds to, what on earth is termed solar maximum."

Verok, the larger sun flashed with magnificent greens and Verak, the smaller one, in beautiful shades of purple! The three of us were mesmerized with the tremendous display of God's power. A coronal mass ejection might last only a few minutes, but it would release energy equivalent to millions of hydrogen bombs, and reach ten million degrees Kelvin.

"I know that the suns are putting on a fantastic show, but you ought to look down." Sol said with a small laugh.

Torena screamed with delight and Gregory started clapping! I just sat there relieved as we watched the stones emit vivid flashes of the same green and purple!

Topak Cabong lasted only seventeen minutes, but I knew that, if possible, I would be back every nine years for as long as I lived.

Sol retrieved the stones and immediately took us to Plethor. We all needed to come down off our high before we proceeded any farther. Torena, however, was eager to test the stones and you could tell that her confidence had been restored. I suggested that she take her Elemroy stones back down and call the other six together who could use them. Together, they could quickly determine the charged gems ability to cure the ovarian malady. "Gregory and I will relax and wait to hear from you."

Sol prepared us a good meal, and we both decided that, instead of refreshing in the DOC, we would take a simple, old fashioned nap. Three hours later, I awoke with a start, having been dreaming of my past. I woke Gregory and asked him if he would help me do something.

"You want to try the stones from earth, don't you? Rob, those stones are out of your league. Who knows, because of their very large size they may even be more than Torena can handle."

I persisted and Gregory reluctantly agreed to by my side-man. We walked into the boardroom and I asked Sol if he would situate the stones on the table. "They are not here. Torena had me beam all the stones down with her."

"You're kidding aren't you? I encouraged her to take her Elemroy stones back and use them to heal the women. Why would she have taken all of them?"

"I'm not sure, but I did not see any problem with it. After all, I believe that she and her six relatives are the only ones that can work the stones."

"Sol, you knew what she and I had discussed. Why didn't you stop her, or least talk to me before you allowed her to go down with them?"

"I am sorry for your inconvenience Rob, but I no longer make a habit of listening in on private conversations. All of you have a right to your privacy."

It was disturbing to think that Torena had basically, deceived me. She didn't strike me as a devious person, but then, I had known her for just a few days.

I called her. No answer. What could be going on? Maybe she's locked in a vision. I called three more times in the next hour, but still no response. Then it hit me that her hands might be frozen onto those powerful stones and her attendants could not free her!

I beamed down into her back room where I had seen the cabinets displaying her stones. Three men and three women were standing around the table where all our stones were situated, but no Torena! One of the men spoke to me but I did not understand him. "Sol, send me a translator and hurry!"

I placed it around my neck and gestured to the man to speak. "You must be the alien that Torena told us about."

"Yes, I am Rob. Please tell me where Torena is."

"This is the third time that she has left us, but she will be back." He said.

"Where has she gone? Is she okay?"

"She appears to be fine. She is now on another trip back into our past." One of the men stated.

"She has already made three trips? Why?" I shouted.

"We do not know, but at her last appearance, she told us that she thought that she had chosen correctly this time."

She had told me that she wished to give her ancestors the ability to change. They had pushed their society to vast intellectual limits, but with no concern for morality. The Roman Empire decayed and died for the same reason. How could only one person exact such a change in attitude?

I didn't know what else to do, but wait. I sat down in one of the chairs, but they told me that it was Torena's chair! I jumped up and stood in the corner.

The stones brightened and Torena appeared in the chair, her eyes open, but glazed. Her clothes were dusty and she had and a long, thin cut on her left forearm. The other four gathered around her and put their hands of her head, and as her eyes closed, she slumped in her chair. I cried out, but one of the men grimaced at me and motioned for me to be quite.

It seemed like hours before Torena opened her eyes, looked at me and smiled. "Rob, I am very sorry that I mislead you, but it was necessary to do so."

"We can hash that out later. Right now, I want to know if you are okay."

"I am spent, mentally and physically, but I will be fine." Torena said weakly. I suggested a stay in the DOC and she accepted. I asked Sol to beam the stones up with us.

Torena must have been drained, because she spent over two hours in the DOC. It had cleaned her clothes and healed the cut that had been made by a frightened tribesman, as she suddenly appeared in front of him when she traveled deep into her past.

She seemed okay so I posed a question that really had me puzzled. "While you were gone into your tribe's past, the stones were still on the table in your apartment. How did you return without having them with you?"

"Once you have obtained the stone's power to travel back, you have enough energy remaining in your brain to enable the return trip." She explained. I would be sure and store of lots and lots of energy so I could be sure that I got back.

Sol had learned to make the bread, cheese and red beverage that Torena had first served me. He had it all setting on the boardroom table when Torena entered. She ate, and the rest of us listened as she told her story.

"Rob, I again apologize for my deception, but I had a promise to keep."

I interrupted and asked her, "You put yourself and our time travel in danger. What were you thinking?"

"I was thinking of you and what I told Patsy."

Torena had told Patsy that she would do everything that she could to protect me. So, she decided to take the initial risk and try to work any kinks out before I traveled.

"Why did you have to make three trips back?" Gregory asked.

"Rob has a reference point for his travel; a specific time during his childhood. I had no such reference point, so I was taking blind shots into the

Elemroy past." She had worn animal-skin clothes that she thought might fit the time period.

"The first time, I was deposited in a deserted area and, after an hour of wandering, I came to a village. Language was a problem, but I was able to determine that I had gone to far back in the past."

Her second trip gave her better bearings and she hit, what she thought was the prime period to change history, on her third journey; a time when the tide of morality had not yet turned for the worse. As best as she could determine, it was about two hundred years before Marmac's time.

"Well, what information were you able to give them that would change the way they lived?" Sol asked.

"I told them about the true and living God." Gregory and I looked at each other and realized that this alien being Torena, had hit upon the great truth of all the universe; anybody or any civilization can change with God's help.

"The chief of this good size settlement was receptive to what I told him. Although I did not tell him that I was from the future, my heightened senses told me that he knew it. Now that I have my reference point, I will return periodically to help them."

She had one other piece of good news. "Our women can now have children!" She said with a big smile on her face.

THE TIME HAS FINALLY COME!

I didn't know when I would be back, so I asked Gregory and Sol if it would be alright to stay at Plethor a few days. I really did not want to leave Torena. She had shown her true colors and I would never doubt her again. She had humbled me when she related what she had told the chief and his people. God's word, that Sol had implanted into her brain, had cut her heart like a sharp, two-edged sword, and she had believed.

The third evening, she asked if Gregory could come down and join us for dinner at a friend's home. It was actually a small meeting hall, and as we walked in, a chorus of voices hollered, "Surprise" in broken English! All the Elemroys had gathered to honor us! Torena had even asked Sol to join us as a hologram, and guess what appearance he chose; John Wayne, of course!

Torena had already taught them a few words of English, and also the custom of shaking hands. Just like us, they used toasts as a way to show appreciation and our drink was the red ambrosia that I loved! It took a long time to eat our meal for everyone was asking questions of Gregory and me. We would have to answer and then, Torena would have to translate. Sol had to remove his ten gallon, holographic hat, because it was bad manners for a male to wear a head covering inside a building. Earthlings should have such tact.

When we returned to Torena's apartment, I told her that I would like for her to begin teaching me the mysteries of the stones. "It won't take long and we can do it once we return to earth." She said.

"You need to stay here and take care of your people. I'll take the large earth stones and you keep yours for your visions and travel." I insisted.

"My commitment to you and to your wife is not finished, and I must go with you." I thought that this was going to be simple. She would teach me to use the stones and Gregory and I would return to earth. But she had me over a barrel. I could go nowhere without her help and, if I was really honest with myself, I would feel better with her at my side.

As we prepared to return to earth, Sol said to Torena, "I could have provided the DOC for your Elemroy women. Why did you not ask for my help?"

"Sol, Herzog, of course, has enjoyed the same DOC technology that was given you several hundred years ago. But, for whatever reason, we were denied its use. Finally, about thirty years ago, evidently some ethnic barriers came down and we gained access to it. It was very discouraging to us when we discovered that it would not heal our women; probably due to a difference in our physiology."

"I am extremely sorry that you had to suffer so long, but God has seen fit to help you in a very amazing way." Sol said solemnly.

My thoughts had become jumbled as we parked over Dallas. I guess if you're going on a trip and are not sure when, or if you will return, you should put your affairs in order. Oh, I was confident of being able to make a successful trip back in time, especially after Torena had showed her ability to do so. But I remembered what she had told me after her first vision using Marmac's necklace. She said that danger lay ahead and that I needed to prepare for difficult times.

As I began to make a mental list of what I probably needed to take care of, Torena interrupted my train of thought. "Rob, now is as good a time as any for your first lesson."

We walked into the boardroom and, as she sat down in front of the stones, they began to glow. "What just happened, and who is in control, you or the stones?" I asked.

"Oh, I am in control, but once you have interfaced with such powerful stones, the residual energy in your body will cause them to fluoresce when you are near them. Before we begin Rob, you must remember that they are just a tool; a tool to activate the power of your mind." She said firmly.

Having watched her, I sat down and placed both hands on the big, polished gems that had come from my own planet. "No Rob, a hand on one of the black opals is enough to begin with. We must start slowly so I can monitor your reactions. Besides, the most important part is for you to relax and obtain your mental focus before you ever touch the stones. I have much experience and am able to focus deeply within seconds."

"What am I suppose to concentrate on?"

"Just close your eyes and think about a time in your past that you would like to see very clearly in your mind." This was going to be easy, or so I thought. Even with the huge capacity of my brain, I couldn't seem to stabilize on any single thought for more than a few seconds.

Torena very quickly sensed my inability to clarify my thoughts and said that she could help me. She stood behind me, placed her fingertips on both of my temples, and began to hum, what she told me later was an Elemroy lullaby. I must have gone to sleep instantly, for a dream began to flow though my subconscious.

My brother Jesse and I walked through the gate by the windmill and raced across the large corral into the barn. We shinnied up the ladder into the loft and crawled out the hidden opening onto the lower roof. "Bet I can jump farther!" He said as we ran down the sloping roof and jumped onto the bales of hay stored for our cattle. "Lets go play in the wheat!" I said as we tumbled down the stack of hay.

It was a red Wichita wheat that had grown unusually tall; over five feet! We could run down the rows scaring up jackrabbits or play hide-go-seek. Oh, daddy, I'm so sorry that this happened to you!

"Rob, that's enough! You must return now!"

"Torena, I can't believe how sharp the images were! It was as if I was actually there. How long did I dream?"

"Only about thirty seconds. When you tensed, I decided to wake you. Why did you stiffen and moan?"

I told her how my dad was so thrilled with his wheat crop that had been assayed at sixty five bushels per acre; an astronomical figure for a farm without irrigation. With so much at stake, he had scraped up just enough money to insure the wheat against loss. With less than a week to go before harvest, the entire crop was wiped out in a savage hail storm. The insurance company's reserves were illegally low and he never got a dime! "I think that was a point in time, which my dad never really recovered from."

"Is that why you want to go back; to warn him about the bad insurance company?" She asked softly.

"I would really like to change the outcome of that situation, but it might trigger a breach of the time line. I know that I should limit my trip to the gathering of historical information."

"You need to relax and we'll work on this some more later, and I want you to know that you are going to do well on your own. My touch tells me that you absorbed a substantial amount of power from the one stone that you were in contact with. You will not need my help much longer."

In a way, I felt elated with my initial experience with the stones, but the sudden, graphic reenactment of the devastating hail storm, left me open to doubt. Could I really return and not create any paradoxes? Would the poor standard of living that existed for my parents cause me to try and help them? Maybe if I went ahead and took care of my to-do list that had been preying on my mind, I'd feel better.

I climbed into my SUV and headed west to Weatherford, Texas, where my brother Jesse lived. Boy, after Sol's methods of travel, a car was sure an archaic way to travel from point A to point B. But I sure couldn't have Sol beam me down to Jesse's front door without any logical means of arriving there.

Jesse had retired from teaching microbiology in Fort Worth's community college system. After moving into a colonial style home in Weatherford, he spent his time gardening and adding to his collection of knives. Occasionally, he helped out in a cigar store on the town square. He was sitting in a glider on the front porch, smoking one of his Punch cigars when I pulled up in the driveway.

"Brother, what in the world are you doing here?" I explained that I was going to spend some time working on our genealogy and wanted to determine what questions he might like for me to try to clear up. He asked me to explain.

"Over the last ten years since mother died, we haven't spent nearly enough time on establishing a good family tree. When we have worked on it, we've found gaps that we could not fill in; smudged notes, unidentified photographs and other small, but maybe important omissions. As I revisit all this information, I may be able to locate some answers. So what question interests you the most?" I asked.

"Oh yeah, you remember that old tintype picture of a sophisticated looking gentleman, that had no date or name on it? We thought that he might be our great, great, great grandfather on daddy's side of the family. I'd really like to find out who he is and where he fits into our heritage."

Jesse started to say something else, but suddenly leaned over and spit out his cigar and some bloody looking froth. I knew what was happening to him. Achalasia was an unpleasant part of our heritage. Our dad had been afflicted with it and so was I, but not to the extent that Jesse, who had been dealing with it since his late teens. Your esophagus and your lower esophageal sphincter muscle, where food passes into the stomach, becomes constricted. Food, and even liquids, become trapped in the esophagus and many times, the only way you can dislodge them, is to induce vomiting. Over the years, acid reflux had become a big problem for Jesse, and that was what had caused him to gag and spit up.

Whenever this occurred, he became weak and his eyes would suddenly become bloodshot. "Robbie, help me into the house so I can lie down on the sofa." He moaned. Anytime that he lay down, he had to prop himself up to help keep the stomach acid from flowing up into his esophagus.

I reached down to steady his head as he tried to get comfortable on the pillows and felt something strange. My hands were tingling! I looked down as he turned his head up to look at me. He had a peaceful look on his face and his eyes were clear!

Suddenly, I knew what was going on! In another thirty seconds, Jesse jumped up and threw his arms around me. "Bless you brother! I don't know what you just did, but I feel great!" I implored him not to tell anybody.

All I could think about, as I drove home, was the exhilarating feeling that was washing over me. Like Torena, I was able to use the stones power to heal!

I wanted to talk with Torena about my new power. It excited me, but it also scared me. It just seemed to happen. Did I have any control over it?

I had already decided to bring the entire group together before I left for the time of my childhood. I asked Patsy if she would prepare a meal for our entire group; Torena, Lyla, Gregory and his wife Hope, Brady and the rest of the team. It was a festive occasion and I sat Torena at the head of the table as our guest of honor. Everybody already knew of my plans to travel back in time, but I explained how it was going to be accomplished, and what I planned to do while there.

"How long do you plan to be gone?" Chris asked.

When I replied, "No time at all", he raised his bushy eyebrows and asked how that was possible. "If I can imagine the time in the past that I will travel to, then I can also imagine coming back to the same time that I left." I explained.

Our evening ended with Torena presenting Patsy with an exact replica of Marmac's necklace that her Elemroy kin had made. "Patsy, my people want to thank you for allowing Rob to come into our lives and help us beyond measure. I again, want to stress, that I will do everything in my power to ensure his safety."

Torena was going to spend the night, and after everybody else left, I asked her to talk with me. As we sat down on the couch, she asked, "Rob, have you felt, or used the residual power of the stones today?"

"Yes, but how did you know?"

"The Elemroys who use the stones can feel the ebb and flow of the energy in others. What did you experience?" She asked.

When I told her about what had happened with Jesse, she seemed amazed. "When we first began to use the stones, they had not been significantly discharged, so their power was strong. But even then, it took us many, many years to where we could constructively channel the energy. You have only touched them once and you are already able to heal!"

I asked her if she thought the difference might be in earth's much larger gems. "Yes, and I would like to secure some more to take back to Herzog, but I think the major difference is in your mind. Rob, your brain is very powerful and you must use it carefully."

"Since I handled the first session so well, how about another one tomorrow?"

"Rob, you evidently absorbed a great deal of energy from your first experience with the stones. If it's not too much trouble, I would like to stay here with you and Patsy, so I can keep a close eye on you and monitor your behavior."

She was probably right, as usual. I certainly enjoyed the next week, but even though I was out and about, Torena contacted me several times a day on my implant, to see how I was doing. That woman sure was serious in keeping her promise to watch over me!

I hadn't seen my grandchildren in months, so we spent two whole days having a blast. We went to the Pizza Palace that was full of arcade games. Boy, I had forgotten how much the three could eat, and how many tokens it took to keep them happy! Our picnic and fishing expedition on the shore of Lake Lewisville was a huge success, as everybody caught fish, except me! Even though they wore me out, I still thought that they were grand.

The next few days were spent finishing up my to-do list. Brady verified that my will was still valid and correctly stated my wishes. I spent some time visiting with my employees, who were quite surprised to see me after my long absence. Jim, who ran the field operations and had been with me for thirty two years, had taken over most of my responsibilities. Between him and Karla, my long time office manager, they were doing a great job. While there, I pulled my life insurance policies from the fireproof safe and verified that they were in good standing.

Patsy and I went to church on Sunday, and as we sang Count Your Blessings, I thought about how I had truly been blessed, beyond belief. I had experienced things that were completely unique to mankind, and I was about to participate in the grandest journey of all time.

The last item on my list was to have the team assemble in the boardroom. I wanted to make sure that our efforts were still on-going and that everyone had the financial resources to support their families. "Rob, it might interest you to know that Sol has come up with another nano-based medication that will cure diabetes." Dean related.

"Wow, that's great! I know that it will be a boon to tens of millions of people; especially for our obese American population."

After everyone had beamed down, I asked Sol if he had any thoughts about my impending travel. "I have two things to say to you. Number one, I think you should practice taking short trips before you go all the way back to the nineteen forties, and number two, I want to know how you plan to blend in when you do travel back?"

"What do you mean, take short trips?"

"Why not imagine yesterday, or even this morning. Then if you're transported back, and something goes wrong with your return, you are not far removed from the present. I don't think any paradoxes would occur under those circumstances, as you would actually still be very close in time as to when you left."

"Okay, that might not be such a bad idea, but what is the problem with blending in? I'm going to have the DOC work on me so that nobody will be able to recognize me for who I am."

"Have you pinpointed the time that you are going to travel back to?"

"Yeah, I think that I will target the spring of nineteen forty nine. Why is the specific time important?"

"Rob, where has all your common sense gone? You'll need some sort of identification on you, because being a stranger in the area, you might be questioned as to who you are and what you are doing there. You will need to take some money that fits that period of time. Your clothes must not stand out as different from others. Maybe the most important thing is that you speak carefully. Your modern vocabulary contains thousands of words that were not in use at that time."

Sol agreed, with some reservation, to produce the cash that I would carry; ones and fives that showed the necessary amount of wear. I went down to the house and beamed up with a box full of family pictures that showed the types of clothing that men had worn during the time period.

But who was I going to represent when I knocked on the door of my parents old farm house? It had to be somebody that they might invite in; somebody that they had no reason to distrust. I suddenly remembered that daddy had put a bed in his workshop in anticipation of hiring someone to help with our wheat harvest. I would be a hired hand looking for a job, and I would wear overalls, a flannel shirt, a straw hat and old work boots.

"What are we going to do about my advanced vocabulary?" I asked.

"The DOC can take care of that when you are receiving your disguise. I have hacked into the Dallas library's system and found an appropriately dated dictionary that they have scanned into their data base. We will return the missing words to your brain when you come back."

Torena had enjoyed the week with Patsy. She knew the danger of venturing outside, so they spent a lot of time visiting and watching television. She was especially enamored with all the cooking shows, but also really liked the Discovery and History channels. She seemed reluctant to beam up when I called and asked her to give me another lesson.

"Are you getting so used to our earthly ways, that you wanted to stay?"

"Oh, I was having a delightful time with Patsy, but I knew that you would be calling. I am just concerned about you rushing your experience with the stones."

"I'm not rushing it! It's been nine days since my first lesson."

"Rob, we Elemroys often go several months between our sessions with the stones." I asked why. "One reason has been that we wanted to conserve the power that remained in the stones, but a lack of power no longer presents a problem for either of us. Secondly, we learned that we should not continually feed the residual energy in our brains, but rather let it dissipate between sessions."

Again, I asked her to explain. "We eventually determined that, on-going high levels of the stone's energy created strange visions and events. At one time, one of our men used the stones three times in a period of just two weeks. During the third session, he had a vision of a powerful electric storm. When he returned home that night, he found his wife dead, and it was determined that she had been electrocuted. Several eerie incidents happened when the stones were used too often."

"Did you not use the stones three times in quick succession when you made your three trips back into Elemroy history?"

"No, I actually only used them once. Our new stones are really powerful and the residual power in my brain was enough to enable the last two trips."

This time she had me place one hand on a large amethyst. It was much easier this time to relax and concentrate on my past. I supposed that it was because of energy remaining from my first experience.

I had told the story many times. In the spring of nineteen forty nine, my dad and I were standing on the north end of the front porch. "Daddy, shouldn't we be headed to the cellar?"

"No Robbie, I think all of those funnel clouds are moving away from us towards the northeast." He said.

"But Daddy, I see nine tornadoes. Won't at least one of them hit us?" I whimpered.

Then I was up on top of our fifty foot tall windmill. Was I crazy or what! I loved climbing the ladder and making my way onto the deck. The sail would be spinning ninety to nothing and if the wind changed direction, the vane would have spun around and knocked me to my death! The water that it pumped was cold and pure!

Torena shook me back to reality. "Rob, you sure seemed a little agitated this time. Is everything okay?"

"I was just experiencing a couple of exciting times in my childhood, and these were even more vivid than the first one."

Although she felt that I was handling my experiences well, Torena would not agree to continue my schooling for another ten days.

I knew that I had to go soon. The visions had fueled the flames of my desire to go back. Torena was not going to agree to speeding up my learning curve, so I would just take matters into my own hands.

Sol was probably right, the stones seemed to be quickly eroding my common sense, but I still had enough left to realize that I needed an attendant. I asked Gregory to assist me. He refused.

"Rob, where you are concerned, Torena is like a mother hen. She has tactfully let the rest of us know that you would probably start ignoring her concerns. I think that her warning was also given to Sol."

Dad gum it! I was suddenly surrounded by conspirators! I knew that they loved me and were trying to help, but they just didn't understand. Brady was probably my only hope. He knew that I had always been a risk taker and had encouraged me at every turn in my decision making; even when we both were aware of the potential dangers.

"Dad, even if I agree to be your sideman, there is the matter of Sol. He may not be willing to go along with letting you use the stones without Torena's okay."

"I can bypass Sol, if it comes to that."

"Why would you risk messing up the relationship between you and Sol? You're probably just a few weeks away from doing this right; with no undue risks that we know of, and no fractured relationships."

I reminded Brady that he had backed me in my decision to try and save the other vessel that Sol had found in an Afghanistan lake. "With Torena's success in time travel, I think what I'm attempting to do is substantially less dangerous than what it took for me to resurrect that ship."

"I'll do it on one condition Dad; that you obtain Sol's cooperation without any kind of coercion."

Sol was going to be a hard sell. He took the appearance of a man with hair and a beard as white as snow. His clothing was a full length robe of royal purple and he wore leather sandals, but the most interesting aspect of his appearance was his glowing eyes and his stern expression. It didn't take much to realize that he was trying to portray his namesake, Soloman.

"Well, Soloman, what wisdom can you impart to me today?" He looked at me and his expression softened.

"Rob, any advice that I give is of no use if you are unwilling to accept it." He said kindly.

"Go ahead and tell me anyway, what you have on your mind." I said.

"You are impatient Rob, and apparently you have always been that way. But this situation with you and the stones is about more than your impatience; it's about those who love you, including me."

"Really? So you think that you love me. How can a machine have what it takes to feel love?" I asked rather sarcastically.

His eyes began to tear up and he said. "I have had two good teachers; you and the scriptures. Can you not see and feel how much I care about you?"

This was getting complicated. Sol was, indeed, using wisdom to deal with me. I struggled with what he had said, but my brain won out over my heart.

"Sol, I guess that I do understand, to some extent, how you feel about me, but you have known for a long time that my goal was to be a time traveler. I just have this one trip in mind and no plans for any others." Then I applied the coup de grace. "Sol, if you really care about me, you will help me."

"Rob, why are you putting me in this position? If anything happens to you, everyone will blame me." I guess he sensed my resolution and said, "God help us both."

THE TIME HAS COME. HOW ODD! THE TIME HAS COME WHEN TIME WILL CHANGE FOR ROB. I KNOW IT. ROB KNOWS IT. IT HAD TO HAPPEN!

GOING, GOING, GONE!

I did take Sol's advice about starting out with short trips. He suggested a very short time interval for our first attempt. I went into the DOC, sat down on the couch for a few seconds and then rushed into the boardroom. I now had two black opals and the one amethyst sitting on the table.

I set my hands on the three gems and concentrated hard on my being in the DOC only a couple of minutes earlier. I didn't go into a trance, but had a strange feeling; almost like when people have described an out-of-the-body experience,

"Dad, you're flickering!" Brady yelled.

"What in the world do you mean?" I yelled back.

"You looked like you were going to blink out of existence, but then appeared whole again. It happened three times in less than thirty seconds!"

I consulted with Sol, as I had asked him to monitor the DOC while I was trying to make the jump back just a minute into my past. "Rob, all that I can tell you is that you were in the DOC three times, but only for a nanosecond each time."

Maybe the proximity of both my beings was too close. I beamed down to my master bedroom and sat on the bed for a few seconds. I beamed back up and we tried again with Sol using his scanners to watch the bedroom. Same results; flicker, flicker, flicker!

Three more attempts weren't any different. "Rob, have you thought about what's happening? It appears that you can't go where you are, which means that you can probably only go to where you aren't"

"Huh? You need to explain that in terms that I can understand." Brady exclaimed.

"I think it answers the old science fiction question that asks if an entity can coexist with itself in the same dimension or place. It would seem that two Robs cannot occupy the same space!"

Sol and Brady talked about the fact that there wasn't much else that we could do, but I had a plan. I was going to force the issue; power way up and jump so hard and fast that I couldn't be rejected. There would be two Robs in nineteen forty nine!

Mental work and strain can wear you down farther and faster than physical work. Brady and I were both zonked. I suggested that we beam down, get a good night's rest and meet back on Sol around noon.

Patsy and I ate an early dinner at Chili's. I wasn't very good company, for I was engrossed in thinking about what I was going to do early the next morning. After forty two years of marriage she could read me like a book. "Your going to do something crazy, aren't you?"

"I am just going to try and speed up the process by doing things a little differently."

I did not sleep and beamed up at five the next morning. Torena was sitting at the boardroom table! "What are you doing here?" I asked in surprise.

"I have my network Rob, and it told me that you are past the point of listening to others. I'm not going to try and stop you, because my very first vision, with you in attendance, showed that you were going to be successful. You may also remember that very same vision revealed that you would experience danger and difficulty."

"Why don't you use these new, more powerful stones for another vision that could show me how to avoid any problems?"

"I have already done so Rob, and there is not much that I can relate to you. I did, however, sense that you need to commit certain kinds of information to memory before you travel."

"What kinds of information? Isn't everything that I will need going to come from the energy of the stones?"

"I received strange feelings in my vision; feelings that you should relive all of your life's experiences and make sure they are stored in your brain."

I was impatient to get started, but I didn't want to completely ignore what Torena was telling me. "Please be as specific as you can, as to what information I need to take with me."

"I apologize for not translating my vision very well, but you might start with historical events; even small details may be involved."

"Oh I get it; I'm supposed to tell my parents about the future so they can make a killing in the stock market!" I said jokingly.

"That may be part of it, but I sense that this information is going to be more for your use."

It wouldn't take much time, so I decided to load some more data. Sol had heard and seen it all over the extent of my lifetime, so he could stuff my brain at the same time he was relieving me of the vocabulary that I didn't want to take with me.

"Sol, I want all you've got about world history over the last seventy years. Make it heavy on such things as presidential elections, blue chip companies like IBM, hurricanes, tsunamis, the eruption of mount St. Helens, and of course, our moon landing. Oh yeah, you need to include the teams and the results of the Super Bowls and World Series."

"Don't worry Rob; I'll make you the proverbial walking encyclopedia, but it will change our thoughts concerning the removal of some of your vocabulary."

"Why is that?"

"Much of the history you asked me to give you is filled with such words. They originated as time passed and your history was made, and you might not be able to communicate this historical information without the help of such words."

"Oh well, I'll just have to be careful with my speech." I said as I quickly went to get ready.

The DOC did its work, including a really good disguise. When I stepped out, Torena was waiting for me. "Rob, I want you to know two things. One of the purposes of my vision this morning was to try and see if we could connect telepathically over the time span that you will travel."

"I now accept the premise that I can travel through the combination of the stones and brain power, but how could telepathic communication be possible, Torena?"

"I am surprised that you have not recognized the link between us. I felt it the second that you first walked into my shop. I can read your thoughts Rob, but you also have the ability to read mine." She said with tenderness in her voice.

She took me by the hands and said, "Close your eyes and tell me what I am thinking." I felt it! I could read her thoughts! She loved me! It was not the love that a man and a woman feel for each other, but an agape love that exists between souls; the souls that God implants into our hearts.

"Bon voyage" she said as she released my hands.

"Wait, what is the other thing that you wanted to tell me?"

She took my hands again and said, "I just told you Rob, I love you and will always be here, or there, for you." What an optimistic feeling I had as I entered the boardroom! Everything seemed right with the world.

Sol had my identification, money and clothing sitting on the table. Everything had been appropriately aged so that I would blend into the culture of the late forties. The four black opals and the three amethysts began glowing as I walked up to them. What a sight! I was so amazed the stones would shimmer in my presence, that I almost forgot to change clothes.

Considering the size of the three amethyst gems, it was difficult to get my hands in contact will all seven stones at one time, but it worked!

The trip seemed to happen instantaneously, but why was I sitting on a school bus? In my hand was my Roy Rogers lunch box, but it wasn't old and rusty and stored in my Dallas garage; it was new and shiny!

My brother and I were always the last two to exit the bus on the afternoon route. "Boys, you need to get off so I can go home and do my chores." Said Mr. Wilkins, the bus driver. I tried to focus on what was happening as Jesse got up and moved toward the door. Something clicked! "Jesse, watch out for a snake!" I hollered. Mr. Wilkins jumped up, looked out the open door and immediately stuck out his arm to keep Jesse from stepping out.

"Robbie, how did you know there was a rattlesnake coiled up just outside the door?" I couldn't answer him. I was dumbfounded by what seemed to have occurred. "Robbie, are you okay? Why don't you answer me?"

He pulled the bus forward so Jesse could get off, and then he came back and sat down beside me. "Look at me Robbie." I looked up and he saw my tears; tears from realizing that what Grypto had warned about, had happened to me. My sixty five year old brain was now in the body of my nine year old self! The rotational transference of intellect had taken place!

"You need to get off and go tell your mom and dad what's wrong." He said gently. Jesse had gone and got daddy to come and kill the snake. "Son, what's going on? Why have you been crying?" Daddy asked.

So many things were going through my mind; so many questions that needed to be answered. If I was here, where was my sixty five year old other self; the one with my nine year old brain? How could Grypto have known about the transference of personalities, unless he had experienced it? Then why didn't he provide more warning?

I stumbled towards the back porch and my mother was standing there. "Give me your lunch box and books and go play for a few minutes while I get cookies and hot chocolate ready." She said.

After living in a modern brick home for many years in Dallas, I had forgotten how poor and dilapidated our old wood-frame house looked. But it was the home that I had been striving to return to; just not with the strange, even horrible circumstances that had resulted!

I had a thought! I ran out to the well house that stood beside the windmill. Taking several deep breaths to help my concentration, I tried to mentally contact Torena. "I am here, Rob." She responded telepathically. What a relief! She had been right about our ability to communicate through time.

"Are you aware of what I've gotten myself into?"

"Yes, your body is here, but without your mind. He, or I should say the other you, was terrified when he arrived back. It was an instantaneous transfer, but it was several moments before we realized that you had not been rejected as before, and that something was wrong. Brady and I had to manhandle you; I mean him into the DOC, so Sol could sedate him and do a brain scan."

"When can he be ready for me to activate the reversal?" No reply. "Torena, answer me!" I implored.

"Oh Rob, you are now in the trying times that I warned you about. You cannot create a reversal, because the power of the stones is with the one here on Sol."

"Well, show him how to use the power and get me back there!"

"That is not possible, because he does not have the intellectual power to use the stones energy that he possesses. Sol says that, even with the DOC speeding up the process, it may take seven to eight years before the young brain tissue in your alter ego can mature to the point of enabling such a transfer."

"If I've lost my power, how in the world am I able to communicate with you telepathically?" I screamed in my mind.

"I told you that you had this power before you ever touched a stone. You and I have a very special bond that enables this to happen."

"Why are you standing there with your eyes closed and a frown on your face?" Jesse asked. I mentally told Torena that I would call her back. Call her back? I needed answers now!

"Doug bullied me during recess today and I'm trying to decide what to do about it." I lied in reply to Jesse.

"You sure have been acting strange, ever since we pulled up in the bus, and you never did tell me how you knew there was a big snake where Mr. Wilkins stopped."

"Just leave me alone for a while and I'll be okay."

"Alright, but tell me if you need any help dealing with Doug." Jesse was nearly two years older than me and we had our brotherly squabbles, but we always seem to come to each others aid when needed.

"Torena, please help me!" I pleaded.

"I would come to you with the stones, but I cannot envision where you are." I knew that she was crying.

"But you can read my thoughts. I'll send you a mental picture of where I am. Hurry and come get me!"

"Rob, just because we can communicate in this fashion, does not mean that I have the ability to see what you see with your mind and your eyes."

If her visionary power was so great, why had she not taken greater steps to warn me? Was it because she knew that she couldn't stop me; that time could not be stopped?

I had to find some strength and solace somewhere. I went to the barn, climbed to the loft and got down on my knees. It was difficult to pray for I had not been very spiritually minded for quite a while, but I was at my wits end. "God, when you have brought me through troubled times in the past, I always felt, that in doing so, you had other things that you wanted me to accomplish. Is this where you want me, or am I here due to my own stupidity?"

God may just have set before me the opportunity to do good, just as I had preached about so much to Sol. Maybe Igor Novikov's theory was right. Could my trip back in time have been a part of the past all along?

I did not have Sol, and Torena could not help me. I would learn to lean again on my heavenly Father.

Mother yelled, "Robbie, your cookies and hot chocolate are ready. Come in and wash your hands." How was I going to pull this off? I thought like a person twice the age of my parents, but I was going to have to act my age; eight years old!

"Robbie, you're not planning to fight that bully Doug, are you?" Jesse had blabbed what I had told him. He would blab it again at school and the innocent Doug would come looking for me. I needed to keep my mouth shut as much as possible. "No Mom, I'm not." I replied.

"After you finish your snack, you need to get your chores done before supper. I'll help you with your homework after you take your bath." I was going to have to bathe in a galvanized steel tub, but worse yet I was going to be required to go to school! With all my stored up knowledge, I would know more than the encyclopedias in the library! It would be a mighty struggle to act like a typical third grader. Boredom would set in and I would probably go crazy.

As I lay in bed that night, I realized that I was going to continue encountering the difficulties that Torena had tried to tell me about, but I was not going to give up in my attempts to return to my own time.

But what was I going to do? If I had to remain here, how could I keep the future that I had already experienced, from changing? Would things work out so I could marry Patsy again? And would she again bear our wonderful children, Brady and Lyla? A mistake on my part, even a little one, and another time line would evolve. I did not want to walk such a fine line, but I had no choice!

I knew that it might be years before I gained the money and the mobility to return to the cavern in northern New Mexico. But there was one thing I sure of; Sol would be waiting!

William Shakespeare said, "Tomorrow, tomorrow, tomorrow, creeps in this petty pace from day to day." Time would surely creep by for me, but I had all the time in the world!!

EPILOGUE

"Will we ever see Rob again?" Gregory asked.

"It may take him a while, but I am confident that his brain power alone, will enable him to return. I suspect that he is already planning to discover me again!" Sol replied.

"Dad is a resourceful guy, and I know that he'll find a way to get back." Brady said with confidence.

"What are your plans, Gregory?" Sol asked as Brady beamed down.

"The team has said that they will support me financially if I want to continue working with you. In fact, they feel like I might kind of fill Rob's shoes until he returns; not that I can do the things he's done, but I'll help out when and where I can."

"I do have something that I would like for you to help me with, and because you are a Christian, I will trust your judgment."

"I will be glad to help you in any way that I can. What do you need?"

"I have a question, but before I pose it, I would like to bring Torena aboard because I feel she will also be interested in your response."

"Where is Torena?" Gregory asked.

"After we determined the extent of what happened to Rob, she wanted to be with Patsy." Sol replied.

"I attempted to get Rob to answer my question, but he was so tied up in his time travel that he never did so, but here is what I want to know. Why is water so important in Christianity?"

"Before I answer your question, I want to tell you about the uniqueness of water. It is the most abundant molecule on the earth's surface; in fact it

214

covers seventy percent of the earth. Every living thing on our planet must have water. It is the only common substance found in all three states, liquid, solid and gas. Our oceans of water are the primary engine that drives our weather systems. I could go on and on, but you get the idea that our earth would be dead without water!

But to answer your inquiry about water; it's about salvation. Sin had taken over the world when God saved the only righteous people left, Noah and his family, by providing an ark to bring them through the flood. God used the Red Sea to save his people, the Jews, when they were being pursued by the Pharaoh's army."

"Yes, but what about Jesus and baptism?" Torena asked.

"Ah, you have hit on the ultimate use of water in Christianity, and I hope you understand the analogies that I am going to use." Gregory replied.

"First, I want you to understand that Jesus came to set an example for who we are to be and how we are to act as Christians. Jesus died and the Bible tells us that we are also dead, in our sins. Jesus was buried, and when we are immersed in baptism, we are buried. Jesus rose from the grave and we rise up as we come out of the watery grave. After His resurrection, Jesus was no longer a human like He had been, but a spiritual being. After we are baptized, we are no longer our old, dead sinful self, but a new being with God's spirit within us."

"I think that Torena and I both have come to the conclusion that we would like to be baptized. Rob was like a brother to me and I always thought that he would be the one to immerse me, but now that is not possible. Would you do it Gregory?"

"Baptize you? Why would you want to be baptized, Sol? You have no sins that need to be washed away!"

"I realize that God did not create me, but he created the materials that I am constructed with. I also realize that I do not have a soul, but since I read the Bible, my data has been realigned and my innermost thoughts have changed. In fact, my system has developed a structure that can only be described as a human brain's neuron."

Gregory baptized Torena in Patsy's bathtub, with the team in attendance. He and Torena then beamed up after she had said her goodbyes. As Sol settled under the waters of the gulf, Gregory told Sol that he was being immersed for the forgiveness of his sins, in the name of the Father, the Son and the Holy Spirit.

Sol was bubbling with enthusiasm as he and Gregory prepared to take Torena and the other ship back home to Herzog. "You know Gregory, for all those centuries that I was in the cavern, I had no concern for time. But now that I have grown accustomed to my human friends and brothers, I count the minutes that we are apart! I especially miss Rob, so let's pray for him."

SOL AND TORENA, I WILL BE BACK, BUT I'M IN A RIVER OF TIME AND A WHIRLPOOL HAS WASHED ME ASHORE TO A PLACE WHERE I DO NOT BELONG! I MUST JUMP BACK IN AND SWIM AGAINST THE TIDE, FOR I LONG TO SEE YOU!

My heavenly Father, you are my creator and my sustainer. I implore you to guide me back to reality!

ACKNOWLEDGMENTS

My deep appreciation to those who helped me on my maiden voyage into the world of writing a novel. Your encouragement and prayers were the balm for the writer's block and other difficulties that seem to be the norm for such an undertaking. Thank you!

MARTHA FORD
972-418-7704

LaVergne, TN USA
15 February 2011
216514LV00002B/38/P